# THE KAMCHATKA INCIDENT

# THE KAMCHATKA INCIDENT

## Robert L. McKinney

DEMBNER • NEW YORK

Dembner Books
Published by Red Dembner Enterprises Corp., 80 Eighth Avenue, New York, N.Y. 10011
Distributed by W. W. Norton & Company, Inc., 500 Fifth Avenue, New York, N.Y. 10110

Library of Congress Cataloging in Publication Data

McKinney, Robert L., 1946–
   The Kamchatka incident.

   I.  Title.
PS3563.C382K3    1985       813'.54         84-23905
ISBN 0-934878-53-6

TO LYNN.
AND PAUL.

Although inspired by an event
that shocked the world,
*The Kamchatka Incident* is an
imaginative work of fiction.

# THE KAMCHATKA INCIDENT

# PROLOGUE

On the night of December 24, 1993, Trans-Pacifica Airlines Flight 18, New York City to Tokyo via the Northern Great Circle Route, took on eighty thousand pounds of additional fuel and seven new passengers in Anchorage, Alaska. The flight was delayed there an hour and forty-five minutes because the captain complained of problems with the radios and inertial systems while passing over Canada. Before he would continue the flight, he demanded that the navigational equipment be inspected.

The avionics technician arrived, appearing somewhat less than eager to brave the elements on this particular Christmas Eve, and sleepily ran a series of routine tests on the airliner's electronics. He reported nothing out of the ordinary.

Although the technician, a young and bearded Air Force veteran identified only as Hardin by his nametag, recognized the first officer and flight engineer as regulars on the New York to Tokyo run, he had never seen the captain before and did not like the gruff way the new pilot ordered him around. If he had wanted to put up with that kind of shit, Hardin muttered to the flight engineer, he would have stayed in the Air Force.

He finished running his tests and was relieved to find himself being hustled quickly off the flight line.

Finally, with the captain still grumbling to the control tower about radio static and the sticky wet snow that had just started falling, Flight 18 taxied out to the end of Runway 2–4 Left, did a quick engine run-up, and took off into the snowy blackness of the Alaskan winter night.

As the airplane passed over its last U.S. checkpoint, just northwest of the small Air Force station on Shemya Island, Alaska, ground radar showed it at an altitude of thirty-nine thousand feet. The duty air-controller on Shemya informed Flight 18 that his radar screen indicated the airplane was twelve nautical miles north of Zulu Corridor and should correct its course to avoid overflying Soviet airspace.

Zulu Corridor cut nearly two hours off a New York to Tokyo flight, but it skirted dangerously close to top-secret Soviet nuclear submarine bases and Soviet Pacific Fleet Headquarters at Petropavlovsk near the southern tip of the Kamchatka Peninsula. Airline executives liked Zulu because of the tremendous fuel savings, especially with the jumbo jets such as 747s and DC-10s, but the route made even old-hand corridor pilots nervous.

The Soviet Air Defense field commanders were understandably sensitive about invasions of their airspace. In 1976 a Korean Air Lines 707 had wandered in and out of Soviet airspace undetected for more than an hour, and the western press had enjoyed quite a field day ridiculing the Soviet Air Defense. Seven Russian colonels were executed when word reached Moscow.

The Russians shot down the next Korean 707 they caught in their territory, forcing it to crash-land on a frozen lake in 1978, causing the death of two passengers and the loss of a seventeen million dollar airplane.

Then, in September of 1983, a Russian pilot flying a SU-15 swept-wing interceptor fired two Anab air-to-air missiles into an off-course KAL 747, resulting in the fiery deaths of 267 men, women, and children.

Notices to airmen and air navigation charts were brutally explicit about what could happen to off-course aircraft, military or civilian, in the Kamchatka area. Emblazoned across the charts in heavy black letters was the message:

### Aircraft infringing upon non-free flying territory may be fired on without warning

To complicate an already dangerous situation, vast mineral deposits made aircraft compasses less than reliable once they neared the Kamchatka Peninsula. The proximity of the North Pole, coupled with the great distances involved, often made radio communications impossible. Among pilots, Zulu Corridor had a worldwide and well-deserved reputation: bad news.

The pilot of Trans-Pacific Airlines Flight 18 doubtlessly had been warned that increased auroral activity had been playing havoc with radio communications in the polar regions for several days, making two-way communications between airliners and the ground practically nonexistent. In fact, Flight 18's reply to Shemya Control during the early morning hours of Christmas Day 1993 was unreadable in a burst of static. However, the ground radar screen showed the airliner slowly start correcting back to course as if the crew had read and copied their instructions.

As the tiny green flashing blip of the airliner approached the outer ring of his radar screen, the air controller wished the crew a merry Christmas and a safe flight.

The only reply was another burst of static.

When TPA Flight 18 became five hours overdue in Tokyo, airline officials finally conceded to the press and anxious relatives that the airliner would not have had enough fuel to last all that time. A tall man, obviously an American, who was waiting to meet his daughter returning from a state-side college, had to have the officials' statement translated for him by a bystander. When he understood, he sank to the floor in tears.

In response to a hail of shouted questions the airline officials admitted the jet had to be down somewhere, but they refused to speculate about the fate of either the airplane or the 246 passengers and crew aboard.

# 1

WASHINGTON—In his traditional Christmas message to the American people, the President said he is ready to go anywhere, at any time, to discuss a lasting peace with the Soviets.

"This is the season," said the Chief Executive, "when men and women of goodwill, whatever their ideologies or religions, should work together toward peace on earth."

The President and his family are spending Christmas at the presidential retreat at Camp David. Tomorrow they plan to fly to Galveston aboard Air Force One for a brief vacation before returning to Washington.

American News Wire Service
December 24, 1993

**P**ete Shafer never really got used to Florida, and Christmas was the worst time of all. Although he tried his best to feel festive, Pete could not get in the Christmas mood when it was eighty-four degrees outside and kids were roller-skating up and down the street in shorts, "Jingle Bells" blasting from their portable radios. The Christmas parades, broadcast on the expensive color television in the corner of the large living room, with their canned speeches and carefully rehearsed Christmas spirit, did little to help.

Retiring to Florida had been Velma's idea. Pete had picked out a nice cabin beside a trout stream in North Carolina and was ready to give the realtor a downpayment, but Velma had insisted they move to Orlando to be near their daughter and two grand-children.

Pete had given in to her wishes with only token reluctance. After all, he owed her. She had followed him around faithfully for his twenty-seven years with INTEL-5, a super-secret intelligence gathering and espionage agency of the federal government. INTEL-5 was an entity Velma knew little about and, Pete realized, liked even less. Being married to an operative wasn't easy on a person.

A couple of times they had been forced to move without his even being allowed to tell Velma why, but she had gone along anyway, abruptly abandoning with little explanation the few friends their transient lifestyle allowed her to make. Pete had always tried to be as up-front as he could with his wife—she deserved as much—but there were a lot of things about his job that it would be safer if she didn't know.

He had actually worked a few years past his fortieth birthday, an INTEL-5 field operative's normal retirement age, staying on until just after he was forty-six. He was now a fit and trim fifty-one. Although he had kept planning to retire, something always came up at the last minute that needed his expertise and experience. It wasn't that he didn't have confidence in the young operatives coming up—he did. In fact, Pete had personally trained many of them. The truth was that he had enjoyed his job with INTEL-5 and feared the boredom of retirement.

Yet the past five years had been good to him. It was as though his and Velma's marriage had started all over again. They discovered a lot of things about each other that they had forgotten or never known. Not only were they very much in love with each other, they were still the best of friends. Pete was especially glad they both had their health so they could do all the things they had put off. True, tennis with the Andersons next door wasn't as exciting as parachuting into East Berlin, but there was a lot to be said for retirement too. Although he would have been reluctant to admit it aloud, Pete was beginning to enjoy playing the part of a retired State Department employee, his retirement cover.

The smell of roasting turkey and cranberry sauce wafted in from the kitchen, signaling that Velma's preparations for her traditional Christmas dinner were well underway. Pete glanced at his watch. It was nearly 11 A.M. Their daughter and her two girls would be arriving soon. In one corner of the living room stood a five-foot blue spruce surrounded by gaily wrapped packages for the grandchildren.

"Pete? Can you help me a second?" Velma called from the kitchen.

"Sure. Be right there." He got up from his chair and flicked off the newscast as he passed the TV. Probably more fighting in the Middle East, he thought. Why couldn't the goddamned idiots lay off fighting, at least on Christmas Day?

Mary, the family's fourteen-year-old basset hound, wagged her tail hopefully, begging to be petted as Pete walked by her. Automatically he bent down and gave her graying muzzle a friendly pat as he passed.

In the large and cheery kitchen Velma leaned over a gigantic brown turkey, which she had just slid out of the oven onto the stove's open door. "Lift this up to the table for me," she said. "I used to be able to lift these things, but they seem to get heavier every year."

Pete stooped over and lifted the roasting pan and its steaming contents. He felt a little tingle of pain go darting up his spine from an old parachuting injury.

"No wonder you couldn't lift it. This darned thing must weigh forty pounds. We'll be eating turkey until Easter."

Velma smiled. Since Pete had retired, life had been good.

He had the turkey halfway between the oven and the table when the kitchen telephone rang.

Velma lifted the receiver from the wall. "Merry Christmas!" she answered brightly, but her smile quickly faded when she heard the voice on the other end. Even after five years she recognized it immediately.

She covered the receiver with her hand and turned toward her husband, who had set the turkey on the table and was sampling the cranberry sauce. "It's for you," she said with thinly veiled apprehension. "It's Bill Murphy."

Velma had never met Murphy face-to-face. She knew him only as a disembodied voice on the telephone and as Pete's former superior at INTEL-5, but she had nevertheless developed an intense dislike for the man. On the few occasions she had expressed her opinion of Murphy to Pete, he had laughed her off, not unkindly, in an attempt to allay her worries. "Oh, Murph's all right," he had said. "He's just a little hard to understand sometimes. Not wrong, just different. That's all."

Velma still remembered that a call from Murphy had usually resulted in Pete's disappearance, which left her alone, often for months at a time, not even knowing where he was. Even though she realized that was her husband's job, she still resented the intrusions into their life together. She was glad Pete was retired now, so there would be no more missions.

Yet Murphy's voice had aroused in her the old fears, the anticipation of loneliness, the dread of waiting. As Velma handed Pete the telephone, she suddenly realized her palms were sweating.

Pete took the receiver from her outstretched hand. "Hello?" he said.

"I'm in D.C.," Murphy said immediately without even identifying himself. "You seen the news this morning?"

"Hey, Murph! I thought you'd retired by now."

Velma looked up disapprovingly in Pete's direction when she heard the enthusiasm in his voice.

"About halfway. Pete, we need to talk. Where's the nearest protected line around there?"

Pete chuckled to himself. Same old Murphy. He had never wasted time on pleasantries or idle chatter. It was as if he had last spoken to his former associate and, in many ways, his best friend, yesterday instead of more than five years ago. He seemed to have forgotten that he had threatened never to speak to Pete again when Pete retired from INTEL-5. Murphy had tried to talk Pete out of retiring and had acted angry and betrayed when he was unsuccessful. Although Murphy had been Pete's superior, it had never seemed that way. They had always functioned as equals and Pete had to admit that they had been, as Murphy often put it, "the best goddamned team in the business."

"There may be one at the Cape I could use, but I'm an hour and a half from there. What's up?"

"Can't tell you much on an open line, I'm afraid, but it has to do with that jetliner that went in last night."

"Where was that?"

"You ought to watch the news more, Pete. Damned tube's full of it. Charlie Sector. Trans-Pacifica. Two hundred and forty-six people."

Pete caught his breath. Charlie Sector was the area around Soviet Pacific Fleet Headquarters at Petropavlovsk near the southern tip of the Kamchatka Peninsula. A few years ago he had known the area better than any man alive, American or Russian. "They buy the farm?"

"Don't have the slightest. Looks like it though."

"Any of our boys?"

"Couple."

Pete groaned. "Why the hell do they keep jeopardizing innocent civilians?"

Murphy did not answer for a few seconds. Then he spoke. "When it comes to the goddamned commies, I'm afraid, civilians, innocent or otherwise, are a thing of the past."

Pete sighed. When Murphy got carried away he sounded like a tape of the McCarthy hearings. His often too intense hatred of communists was one of his few weaknesses, the others being nothing more serious than an over fondness for Irish whiskey and cheap prostitutes—the cheaper the better. Still, if there was ever a man you could count on to do the right thing in a pinch, it was Murphy. "So, why you calling me?" Pete asked, after a moment. "I'm officially out to pasture."

Murphy laughed. "Pete, you're never out to pasture when you

work for this outfit. You know that. Look, we lost something on that airplane we need to get back real bad before the Soviets find it and I need your expertise. You're probably the one man in the world I can really count on to get the job done. You with me?"

Pete glanced over at Velma, who was frowning as she nervously arranged tiny marshmallows around a plate of candied yams. She had known for some time now that her husband was getting bored with retirement. She steeled herself for what she knew was coming next.

"What about some of the younger men—"

"Those goddamned kids don't know the north Pacific from cold piss."

"I don't agree. We've got some damned good people coming up. In any case I'll need a few more details about this thing before I commit."

"If this was something I could talk about over an unprotected line, they'd be using the CIA or the Boy Scouts or something. They wouldn't be needing you or me."

Pete nodded. "I guess you got a point."

"Good. I knew I could count on you. I'll have a jet in Orlando for you by noon. Or do you need till one?"

Pete looked apologetically at Velma, who raised her eyebrows in a gesture of defeat. "One'll be okay."

At precisely 1400 hours Pete stepped off an unmarked white business jet onto a narrow asphalt airstrip chiseled out of the thick pine forests on the Virginia side of the Potomac, less than twenty miles south of Washington, D.C. Orlando had been warm and pleasant. Virginia, as usual in the wintertime, was cold and rainy.

The tops of the tall, skinny loblolly pines were barely visible through the heavy, wet ground fog with visibility near zero. The seemingly deserted airstrip was hardly the sort of place one would have expected to see a small business jet making what appeared to be a routine instrument landing.

Pete stepped out of the airplane and walked quickly toward a low, white metal Quonset hut set just off the tarmac at the edge of the pines. He carried with him only a worn, brown leather flight bag that held a few clothes and his shaving gear. He had eaten his Christmas dinner, which Velma had hastily packed for him, on the flight from Florida.

Written across the front of the Quonset hut in faded red hand-painted letters were the words OLD DOMINION FLYING SERVICE and a picture of a bi-winged cropdusting airplane.

Pete neared the double doors of the hut and the bi-plane burst apart as the doors slid open. Out rushed a short, stocky man in his middle fifties. He was ruddy complected and wearing a belted, tan, double-breasted trenchcoat against the drizzle. Although he seemed to have aged considerably in the past five years, Pete recognized Murphy immediately. He was hatless and Pete could see he had abandoned his use of hair dye, allowing his thin crop of medium-length hair to go mostly gray. It still had enough of the original Irish red left on the sides, though, to give him a fiery appearance. Murphy always had a temper.

"Pete! Glad to see you could make it," shouted Murphy, as he rushed up, quickly shaking Pete's hand, for Murphy a rare show of affection. "Sorry to drag you away and all that, but we got ourselves one hell of a problem this time, I'm afraid." He rapidly ushered Pete inside the Quonset hut and pulled the door shut behind him.

They were immediately plunged into a gloomy darkness, broken only by a weak shaft of light filtering through a dirty and yellowed skylight. The smell of motor oil, stale aviation gasoline, and moldy rags nearly overpowered Pete. The shadowy form of a partially disassembled Steerman bi-plane sat in the middle of the cavelike space; pieces of its dismantled engine lay scattered about the concrete floor. As Pete's eyes adjusted to the darkness, he noticed that the nearly antique airplane's left tire was flat and its fuselage was covered by a thick layer of dust and pigeon droppings.

Bags of fertilizer and powdered pesticide lined one wall of the hut. Even in the weak light, he could see some of the bags were labeled 2-4-5-T, a pesticide banned for at least a decade. The acrid smell of the fertilizer and pesticide combined with the heaviness of the uncirculated air made Pete sneeze.

Murphy quickly led Pete around the right wing of the airplane and into a small, screened-in area that had once been a tool crib. A few rusty tools still hung forlornly above a workbench cluttered with rusty airplane parts and other trash. Murphy bent down and reached beneath the workbench. Suddenly there was a hiss of hydraulics and a flash of brilliant white light as a wall to Pete's left swung away, revealing a gleaming stainless steel elevator door and a row of brightly pulsating red and green buttons. Pete blinked rapidly, momentarily blinded by the glare. Murphy quickly punched in a four digit code. The door to the elevator silently slid open.

The two men stepped inside the brightly lighted compartment. The doors closed behind them. As it began its descent, the elevator car jerked slightly. Pete reached for a handrail.

"Don't lose your balance there, Buddy," Murphy chuckled.

Pete laughed; then he asked the question that had been bothering him since early that morning. "What the hell's important enough for the outfit to take a couple of old goats like us out of mothballs, Murph? They get tired of paying us our pensions or what?"

Murphy smiled. "Bastards tried to retire me," he said, "but I wouldn't hear of it so they made me take a promotion to a desk job. Over my mild protest, of course." He pulled a pack of the old-style, short, unfiltered Camel cigarettes from the pocket of his trenchcoat as he spoke, shook out one, lit it with a battered silver Zippo, and took a long draw, chuckling to himself.

Pete also chuckled lightly. He remembered that in Murphy's younger days he had considered a full-fledged barroom brawl with twenty marines a minor diversion.

Murphy put the pack of Camels and the Zippo back into his pocket and blew a perfect smoke ring at the ceiling of the elevator. "You remember Red Tango, don't you?"

Pete nodded. Red Tango was a grid of underwater monitors the United States had secretly planted around the Russian Pacific Fleet Headquarters at Petropavlovsk when U.S. intelligence learned the isolated harbor on the east coast of Russia was to become a major nuclear submarine base. Each of the six monitors or sensors was about the size of a small automobile, shaped somewhat like a torpedo, and heavily armored to withstand being air-dropped into the ocean. Once they hit the ocean bottom, the sensors were designed to burrow into the sea floor to escape detection before they started transmitting a constant flow of data about Soviet submarine and ship movement into and out of Petropavlovsk. Each contained elaborate mechanisms to avoid detection and transmitted their data via extremely long-waved subterranean signals very similar to the Navy's Project ELF submarine communications system. Each was powered by its own miniature atomic power plant.

Murphy went on. "Sensor A-three quit transmitting in September. We don't know why. The Russians could have found it, but we don't think so. They'd have probably raised one hell of a flap by now or worse yet, they'd have gone looking for the others. The compromise of the atomic and transmission technology alone on those things would threaten the free world if the Russians found it, not to mention the propaganda value to the dirty bastards. In any case the loss of A-three left one hell of a big hole in the net around Petropavlovsk. We knew we had to replace it somehow."

"So you were trying to drop in a new sensor from an off-course airliner?"

Murphy nodded. "Yeah. We considered all the options, of course. Boats, military airplanes, even subs. With those sensors weighing in at twenty tons a copy our choices were limited. Not to mention all the Russian radar and other detection devices. We couldn't just use a B-twenty-nine like with the originals, but whatever we used had to be big, therefore noticeable. We finally decided an off-course airliner had to be it. Even there, it takes a seven forty-seven or an L-ten eleven to carry that much weight without major modifications to the airframe. We jerry-rigged a drop-door on the cargo bay that could be operated from the flight engineer's station in the cockpit."

"He's one of ours?"

"Uh-huh. Him and the co-pilot."

"Not the pilot?"

"No. Too risky. Man makes captain, he starts putting the safety of his airplane above more important considerations. The regular pilot somehow or other got wind of what we were planning and threatened to raise hell. He was removed before he could broadcast our intentions."

Pete was surprised at the tiny shiver that shot up his spine when Murphy said the pilot had been *removed*. He knew Murphy wasn't talking about a simple transfer. Maybe he had been out of the espionage game too long after all, he thought. His conscience was turning civilian on him.

"And you think the Russians might have forced the plane down before it could make its drop?"

Murphy shook his head from side to side. "We hope not. Our people had orders to ditch the bird and blow it up if the Soviets tried to do that. What we're afraid of is that the Russians might have blown Flight Eighteen out of the sky before the sensor could be either dropped or properly destroyed. If that's the case, and we think it is, it might be laying around where they could find it, probably underwater."

"But they haven't shot anybody down out there since 1983 when they shot down the Korean airliner. They took one hell of a propaganda beating on that."

"Right, but we think they may have somehow found out what was coming their way this time and were willing to risk another beating or even a confrontation with the U.S. to get it."

Murphy leaned close to Pete and whispered, although they were now nearly five hundred feet below the ground, "I don't like the way INTEL-five is going lately, Pete, full of damned liberals, no proper direction from HQ, new regulations. Morale's gone to hell. Leaks everywhere."

"You really think so?"

"Yeah. You can't trust anybody these days. Kids and computers making all the decisions. The people we knew, on both sides, dying, retiring. Christ, Pete, nobody knows who's working for which side anymore. It's sure as hell not like the old days."

Pete shook his head. "I don't guess anything ever is."

# 2

A 747 jumbo jet, Trans-Pacifica Airlines Flight 18, is reported overdue in Tokyo and presumed down with 246 passengers and crew aboard. The flight originated in New York with a fueling stop in Anchorage, Alaska.

Airline executives refused to answer questions from reporters, saying only that the flight was last heard from early this morning.

The airplane's route took it close to Soviet airspace where another 747, Korean Air Lines Flight 007, was shot down by the Soviets in 1983, resulting in the death of 267 people.

WUSA Radio News Report
December 25, 1993

**P**ulsing white and blue lights flashed through a tiny crack between the elevator doors as the car slipped smoothly downward past the first occupied floors of the gigantic INTEL-5 underground complex deep beneath the Virginia countryside. There was a slight jerking sensation as the car began to brake. Pete felt the g-forces still pulling at his guts even after the elevator car had come to a complete stop. For a brief second the blood rushed away from his brain, making his feet leaden, and he felt light-headed. He staggered slightly and reached for the wall to steady himself as he followed Murphy out of the elevator and into a brightly lighted corridor.

Murphy, naturally, gave no signs that the descent or the rather sudden stop had affected him in the least. It seemed to Pete that nothing ever bothered Murphy, although the man was his senior by a couple of years, smoked almost constantly, and nearly always drank to excess. Murphy's face had put on a few more wrinkles and he seemed to be a little more nervous than Pete remembered, but other than that there were no outward signs of change. Murphy still looked hard, muscular, and ready, even anxious, for a good scrap.

The corridor was glaringly white except for the floor, which was gray. Overhead, two parallel lines of naked blue-white flourescent lights stretched away into the distance until they merged and formed a single column, then disappeared.

Twenty feet from the elevator was a guard station behind bullet-proof glass. Three uniformed guards, all with holstered, chromed military-style .45s and two with 30-caliber machine guns stared at Pete and Murphy through the glass. The guards were relaxed, but vigilant. The guard without a machine gun, a slightly older man, who was identified as a garrison commander only by a tiny gold fleur-de-lis on his right lapel, stepped out from behind the glass, followed closely by the others. He carried a black electronic clipboard in one hand and a light-pen connected to the clipboard by a coiled optical fiber in the other.

The commander glanced at Pete and Murphy, made a quick

notation on the clipboard's glass screen, and nodded. "Operatives Murphy and Shafer," he said. His voice was pleasant enough, but crisp, military, obviously accustomed to holding familiarity at arm's length.

"That's us," Murphy said, automatically presenting his right hand, palm up. The commander ran the light pen over Murphy's fingertips. The instrument would, in a matter of microseconds, read Murphy's fingerprints, blood type, and body chemistry, transmit the data to a giant Cray mainframe computer buried somewhere deep inside the complex, and receive a positive identification. Although not routine, the computer system could also instantly analyze the subject's body chemistry, detect drug or alcohol use, and provide a polygraph readout.

A message flashed across the clipboard's tiny screen. The commander nodded. "Welcome to INTEL-five HQ, Mr. Murphy. You are to proceed to Command Central. Your other two team members are expecting you there."

Murphy stepped aside and Pete held up his right palm as Murphy had done. On the first try the screen flashed a numerical code that quietly informed the commander that something might be amiss. The other two guards, also noting the code, tensed slightly and raised their machine guns almost imperceptibly in Pete's direction.

By touching a button on the side of the clipboard, the commander calmly ordered the computer to re-enter the data. For a few tense seconds he poised his right index finger over another button that would seal off the section of corridor and summon assistance. His precaution proved unnecessary. He glanced up and smiled slightly. "Sorry, sir. Your file was still in our inactive banks and had to be updated before it would clear. You're to proceed to Command Central with Mr. Murphy."

"Quite all right," Pete said. He scrambled to catch up with Murphy, who had strode briskly away the second he knew Pete had cleared security. The entire procedure, including a complete update of Pete's files, had taken less than thirty seconds, one third the time it would have taken five years earlier. In another minute the two men turned into a doorway marked COMMAND CENTRAL in small black stenciled letters.

Pete stopped two steps inside the door to let his eyes adjust from the brilliant white light of the corridor to the subdued gloom of the cavernous room they had just entered. The room was large with a high ceiling. Backlit, glowing multi-colored maps and charts covered the walls from floor to ceiling. Rows of digital clocks gave the time, down to the second, for various zones around the world. Colored television screens displayed columns of data.

A large, horseshoe-shaped bank of computer screens occupied most of the room's center. About a dozen people, men and women, sat in front of the amber-lighted computer screens, intent on flickering displays. At least half the operators wore uniforms similar to those worn by the guards. Five years ago, Pete remembered, INTEL-5 had been strictly a civilian operation and only guards and janitors wore uniforms of any sort.

Two young people, a man and a woman standing at the far end of the room, looked up from a map as Pete and Murphy entered. The two young operatives walked toward them. Neither looked any older than Pete's daughter in Orlando. In fact, Pete noticed somewhat self-consciously, he and Murphy stood out in stark contrast to the youth of everyone else in the room. Even those people Pete identified by either their manner or insignia as filling supervisory positions were at least a decade his junior.

The woman approaching them, although as young as any of the others, stood out in her own way. To begin with she was six feet tall if she was an inch and had a stately air about her, as if she were a person sure of herself and her abilities. Even in the dim light of the Command Center, Pete could see she was beautiful. By her carriage and movements, it was also quite obvious that she was the senior in rank of the two young operatives. She thrust out her hand, first to Murphy, then to Pete. "Good afternoon, Mr. Murphy, Mr. Shafer," she said in a businesslike, but pleasantly feminine voice. "I'm Sheena Lawrence and this is Larry Jones. We're your team."

Murphy quickly shook hands, first with Lawrence, then with Jones. Pete noticed Murphy's slight discomfort at Sheena's tone and manner. When it was offered to him, Pete took Lawrence's hand. Her handshake was firm and confident. Yet, despite her position as an INTEL-5 operative, Pete could not help but imagine that the slim, muscular brunette would look more in place turning heads on a country club tennis court than she did in the Command Center of the most secret organization in the Free

World. Her green eyes were laced with gold flecks that flickered when they caught the light. Pete suspected, no, he *knew*, that there was bound to be much more to this beautiful woman than met the eye, pleasant enough though it was. He hoped that what he couldn't see was of the same caliber as what he could. He was sure it was. Pete also anticipated Murphy's reaction to such an obviously capable female operative, given Murphy's generally traditional opinion of women agents and their uses.

"Please call me Pete," he said. "I've never been much for formalities." At least, he thought, she wasn't wearing a uniform like many of the other young people in the room. Both she and Jones were dressed in simple, casual clothes—slacks and conservative pullover sweaters.

Sheena Lawrence smiled. She had perfectly even white teeth. "Sheena," she said.

The rest of the introductions quickly out of the way, Murphy strode to one of the illuminated maps and pointed to a depiction of the northern Pacific, then tapped the coastline of Russia with a chromed telescoping wand. He moved the pointer to Alaska and traced a broken red line that began in Anchorage. It swept in a long curve past the Aleutians, then continued southward, staying a few inches off the coast of the Kamchatka Peninsula, until it ended abruptly just before it reached the first of the Kuril Islands, about two-thirds of the way from Anchorage to the northern tip of Hokkaido Island, Japan.

"Briefly, here is what we know for sure," he said. "Trans-Pacifica Airlines Flight Eighteen departed Anchorage at approximately seventeen minutes after midnight, their local time, this morning. In addition to two of our people, there were two-hundred forty-four passengers and crew aboard. The last civilian contact occurred about two hours later.

"NORAD kept Flight Eighteen on their radar for another hour after that, then lost radar contact because of interference from aurorean activity, which has been especially heavy for the past few days. Frankly, conditions couldn't have been worse. One of our clandestine listening posts on the Kurils picked up and relayed a few garbled bits of an FM transmission from the plane, which said nothing about trouble. That's all we know. The Japanese may have heard something with their equipment on Hokkaido, but if they did, they're keeping tightlipped about it."

"Excuse me," said Sheena, "but then we aren't even completely sure that the airplane was actually destroyed?"

Murphy turned from the map and shook his head. "No, we aren't, and that's the problem. We had a couple of our own vessels, disguised as Japanese fishing boats, offshore to direct the drop, but right before Flight Eighteen arrived the skies suddenly got busier than hell for no other apparent reason. Our people had to shut down their radios to keep from compromising themselves.

"It appears Flight Eighteen hit wall-to-wall MiGs. They may have been tipped Eighteen was hot, but we can't prove it. The Russians don't generally go shooting in the dark. It could have been nothing but a trigger-happy Air Defense commander out to save his own ass—couldn't say I'd blame him—but I doubt it." Murphy caught his breath, then continued. "If the goddamned Russians get their hands on that airplane, it would be a major breach of security, not only for the United States but, worse yet, for INTEL-five. Those jealous bastards over at the damned CIA would see to that."

"Which," interrupted Jones, "could tear hell out of INTEL-five funding." Jones was short and squarely built, much like Murphy. His hair was clipped close, military-style, and he had a small, thin mustache chopped off abruptly at the corners of his mouth.

"Yeah," Murphy grunted, disdainful of the younger man's dry attempt at humor. "That's part of it."

Jones smiled coldly at Murphy. "And they dusted you off to help us find Flight Eighteen. Is that it?"

Pete's heart sped up. Although he realized Jones was probably only joking, he'd have to get the young man aside and fill him in on Murphy's temper. Murphy was one hell of an operative and he expected no less from the young people who worked under him— no dissension, no deviation—just results. And that is what he got.

Murphy breathed out heavily. "Our mission, Mr. Jones," he paused, "is to destroy the airplane—if there's anything left of it— and its contents." Murphy went silent for several seconds as he and Jones stared at each other. Finally he broke Jones's stare and turned to Pete and Sheena. "Lawrence will brief you on our travel plans."

Murphy pulled out a Camel and lit it as Sheena quickly began. She was visibly glad for a break in the too obvious tension. She stepped to a large Mercator projection of the United States and most of the northern Pacific. Taking Murphy's pointer, she tapped a large red dot located at Washington, D.C. "We have a business jet and crew at Washington National waiting for us," she said. "They will transport us to our facilities near Wrangell, Alaska. The jet has auxiliary fuselage tanks and tip tanks so our flight will be non-stop direct, approximately six hours.

"At Wrangell we will pick up our insert equipment and board another small civilian-styled jet, a Lear twenty-five, that has been extensively modified for STEALTH operations and high altitude drops, including an underbelly jump-door. We refuel on Shemya Island, then fly directly to where Flight Eighteen was last estimated to be. We will, of course, fly in under Soviet Air Defense radar, aided by multi-image generators, radar jamming devices, and other little STEALTH goodies aboard the Lear.

"Then, while the crew gives the Soviets an interesting diversion or two, we will parachute in, locate our monitor, dive to it if necessary, blow it up, make contact with a Japanese squid fishing boat named the Geisha Lady, and beat it to Hokkaido. With any kind of luck at all, we'll be sipping saki in Tokyo by New Year's Eve."

Sheena smiled and caught her breath, aware that all of them knew the mission was much more involved and dangerous than she had so lightly indicated. Each would be supplied with a complete package of concise, but highly accurate, intelligence data and maps to study on the way to Alaska. "Any questions?" she asked.

"Thank you, Lawrence," Murphy said. "Now, as you can see, all of you, time is of the essence. There's food and your personal gear aboard the jet. If we hustle, we can hit Wrangell by oh-five-hundred local, which leaves us time to switch airplanes and be in the Kurils before daylight. Sleep on the way to Alaska if you think you're going to need it. You may not get another chance."

Without waiting for comments Murphy led the way out of Command Central. Pete, Sheena, and Jones were caught off-guard by his sudden departure and had to hurry to keep him in sight. Pete shook his head to himself. He had been right. Still the same old Murphy. Still the same old warhorse raring for a fight.

As they strode down the corridor, Sheena fell in beside Pete. He looked over at her jogging along beside him, easily matching her stride to his. He suddenly became aware that he was breathing rapidly. "I'm not in the shape I once was," he apologized.

"Neither am I," Sheena laughed. She nodded toward Murphy's back. "He always run like that?"

Pete glanced over at the beautiful young woman hurrying along beside him. If she wasn't in shape now, he didn't think he could have stood seeing her when she was. He smiled. There was something about being on a mission again, about being with young, enthusiastic people that he liked. "No," he said. "You haven't seen anything yet. Wait'll you see ol' Murph get scared or mad and *then* watch him go. That's—how do the kids say it?—goddamned awesome!"

# 3

Trans-Pacifica Airlines officials have announced that the missing jumbo jet with 246 passengers and crew aboard, TPA Flight 18, is reported to have landed at a Soviet airfield on the Kamchatka Penninsula, ending fears that the jet had crashed at sea.

The details are not yet clear, but it appears that the airliner strayed into Soviet territory and was forced to land. There is no report of any injuries to either passengers or crew.

The news was greeted with a mixture of jubilation and relief by the relatives and friends of passengers aboard the flight—some of whom had been waiting all night for word of their loved ones.

IND-TV News Bulletin
December 25, 1993

The black Cadillac limousine hurrying along Pennsylvania Avenue had the street almost entirely to itself. Its glistening metal surface contrasted starkly with the dull gray and mottled browns of the capital's deserted streets. Even yesterday's papers, old news that nobody cared about anymore, lay in sodden masses in the gutters.

The car's windshield wipers slapped back and forth slowly, beating out a melancholy rhythm, which only added to the omnipresent gloom that enveloped the city in cold, dripping flannel.

A few soggy and forlorn-looking Christmas decorations, shop-worn from having hung in place since before Thanksgiving, dangled limply from the poles of still-burning streetlights. At intervals along the famous avenue rain-darkened billboards pictured idealized Christmas scenes, both urging the consumption of cheap Scotch and the keeping of Christ in Christmas.

Inside the tiny womb of warmth and dryness afforded by the limousine, the chauffeur raised his face and glanced in the rearview mirror. His passenger was a large, elderly woman in a dark woolen overcoat with a black hat pulled low over her eyes. She had an open briefcase on her lap and several maps spread out beside her on the seat. She studied the maps intently. Her rounded, wrinkled face had a worried look.

She looked up and frowned when she noticed the chauffeur watching her in the mirror, her hands automatically reaching out to shield the maps from view. The chauffeur quickly dropped his eyes to the street, wondering what the hell was so important that he had been dragged away in the middle of his Christmas dinner.

The car turned down a side street when it neared the Capitol, then circled a dozen or so crumbling burned-out tenement blocks—stark relics still remaining from the sixties' race riots. The streets and sidewalks were nearly covered by piles of trash, blackened snow, and dead weeds. No amount of federal subsidies or incentives, even thirty years later, had yet convinced white investors to sink their money into the overwhelmingly black city surrounding the nation's capitol.

As it neared the entrance to an underground parking garage the Cadillac turned off the street and slowed slightly. A bored and sleepy-looking gate guard, dressed in a plain blue police-style uniform, sitting alone in a glass-enclosed shelter, lifted his head as the limousine approached. He glanced at the license plate that identified the vehicle's occupant as a United States senator and waved it past without expression.

A wide steel door slid open in the side of the building and the limousine disappeared. The door closed silently behind it. The guard picked up the telephone receiver at his elbow and dialed a short series of numbers. He listened for a few seconds, then spoke quietly into the receiver. "The senator has just arrived," he said.

Any of the five people seated around the shiny walnut table would have been recognizable to a regular reader of any major daily newspaper in the country, although two of them held secret posts. There was the senator, of course, white-haired, dignified, and generally considered the spokesperson of the rich eastern-liberal establishment, although her popular support transcended many social and economic divisions, more because of her skillful rhetoric than anything she had ever actually done.

Seated on the senator's immediate left and right were the actual heads of the Central Intelligence Agency and the Federal Bureau of Investigation—although other, lower-ranking men filled the slots publicly.

The fourth person, wearing his thick, metal-framed trademark glasses halfway down his large, almost comical, nose, was a famous international diplomat and arms negotiator. He held no publicly recognized government position, but he was known as a man with world-class political power.

The fifth, chairperson of the group, also claimed no elected or appointed office. He was usually identified by the press, of which he was once a part but now renounced it as detrimental to government, as "very close to the White House."

Together the five made up the governing board of the super-secret, all-encompassing, all-powerful spy and espionage organization known simply—to those who knew of it at all—as INTEL-5.

Each of the five watched the other four cautiously, making only the barest, most superficial conversation about plans for Christmas and the holidays. The CIA representative was muttering something to the presidential advisor about his displeasure that he was going to be unable to join his family who were spending the holidays skiing in Wyoming. The presidential advisor was pointedly ignoring him. When all were seated, the presidential advisor cleared his throat very quietly for attention. When he spoke, his accent hinted vaguely at his southern childhood although he had not lived farther south than Georgetown in over a quarter of a century.

"I believe you all realize why we are here," he said. The others nodded, as one, and the advisor continued.

"This is the third time that our people have been unsuccessful in replacing the monitor at Petropavlovsk. As you recall, on the first try, in late November, we merely had to abort the mission when it was intercepted well before it got into the drop zone. The first failure could have been, and probably was, merely blind luck on the Soviet's part.

"On our second attempt, four days later, the Russians also scrambled their interceptors before we could get within range, and our people had to retreat to international waters. This time, though, I began to suspect the Soviets were getting inside information.

"Just to see if my suspicions were correct, I very quietly arranged, on my own, for two genuinely innocent airliners to stray off course. Neither was intercepted until it was well past Petropavlovsk into the Sea of Okhotsk. Either one could have easily made the drop, but somehow the Russians knew the airplanes were flying clean."

"I certainly don't approve of your unilateral action," said the negotiator, "but if your theory is true, they must have known, somehow, about the cargo on Flight Eighteen."

"Just my point," replied the presidential advisor. "There's somebody in INTEL-5, itself, tipping them off. We've kept knowledge of this project down to the fewest possible people. The damned frustrating thing is that it could still be any one of a hundred individuals all the way from the top down." He looked around the table, deliberately staring at each of the other four. All met his gaze squarely. "Even one of us."

His statement drew only silence.

The presidential advisor shuffled a few papers he had spread in front of him, then continued speaking.

"All indications are that the Soviets were expecting Flight Eighteen and knew exactly what it was carrying or they wouldn't have risked an international incident like this thing is likely to be. They've been having a lot of luck in the Third World, lately, portraying themselves as the peace lovers and us as warmongers."

He paused, then continued. "Our picture is still pretty sketchy, but it looks like the Russians allowed Flight Eighteen to get within a few minutes of the drop zone before they scrambled their fighters. Using near-total radio silence, I might add. It looks very much like they were actually letting their defenses appear to drop, like they were luring the airplane into a carefully set trap."

The senator cleared her throat. "Now, this monitor on the airliner, do you think the Russians have it? Couldn't the crew have destroyed it if they knew they were about to be forced down?"

"No," said the advisor. "Destroying the monitor properly, in the air, would have taken at least three or four minutes. It appears the crew didn't have near that much warning. We think the Russians knew they had to hit the airplane so quickly and decisively that there would not be time for the monitor to be deliberately destroyed. The cockpit crew probably never knew what hit them. Neither did the other two-hundred forty-three people on board, thank God. They all probably died instantly from the blast or nearly so from rapid depressurization."

"At least that's a relief," sighed the senator.

"Damned little," said the negotiator.

The advisor ignored his remark, quickly continuing. "If the goddamned Russians retrieved the monitor, they would probably have let it be known by now.

"They're already taking a hell of a beating, world-opinion-wise for shooting down an unarmed airliner with all those innocent people on board. Right now, of course, they're claiming total ignorance of the whole affair, literally saying, 'What airliner?'"

"But they won't be taking half the beating we'll get, especially from our own damned press, if they produce that atomic monitor we were trying to drop on them," said the negotiator.

Everyone around the table heartily nodded their agreement. "Can we assume our people are doing all they can to see the Russians don't find it?" asked the representative of the CIA.

The advisor looked around the table nervously. "I admit we were almost caught with our pants down," he replied. "It somehow wasn't properly reported that our two best men on that area disappeared three days ago under what now seem very suspicious circumstances. If we had known, we would have postponed the mission. We suspect the foul-up in communications might have also been less than accidental."

A murmur swept around the table.

"We had a couple of young operatives who were being trained to assume north Pacific responsibilities, but we didn't feel they are ready to handle a mission of this magnitude by themselves, so we've pulled in a couple of old operatives, one retired, one semi-retired, to go along with them and run the operation."

The CIA representative snorted loudly. "Retired? Was that the best you could do?"

The advisor drummed his fingers on the table impatiently, staring straight ahead. "Under the circumstances, yes. These two guys are a couple of old-school spooks and damned good at it. They were our top field operatives when they left active service five years ago. The one who's totally retired was our leading expert on the north Pacific, especially the Kurils and the Kamchatka Peninsula. He knows the area better than any man alive. The other is a master planner par excellence. We've kept close tabs on both of them, as we do on all our people, and they're still up to it."

"But they must be in their fifties. Isn't that pushing it a little bit for a field operative?"

The advisor nodded and glared coldly at the CIA representative. "Fifty-one and fifty-three respectively, but either one of them could still kick the shit out of any ten of your boys over at the company."

The representative tensed, sliding forward slightly in his chair.

The advisor regarded him coolly.

The representative started to speak, but seemed to think better of it. He settled back down into his chair. "If you say so," he growled into his fist.

The negotiator spoke again, partly to lessen the tension he knew existed between the CIA and the White House. "Is our team in the area yet?"

The advisor shook his head. "The two older men are meeting

the rookies, then flying to Alaska this afternoon. From there they'll proceed to the Kuril Islands during the night."

The CIA representative grunted again. "I still don't like it," he said to no one in particular.

The presidential advisor pretended to ignore him. "I have to admit it's not the best possible arrangement," he conceded, "but it's the best we could put together in so short a time—which is, of course, of the essence. Believe me, I have authority from the highest levels of the White House on this."

The negotiator pushed his chair back from the table. "So, is there anything else you need from us?" he asked, looking at his expensive gold wrist watch. "I'm having guests over at two for dinner."

"No," said the advisor. "The President just wanted you all to be informed in case we have to make any further decisions. I'm sure I don't need to reiterate that he's damned upset about this whole thing. Right now, we don't know what might come out of it, but I'm sure that you agree with me, and the President, that it is imperative we reach that monitor before the Russians."

The meeting of INTEL-5 had taken less than half-an-hour from start to finish. As the five vehicles of the participants rolled out of the parking garage the guard noted each carefully, but did not raise his head from a comic book he appeared to be reading. As each car passed he compared its license number to a list taped inside the comic's cover.

The senator and the negotiator, each in chauffeur-driven Cadillacs emerged first, followed by the FBI liaison in a rusty, unmarked blue Mercury. About a minute behind them was the dark metallic-blue Mercedes 450 SEL of the presidential advisor and the small white BMW belonging to the CIA representative. The last two cars turned in opposite directions on Pennsylvania Avenue.

The Mercedes drove several blocks until it was well out of sight of the others, turned onto a narrow sidestreet, then stopped beside the curb. A few minutes later the white BMW came from the opposite direction down the same sidestreet. It stopped beside the Mercedes so that the drivers were next to each other, facing in different directions.

Each driver lowered his window a few inches. The two men

looked at each other and shook their heads, then the CIA representative spoke. "I sure as hell don't like this," he said. "The damned thing should have gone off. Suppose that team does find the wreckage of Flight Eighteen? If they're expecting to find a submarine monitor, they're in for one hell of a shock. Is there any way they can be called back without the rest of the board getting wise?"

The presidential advisor nodded. "Certainly, but we don't need to. Half that team is taking its orders from us—not INTEL-5—and they can deal with the other two when they've served their purpose.

"We can still make sure it looks like the Russians fire the first shot and our people in the Pentagon are ready on their end."

"How long you think it'll take?"

The advisor stroked his chin. "A week, maybe two, before they surrender."

The CIA representative chuckled. "The Japanese could have used a man like you at Pearl Harbor."

"You're not so dumb yourself. Getting your family out of Washington to Wyoming was a good idea."

The representative smiled. "That was about the safest place I could think of. We have bunkers there and Peg knows where they are."

The advisor started. "You told her?!"

"Of course not. I just let it slip 'accidentally' a few days ago that the CIA had fallout bunkers near where we'd be skiing. Peg's got sense enough to put two and two together when the missiles start flying."

# 4

TOKYO—Searchers have reported spotting an oil slick on the water just south of Petropavlovsk, the area where the Trans-Pacifica Airlines 747 is believed to have gone down. There are no reports of survivors.

Apparently, earlier reports that the airliner had landed safely at a Russian airfield on the Kamchatka Peninsula were unfounded.

Amid growing speculation that the jumbo jet with 246 people aboard may have been shot down by the Soviets, the President of the United States has summoned his top security advisors to the Camp David White House. They are expected to meet this afternoon.

There has not yet been any reaction at all from Moscow.

*The Washington Chronicle*
December 25, 1993

**M**urphy stopped the ascending elevator at the two-hundred-fifty-foot level, then led Pete, Sheena, and Jones into a corridor much like the one they had just left.

The four operatives walked briskly to an unmanned stainless steel, glass-enclosed, bullet-shaped shuttle train consisting of two connected cars, which sat on a small spur track. As they approached the doors, triggered by an electronic sensor, automatically opened for them. Murphy punched in a code that gave the train's computer their desired destination, and they were whisked silently, on an air-cushioned track, into a main artery that led through eighteen miles of a lighted tunnel cut through solid rock. They were the only passengers.

The tunnel ran almost arrow-straight from one side of Washington, D.C., to the other. In addition to being a passageway for the train the tunnel also served as a secure route for electrical conduits and thick bundles of fiber optic cables that allowed speed-of-light voice and data communication between units of the sprawling underground complex. And the tunnels were designed to act as a blast shelter and route of escape for selected federal officials in case of an imminent nuclear strike.

Only once during their passage beneath Washington did they pass another train. Their passing was little more than a brief flash of light and Pete realized he could not see into the other train, nor could the passengers inside it see him. One-way glass was just another little touch of security to keep INTEL-5's left hand ignorant of the right hand's movements.

The trains, of course, like all the INTEL-5 complex, were subject to constant monitoring by a variety of methods, yet they were not foolproof. At one point Pete noticed that someone with a sense of humor, a maintenance person most likely, had used a can of black spray-paint to draw an arrow pointing straight up on the rock wall of the tunnel and had written, in large letters, POTOMAC RIVER—250 FEET.

The train automatically switched to a siding and stopped

smoothly at a small boarding platform. A small LED sign attached to the train's forward wall gave their position as directly beneath Washington National Airport. The car's door slid open and the four stepped onto the platform.

Two guards, uniformed much like the others Pete had seen, looked up from a video monitor as they approached. Pete knew the guards had been watching them via hidden cameras. It was next to impossible to go anywhere in the complex without being constantly monitored, although a few people, like the arrow-painter, enjoyed making a game of it.

"Good afternoon," said one of the guards, snapping to attention. "Your aircraft is ready directly above us. You are familiar with the ground ID procedure."

"Thanks." Murphy gave the guard a quick salute as they stepped into the open door of an elevator. The car shot upward.

Within seconds they stepped out into what appeared to be a walnut paneled executive meeting room. When the elevator door closed behind them, there was no evidence that it had ever existed. Murphy crossed the room and unlocked its one door. It opened into a dining room for lower-level management employees of a major international airline. Most people would have been shocked to know that particular airline was involved in espionage, yet Pete knew that a large number of airlines, probably most, cooperated explicitly or implicitly with the government. The government's cooperation through subsidies and route assignments was, after all, necessary for their survival.

The team strode across the nearly deserted dining room and out into an aircraft maintenance hangar where they were met by a man dressed as an airline mechanic, although his clean fingernails were clearly not those of a mechanic. He quickly led them past a Boeing 707 that was being readied for repainting, then out of the hangar onto a concrete apron. A sleek white twin-engined business jet sat waiting with its engines running. It was unmarked except for FANCO CHARTERS written in small red letters across the vertical stabilizer. A couple of extra radio antennas were the only telltale signs that this was no ordinary business jet.

Pete followed the three others aboard the rapierlike airplane. He noticed that Sheena had to duck low as she climbed inside the jet's low doorway. Only five-nine himself, he had always been attracted to tall women.

Murphy checked the lock on the door, then signaled to the two pilots that the team was ready for takeoff. Almost immediately the plane began to roll. It taxied to the downwind end of the runway, bypassing a line of commercial jets and general aviation aircraft impatiently waiting in the freezing drizzle for their turn to take off. The weather had not improved. D.C. was as Pete had remembered it: rain, rain, and more rain. The jet paused only momentarily for a run-up check. Then there was a quick burst of power and it was airborne. As he felt the wheels clear the pavement, Pete peered outside through one of the jet's tiny round windows. He got only a quick glimpse of the capital's forlorn-looking monuments before they disappeared beneath the charcoal gray layer of rain clouds that now looked as if they might turn to snow at any second.

The jet rapidly climbed at a steep angle and in two minutes had broken through the clouds. As it leveled out at a cruising altitude of forty-two thousand feet, the clouds fell away below them until sunlight and distance turned the dark layer of clouds into a snow-white blanket of fluffy cotton stretched from horizon to horizon. The sky around and above the airplane was a deep, sapphirine blue and the brilliant winter sun made little dancing crystalline reflections in the curved Plexiglas of the jet's windows. The noise of the engines behind them, only the smooth rush of air across the airplane's glassy skin betrayed that they were traveling at nearly the speed of sound.

Pete's mind went to all the other airplanes he'd known throughout his life—the C-47s and B-24s, the Connies, the Hercs, and the Boos. They'd carried him millions of miles, to places most people had never even heard of, and, usually, they'd even brought him back. The other times he'd always made it back somehow or other. Coming back was seldom part of the assignment, just something you did for yourself when the work was over.

He turned his attention to the inside of the jet. The passenger cabin contained eight seats, arranged side-by-side with a narrow aisle down the middle. Murphy and Jones sat in the two forward-most seats while Pete and Sheena occupied the aft two.

Murphy swung his legs out into the narrow aisle and cleared his throat for attention. "I don't anticipate that we'll need a cover for this mission," he said, "but just in case we do, HQ has prepared us one."

He produced four thin manila envelopes and passed one to each of them, keeping the last for himself. "I suggest you read the material inside very carefully. In addition to mission particulars, you will find in your individual packets, passports and other identification papers, which prove conclusively that we are a scientific team studying the wintering habits of northern Pacific marine mammals." He laughed. "Of course, the Russians wouldn't buy this shit for a minute. It's mostly for domestic consumption should the need arise. If you have any questions after going over the material, I'll try to answer them. Okay?"

"Can we assume this stuff is verifiable?" asked Pete.

Murphy nodded. "Absolutely. Just for simplication, we're keeping our real names, but we've all been granted Ph.D.s in various forms of science from leading universities. The identities in your hands are backed up so completely that there are scientific papers actually on file in several major libraries across the country under your names, even though it's a holiday and this mission was launched less than six hours ago. There are even books by each of you in various libraries around the free world." Murphy chuckled.

Pete whistled. "That's pretty damned impressive," he said.

"The outfit's really expanded since we were active operatives, Pete. It's almost enough to make me wish I was young again and just starting out.

"Of course, there was a lot to be said for the old days, too. We've got young people now, been with the outfit for five, six years and still haven't been in the field. Just do all their work sitting in front of a goddamned computer."

Pete laughed. He knew how Murphy felt about computers. "I assume the computers can make us disappear as fast as they can make us appear?" he said.

"Uh-huh. In an hour or two it could be like we never existed at all. Really Orwellian nonpersons. No birth certificate, no service record, no addresses, no nothing. Not even an obit in the local paper, or a grave, or even a family or anybody that remembers us, if necessary."

Pete glanced over at Sheena, curious to see the effect of Murphy's words on her. Her face was expressionless until she noticed Pete looking at her. She understood his unspoken question and smiled slightly as a reply. Pete wondered why such a beautiful woman would be drawn to this dangerous and usually lonely line of work when, with her brains and body, she could obviously have anything she wanted. He felt a fatherly protectiveness for her, although he suspected she would strongly resent his feeling if he were to express it. Besides he had already assessed Sheena as a capable operative, perfectly willing and able to take care of herself.

Pete realized he had been staring at Sheena. He somewhat self-consciously turned his attention to the material inside his packet. He quickly read through the three single-spaced sheets that gave him his background cover information. He quickly memorized a few things such as his fictitious date of birth and education. Then he pocketed his identification papers, consisting of a passport, a Maryland driver's license, and several miscellaneous cards and papers. Across the narrow aisle from him Sheena did the same.

The next six hours passed slowly as Pete tried unsuccessfully to sleep in the too-narrow seat. Thoughts of his wife, his daughter and granddaughters, even Mary the basset hound ran through his mind, keeping him half awake.

He recalled hundreds of other holidays, Christmases, birthdays, anniversaries, that Velma had been forced to spend alone while he was out chasing around the globe on some mission or other—and for what? What had he ever proven? For what had he endangered his own life and the lives of his family? Was the world any better off for his sacrifices? Any freer? Not for the first time in his life, Pete doubted that it was.

He thought that INTEL-5 was a perfect example of what was happening to the whole country. While he and all the other operatives like him were out combating the foreign enemies of freedom all over the world, INTEL-5 was fast threatening to become just such an enemy itself as it grew and grew, cancerlike, gaining a stranglehold on the government, the economy, the military. Pete knew that what Murphy had meant as a joke, about nonpersons, was true. INTEL-5 had actually become Big Brother. It could create and destroy people almost totally at will, even to the point of eliminating families and friends from the face of the earth just to erase a single person or idea that it disagreed with. To title his book George Orwell had only reversed the year he wrote, 1948, to get *1984*. Then 1984 passed without the general public being fully aware of what was really happening in such organizations as the CIA, FBI, and INTEL-5, and Orwell's predictions were roundly criticized. But he hadn't missed his mark by much.

Pete glanced over at Sheena, already sleeping peacefully in her seat as if she were on a pleasure trip to Nassau rather than a clandestine insert into hostile and dangerous territory. Was she so innocent, he wondered, or already so hardened? And why? Or was she just the way everybody would be someday? She couldn't be more than twenty-five. And she was beautiful. Oh, God, was she beautiful.

It seemed to Pete that he had just managed to drift off into an uneasy sleep when he was abruptly jerked awake by the changing sound of the jet's engines as the pilots cut the power to begin descending. A short time later Pete felt the airplane's nose being raised and the slight drag of the first eight degrees of flaps. He looked at his watch. He had been asleep longer than he thought.

Outside the airplane's window the sky was already dark, glittering with a million cold pinpoints of starlight. Pete glanced toward the front of the dimly lighted cabin. The door into the cockpit was standing open. Murphy, or one of the others, must have been forward talking to the pilots. From his seat Pete could see the green glow of the instrument panel and the silhouettes of the pilots' shoulders as they started their let-down checklist. Across from Pete Sheena still slept, breathing smoothly and evenly. In the faint light of the cabin her breasts rose and fell in a gentle motion that would probably have sent a younger man than Pete into a fit of passion. Pete found his heart speeding up slightly as he watched her. He had never been the kind of operative that had a mistress in every backwater but there had been times . . . there had been times.

As the jet descended through the first clouds the glow of the cockpit instruments and a dim exit sign above the outside hatch kept the cabin from total darkness. There were interior lights, of course, but no one bothered turning them on. Outside his window Pete saw a faint green reflection against the clouds from the right wingtip's running light. Somewhere out there, he knew, hidden in the darkness, were mountains that soared thousands of feet above the airplane, embedded like deadly gray granite spikes. If they hit one of those, even at approach speed, it would be a death without suffering for all of them.

The pilots put in another notch of flaps and assumed a higher nose-up position to slow the jet still further as they entered the downwind leg of their approach pattern. The airplane banked steeply and Pete knew they had turned across the wind to line up for the final approach. Pete knew he would feel the landing gear any second now. There, the gear was coming down. From the cockpit the voice of approach control over the radio droned on slowly, confidently, giving path and glide slope information to the pilots. Out of habit Pete checked his seatbelt and tried to wake up for landing.

Suddenly the engines, which had been nearly silent as they descended, roared into life. Pete was pushed back into his seat as the airplane accelerated. The nose lifted sharply and a whirring noise outside the cabin told him the flaps were being retracted. Although the sudden change knotted his stomach, Pete told himself the pilots had only somehow miscalculated their approach and were going to have to go around the pattern and make another try.

In the front of the cabin the dark, unmistakable figure of Murphy moved toward the cockpit, leaning forward against the airplane's acceleration. Pete knew Murphy would be furious with the pilots for wasting his valuable time, although a missed approach, especially at night in Alaska, was not an unusual occurrence. Murphy could be an asshole.

Then Pete realized he had not felt the landing gear come up. He'd done enough flying himself, all in small, single-engine airplanes, to be sure that retracting the gear was an essential part of a go-around clean-up. His question was immediately answered when Murphy stomped away from the cockpit. Jones, who had been sleeping during most of the entire flight, suddenly snapped awake at the noise and leaned out into the aisle. "Goddamned gear's stuck halfway down," Murphy announced to no one in particular. "If it won't come unstuck, we'll have to crash this bitch and that's going to throw our whole schedule off." In spite of the potential seriousness of their situation, Pete appreciated Murphy's gift of understatement. When one crash-lands a Learjet, keeping to one's schedule is hardly the greatest concern. Murphy turned and stomped back to the cockpit.

Sheena had been awakened by Murphy's announcement, but

had only caught part of it. She leaned over and tugged at Pete's sleeve. "What'd he say?"

"Gear's stuck halfway down. Probably just cold hydraulic fluid. Must be seventy below out there. We're making another go-round so the pilots can try to recycle it."

"First go-round?" Sheena asked without much inflection.

At first her calmness amazed him, but he would have been surprised if she had been anything else but calm.

"Yes. Probably no big deal," he found himself saying. "Of course, if it won't move, it could be trouble. Coming in with gear halfway down is worse than no gear at all. If either side decides to collapse before the other, it'll send us cartwheeling, and at the speed of this soap box that could be bad news."

"What'll we do in case it doesn't respond?"

Pete wondered at his own jittery stomach as opposed to Sheena's calmness. After all he had survived at least four crashes and a couple of decidedly rough landings that would have counted as crashes in any other business. Maybe that was why he suddenly felt hot and flushed under his light shirt. There was a rule among operatives that everyone's number came up sooner or later. Parrish's had come up in East Berlin, Smith's in Africa, "Mad Dog" Charlie's in Moscow, all of them damned good men. Would his be next?

It was funny how, when he was an active operative, he'd never thought much about getting killed. Maybe it was thinking he'd made it through alive—that he'd beaten the system—that had given life meaning again. Maybe that was it.

To the fictional spy, the spy of cheap paperback thrillers, fear did not exist, but to the working operative it was an everyday occurrence, something that was as much a part of their lives as shaving or taking a crap. There were the fears of being exposed, of endangering fellow operatives and innocent family members, of falling, even the fear of losing one's job in agency cutbacks, but the fear of being killed very seldom entered into it at all. The real operative and the comic book spy had at least that much in common, but for different reasons. When real spies stopped being scared they were dead.

Trying to hide his concern about the airplane's condition, Pete answered Sheena's question about Lear crash procedures. He knew he sounded a little more flippant than he should. "Oh, strap in, pad ourselves if we can, pray if you got 'em. But you probably won't need to." He laughed nervously. "Hell, they got snowdrifts down there that'd stop a Mack truck. Of course, we may have to sit there till spring before they dig us out." Sheena laughed quietly, but Pete knew his attempt at humor had fallen flat.

The jet went into a high bank and had started a turn back to line up for another try at final approach when it abruptly began to shudder. Pete felt it start skidding through the sky sideways like a car out of control on glare ice. "My God!" he said, loud enough for everyone in the cabin to hear him, "We just blew an engine!"

Pete could feel the pilots fighting the controls to get the airplane leveled and coordinated. With one engine flaming out in the middle of a high bank, the jet could have lost all forward momentum and boomeranged across the sky, ending up in a dead-stick tailspin, if it didn't crash into a mountain first. The pilots, however, through some super-human effort, straightened it out and regained some degree of stablization. But, with the gear still stuck halfway down and one engine gone, the possibility of a messy crash landing had now become a very real possibility.

The weather on the ground would play a big part too. Pete had caught swatches of the pilot's conversation with approach control and the weather sure as hell wasn't the best. Even without additional problems, blowing snow, an eighteen-knot crosswind, and patches of glare ice on the runway hardly were conditions to land a speedwagon business jet in the dark. And, Pete remembered, jet engines have a nasty habit of flaming out in pairs.

Taking advantage of the airplane's momentary smooth glide, Pete unbuckled his seatbelt and felt his way in the darkness to an emergency-gear compartment above Sheena's seat where he knew life jackets would be stored. With one hand he tried the door. The goddamned thing was locked! Typical government move! He grasped the handle tightly and gave it a hard jerk. There was a crunching, ripping sound as the lock gave way.

Pulling out an armful of life jackets, Pete tossed them to Sheena. "Strap yourself in so tight it hurts," he ordered her, "and keep these in front of your face for padding." He tossed a couple to Jones and took one for himself before sitting back down and buckling in. Pete couldn't see Murphy in the darkness of the cabin, but there wasn't time to hunt him. Besides, Murphy knew what to do.

Pete had just clicked his seatbelt when he heard a muffled explosion outside and the airplane rocked sideways like it had been hit. As he had suspected it would, the other engine had just flamed out.

Instantly the cabin went deadly silent except for the rush of the wind over the airplane's skin as the pilots valiantly fought for control. Pete was nearly lifted out of his seat as the jet rolled on its side and started to fall.

From the cockpit came the harsh bleating of the stall warning buzzer as the pilots tried to fight the airplane level into a straight glide path. There was no way for Pete to tell how close they were to the mountains now or how close to the ground. The cockpit instruments would still operate on batteries and the APU, the auxilliary power unit, would still supply hydraulic pressure to run the controls—for a while, at least. With their rapid rate of descent Pete knew that a while would be long enough.

After an interminable fifteen seconds, Pete felt the nose leveling out as the jet reluctantly came back into some semblance of coordination, but they were still falling fast.

It is a common joke among their pilots, Pete remembered, that small business jets glide like a rock. And while the engines are running the joke is funny. Their short stubby wings are built for speed, not efficiency of glide. Under normal conditions that works well enough.

Normal conditions being when everyone involved wants the airplane to keep flying.

These, Pete knew, were not normal conditions.

Except for the sound of the rushing air outside, it was totally still inside the cabin. Even Murphy, who had been robustly cursing the pilots and the airplane, was silent. Everyone aboard was listening for the flaps to slow the airplane for landing, but there was no sound except for the repeated clicking of the flaps control switch in the cockpit. The explosion of the second engine had ruptured the hydraulic lines, causing a complete loss of fluid. The entire system was gone.

Pete heard the co-pilot quietly talking to ground control on the radio. He was calmly asking for a crash truck and ambulances to stand by and informing the ground that there were six souls on board. The co-pilot's use of the word *souls*, proper language for an emergency report, morbidly underlined their desperate situation.

Pete had often heard flying described as thousands of hours of boredom, punctuated by seconds of stark terror. The hours were over.

It was going to be a dead-stick, no-flaps, crosswind landing with gear that would probably collapse the second it had weight on it. And the field, at fifty-eight hundred feet, was just barely long enough for a small jet under the best of conditions. Any one of the three mechanical elements, taken without the crosswind, darkness, and ice, would have been cause for major alarm. There would not even be time enough to foam the runway for fire control.

From his seat Pete saw the flashing strobes of the runway rushing at them. He sucked his lap belt down as tight as it would go and buried his face between his knees, holding the life preserver over his head.

It seemed like he kept the crash position for hours, but in reality it was only a few seconds until he felt the jolt of the wheels slamming into the concrete strip at nearly two hundred knots.

The hard frozen tires screamed as if in agony as they hit the ground, sliding forward in clouds of smoke, before the frozen wheel bearings broke loose allowing the wheels to roll.

Pete felt the slight jerking as the pilot tested the brakes, tapping them, daring not use them until the airplane slowed more. Pete could only guess how much runway would be left. Even if they had touched down on the exact end of the runway, which was unlikely, at this speed it wouldn't last long.

He tried to remember what was at the other end of the field. Trees, he thought. Nothing but snowdrifts, he hoped.

Pete's thoughts were cut short when the left side of the airplane abruptly dipped as half the landing gear collapsed beneath it. The auxillary fuel tank on the left wingtip caught the concrete in a shower of sparks. It broke away and spun off to one side, bursting into flames—ignited by the sparks thrown up as the aluminum ground against the concrete runway. The airplane spun around and across the runway like a toy top before the flames from the tip-tank could spread to the main fuselage. The airplane rocked and threatened to overturn but the right gear also broke off before the plane could flip and start flopping end over end, which would have been sure death for all of them.

The airplane, now sliding completely on its belly at just over a hundred knots, skidded off the side of the cleared airstrip and into a hard-packed, ten-foot high wall of snow and ice thrown up by the snow plows.

As the airplane crashed into the snowbank both wings and the tail section sheared off. The fuselage rolled over twice before snapping in half just as it came to a stop, resting on its left side, nearly buried in six feet of soft, powdery snow.

Pete lay stunned. He did not know for how long. It was finally the penetrating kerosene smell of jet fuel that snapped him awake.

He lay on his side, still strapped in the seat and clutching the life preserver. He held onto his position for several seconds, not sure if the airplane had stopped rolling completely or not.

Below him in the pitch-blackness he heard Sheena softly groaning.

For the first time Pete noticed that his clothes and hands were soaked with jet fuel from the ruptured tanks. "Don't anybody light a match," he whispered. "Please, God, don't let anybody light a match!"

Through the ragged two-foot crack between the halves of the fuselage, Pete saw the first flashing red lights of the approaching crash vehicles, still about a half-mile away, and heard the wail of approaching sirens. In the flickering light he saw Sheena hanging by her seatbelt, nearly unconscious and squirming around helplessly, trying to escape. Her head had apparently hit the seat in front of her.

Jones hung limply in his seat and Pete could see a piece of flying metal had cleanly taken off the top half of his skull. Obviously he had tried to sit up during the crash, paying the ultimate price for his failure to assume crash position. Pete couldn't help thinking the whole scene, illuminated as it was by the flickering red lights, had a surrealistic air to it like a French art film his daughter had dragged him to once. The pilots or Murphy were nowhere to be seen.

Slowly Pete pulled the release on his seatbelt and let himself fall free, feeling his way to Sheena's unconscious body below him. She was also soaked in jet fuel, as was the entire airplane. Why it hadn't exploded instantly was almost beyond his comprehension.

Pete managed to free Sheena from her seatbelt, then holding

her beneath him in a sort of fireman's carry, crawled toward the crack in what had been the airplane's ceiling.

The biting cold of the night air hit Pete in the face like a stunning hammer as he dragged Sheena out of the fuselage into the snow.

His left hand came down on a piece of jagged aluminium, so cold that it seared his exposed flesh like red-hot metal. He instinctively jerked his hand away, leaving a bloody fragment of skin and flesh sticking to the metal. A lightning bolt of pain shot up his arm from the torn skin. He cursed, but at the same time the shock of cold and pain cleared his head and snapped him to his senses.

He stumbled to his feet, still carrying Sheena pressed close to his chest, and ran, stumbling repeatedly, away from the airplane. He staggered back along the path of packed snow the jet had made as it skidded off the runway. He was going downwind from the plane, not the best way to go should it explode, but it was the only route possible. The smell of jet fuel was overpowering.

About a hundred yards from the twisted and broken fuselage he fell to his knees exhausted, lowering Sheena's body to the snow beside him. For the first time, he realized neither of them was wearing a parka. In the sub-zero Alaskan air they could both die of exposure in minutes. But he had no time to think about it. There was a flash and then a roar, as the entire fuel-soaked fuselage exploded into flames behind him, ignited by some spark, or piece of hot metal. The concussion of the explosion knocked Pete facedown and rolled him sideways as though he weighed nothing at all. As he rolled, he threw up his arms to protect his face.

There was a loud groan, close beside him, and Pete wheeled to see fire quickly spreading on Sheena's fuel-saturated clothing.

Without thinking that he was also soaked in fuel, Pete lunged forward, throwing himself on Sheena to extinguish the fire. Instantly they were both engulfed in roaring orange flames. Holding Sheena tight against him, Pete rolled over and over in the snow until the fire was gone and only the sizzling of their still-hot clothes competed with the distant roar of the burning airplane and the sirens' wails.

Sheena snapped awake. "What's burning?" she demanded.

Then she saw the airplane and her own smoking clothing. She sank back to the snow, breathing heavily.

Only the sound of shouting, somewhere in the distance, kept Pete from sinking down beside Sheena as the flames roared overhead. He groggily forced himself to his feet and ran unsteadily, stooping, tripping, toward the sound. When he rounded a pile of snow thrown up by the sliding airplane, he saw Murphy and the two pilots.

Lying on the snow in a pool of steaming blood, his face and part of his forehead torn completely away by crashing into the instrument panel, was the pilot. Kneeling close beside the pilot's body was the co-pilot, his orange flight suit tattered and covered with blood, his left leg sticking out at an odd angle that showed it was badly broken.

His face was a horribly twisted mask of pain, the effect heightened by the yellow light of the roaring fire. He was desperately clinging to one of Murphy's legs, holding him back, ignoring Murphy's loud cursing and efforts to disentangle himself by kicking the co-pilot. "You can't go back in there!" the co-pilot was shouting. "It's too late!"

Murphy had lost his jacket in the crash. There was an ugly gash across his right cheek and his face and hands were covered with a mixture of blood and soot. "Let me go, you son-of-a-bitch! Let me go, goddamn you!"

Murphy's eyes glared yellow and hard like those of a cornered wolf. The fire of the blazing airplane made his face look even more demonic. He was starting to reach for the automatic pistol he wore in a holster attached to his belt.

Pete lunged forward and grabbed Murphy's wrist, preventing him from removing the pistol from its holster.

"Damn you!" yelled Murphy as Pete clamped down hard on his wrist, forcing him to drop the pistol into the snow. "You'll pay for this!" Then a flash of recognition swept Murphy's face. "Pete!" he shouted. "Pete, you made it out!"

Then Murphy wheeled around. "We've got to go back in, Pete!" he cried out. "Jones and the girl are still in there!"

Pete tightened his grip on Murphy's arm, holding him back. "I got the girl. Jones tried to sit up. He's dead."

Pete and Murphy stared at each other for a long while, Murphy still trembling with frustration. A look of understanding passed between the two men and Murphy relaxed. Pete shook his head sadly. "You did all you could, Murph."

Neither man said anything more. They just looked at each other for several seconds. Only the approach of the rescue vehicles rumbling toward the crash site and the shouts of medics and firemen interrupted them.

Pete and Murphy allowed themselves to be led away from the crash site by the medics. Murphy was placed aboard a tracked snow vehicle while Pete, the co-pilot, and Sheena were loaded into a four-wheel-drive ambulance.

As the ambulance pulled away, Pete could see the pilot's body being covered with a tarp and rolled onto a stretcher. Beside Pete the co-pilot, strapped to another stretcher, sobbed quietly for his fellow aviator. Firemen swarmed by them with hoses and foam, shielding their faces against the heat of the blazing airplane.

Pete knew that Murphy, had he not been held back by the co-pilot, really would have run into the blazing wreckage in a desperate, hopeless effort to rescue his other team members, including himself. It was a damned strange feeling to know another person had just been willing to die for you. Not that, for either Pete or Murphy, it would be the first time they had risked their lives for each other. And Murphy would have probably slugged anyone who tried to thank him, even Pete—especially Pete. The goddamned man was like that. His own safety was the very least of his concerns. Murphy wasn't usually easy to like, but he was damned impossible not to respect.

As the ambulance picked up speed, siren wailing, Pete and Sheena braced against each other and an inside wall.

"What the hell got into him?" gasped the co-pilot hoarsely between grimaces of pain as a medic started putting his leg into a temporary splint. "He was really going to shoot me just because I was trying to keep him from killing himself. He dragged me and Frank out—one of us under each arm for Christ sake—then he started back in when the fuel exploded. He saved my life by dragging me out of that airplane, but I really think he was going to shoot me if I didn't let go. You may have saved my life too."

Pete reached out and patted the young co-pilot's shoulder. "Then we're even," he said. "You guys did some damned fine flying tonight."

Pete steadied himself as the ambulance bounced across the

broken concrete of a cross taxiway. With his uninjured hand he held onto Sheena. She still appeared a little confused from her experience. A large bruise had appeared on her forehead where it had hit the seatback.

"No," said Pete, shaking his head slowly while hundreds of memories flashed through his mind. "He wouldn't have shot you. I've known Murphy too long. He's a damned crazy bastard sometimes but he wouldn't risk the life of a team member without a damned good reason."

Suddenly Pete laughed out loud, causing the medic who was working on the co-pilot's wounds to turn and look at him in alarm. "More like him to feed you the pistol. I'd trust Murph with my life any time, and have, but I'd be damned reluctant to get in his way when he sets his mind to something."

"It's good he's on our side," muttered the confused co-pilot as a shot of morphine he had just been given rapidly started to take effect.

"He is," said Pete, "and that's a damned good thing. If he were on the other side, we'd probably all be speaking Russian by now."

Sheena buried her face in her hands.

# 5

Early yesterday morning a Soviet fighter shot down a Trans-Pacifica Airlines jumbo jet with 246 people aboard, the U.S. State Department has announced.

An angry Secretary of State demanded a Soviet explanation of why the unarmed jetliner was attacked after it accidentally strayed into Soviet territory.

The incident has produced a furious reaction in the United States and around the world. The Secretary of State said the official reaction of the United States was one of "revulsion."

"We can see no excuse whatsoever for this appalling act," he said.

At least fifty Americans were believed to have been aboard the airplane, many of them Americans of Japanese descent, going to visit relatives in Japan during the Christmas holidays.

*AM-American Newshour*
December 26, 1993

**W**hen Pete awoke, for a few seconds he wondered where he was then the events of the previous day and night came rushing back to him. The crash, the deaths of the pilot and Jones, the near altercation between himself and Murphy, all seemed like a half-remembered nightmare, but he knew it had been all too real.

He glanced around the room. It was spartan and motellike, furnished with only a single bed, a nightstand and lamp, an old plastic-cased black and white television set, and two plain wooden chairs. A two-week-old copy of *Time* lay open, facedown, on one of the chairs.

After the team left the blazing wreckage of the airplane, they were taken to the secret underground complex a few miles from the runway where they had nearly died. The complex was one of several that INTEL-5 used to monitor Soviet communications. It was also a staging area and jumping-off point for operatives penetrating Russia's eastern frontier.

Pete, Sheena, and Murphy were physically examined and treated by the complex's small medical crew. Other than a few stitches in Murphy's cheek and a bandage for Pete's hand wounded from the piece of cold metal, all three seemed to have survived the crash, discounting bruises and scrapes, in better shape than they had any reason to hope for. Murphy had escaped with only the cut on his cheek, although he had ridden the jet down braced between the pilots' seats. Murphy had always lived a charmed life. In the nearly twenty years that Pete had known him well, Murphy had never been badly injured, although he was always in the thick of the action, be it a midnight firefight on the wrong side of the Berlin wall or adventures of an entirely different sort in the whorehouses of Prague.

The co-pilot's left leg, as Pete suspected, was broken in several places. Jones was incinerated with the fuselage. The pilot bled to death within minutes, despite being dragged outside by Murphy's super-human effort. Most of his face was sheared off and nothing could have saved him.

— **57** —

Already the mission had cost the team two lives, not counting all the people lost aboard the airliner. Pete wondered how many more would be sacrificed before it ended; how many more innocent men, women, and children would be killed in the name of nationalism where their individual lives meant no more to world leaders than plastic pawns on a chessboard. What Pete knew—and the public did not—was how much force is used every day between the super-powers and how close the chance of global holocaust is. Even the worst doomsayers of the antiwar movements have no idea how near to nuclear war we are. The power of thousands of megatons of nuclear destruction mere millimeters beneath the shaky fingers of frail, bitter old men was something Pete had to forcibly not contemplate.

Pete knew the crash of the small jet had been no accident. What he didn't know was who or what it was that had somehow got to the jet in the few hours from the inception of the mission until the team departed for Alaska. It had been sabotage, no doubt about it.

He flipped on the bedside lamp and blinked as its dim yellow bulb shone down in his face the way the sun shines through a desert sandstorm. He instinctively threw up his hands and closed his eyes to protect them from the blowing sand and blistering heat.

When he opened his eyes again, through the tiny blistered slits he saw Murphy standing over him. Murphy's face was red and blistered from nearly a week's trekking across the Iranian desert with no shelter from the sun. Their water had run out two days before. Murphy's lips were swollen twice their normal size, and blood was oozing slowly from where they had cracked.

"Get up, goddamn you!" Murphy was shouting. "Get up!" When Murphy got no response from Pete but a blank stare, he tried to kick him in the thigh to arouse him but Murphy was so weak from the sun and lack of water that he fell over himself.

Pete and Murphy had successfully stopped the hastily planned and ill-conceived Iranian hostage rescue mission but, in the rush to escape the approaching Soviet MiGs a giant Sea Stallion helicopter had crashed into a C-130 transport airplane. Eight Americans had died in the resulting inferno. Although it was Pete and Murphy who had daringly intervened to prevent a global nuclear confrontation between the United States and the Soviets, they had somehow been left behind in the desert.

"Goddamn you, Pete! Get up!" Murphy's voice was weak, but angry.

"Go on, Murph," Pete begged him, knowing he was unable to even crawl another foot, much less face miles of barren desert.

"Bullshit, you bastard! Get up!" Murphy was insistent. Pete tried to struggle to his knees, but made it only to his elbows before falling back. Twice more he tried with the same result. When it was obvious that he could not arise under his own power, he felt Murphy's arms wrapping around him, lifting him up; then felt Murphy stagger as his shoulders took Pete's entire weight.

How long Murphy carried him, struggling through knee-deep sand, Pete did not know until much later. In his delirium all he could sense was the sun, then the cold of the desert night, and then the sun again. How many times the cycle repeated itself, he lost count. Once he woke up choking and saw Murphy leaning over him, wringing the bitter sap from some desert plant he had found into his mouth, covering Pete's blistered face with his own shirt. And then he knew he was being carried again.

Somehow or other, Murphy managed to evade the searching Soviets for nearly a week after the water ran out, eventually finding his way to a small band of nomad goat herders who nursed the two of them back to health from much nearer death than he liked to recall. The first thing Pete remembered was being awakened in a goatskin yurt by two staccato knocks on the doorframe. His head was resting on a pillow of some sort made of dried skins. Thinking the Russians had found them, he frantically dug under the pillow with his hand for the tiny 7mm German automatic pistol he always slipped beneath his head before he went to sleep. The cold steel of its barrel against his palm snapped him alert. He groped to fit his finger into the triggerguard.

"No need for that!" Murphy waved his hands in front of him and forced a smile. "It's only me."

Pete dropped the hand holding the automatic and stared blankly around him. Murphy was standing in the door of the motellike room in Alaska. Suddenly Pete wanted to laugh, but his body ached too badly. He quickly checked the weapon and slipped it into its holster. "I guess I was asleep," he said.

Murphy scanned the room in a glance and then spoke. "I've

come to apologize for my behavior last night. I think I got a little carried away. This whole damned thing's got me nervous as hell, Pete. You and the co were right to stop me from trying to get back inside the airplane. I guess I just sort of flipped out there for a second or two. I went by the co-pilot's room, but he was still sleeping it off. He's going to be okay. I left word I'd been by."

Pete shook his head, then laughed. "I haven't seen you go nuts like that since Algiers," he said.

Murphy smiled. "Goddamned Arabs!" he snorted. "Nineteen seventy-seven, wasn't it? How the hell was I supposed to know those twenty-seven belly-dancers were the private property of King Assaud? You kept me out of trouble that time too. I owe you a lot, Pete." Murphy glanced at the floor, paused, then spoke again. "I want you to go home, Pete."

"I will when the mission's over."

"I mean it."

Pete swung his legs stiffly to the floor, found his clothes hanging across a chair, and started putting them on. Murphy's mood worried him, but he attributed it to the sabotage. It was not the first time in their careers that Murphy had tried to shield a fellow-agent from an assignment that had suddenly turned more dangerous than had been expected. Murphy seemed to never think about himself, but he would get madder than hell if anyone ever accused him of altruism. Pete decided to ignore him.

"Any word on what happened out there last night, Murph?"

Murphy shook his head. "Nothing. Damned little left after the fire."

"What about the wings, the tail section? They wouldn't have burned."

"Nothing there either. Whoever fixed our gear and hydraulics did a damned good job."

"KGB, you think?"

"Probably. Could've been anybody though, from the Russians to the Syrians to the IRA. America doesn't have a lot of friends anymore."

Murphy looked uncomfortably around the bare room again as Pete dressed. It was obvious he had something on his mind more than just a crashed airplane. He cleared his throat and started to say something else, but stopped. He pulled out a fresh pack of Camels, shook out one, and lit it.

After a pause he tried again. "Pete, I'm worried as hell. I really did damn near lose it last night. I've never done that before. I damn near panicked like a greenhorn." The trace of helplessness in Murphy's voice when he spoke surprised Pete. One thing Murphy had never considered himself was helpless, even in the face of overwhelming odds.

Pete shook his head. "No, Murph, it's not just greenhorns who lose it. We all slip sometimes. Even the best. Even you. Anybody's been in this business as long as we have has lost it more than once. They just show it different ways. Some people panic in action; others just get so they can't sleep anymore. When I first retired, I couldn't sleep for over six months, always afraid something was going to catch up to me."

"But you got over it."

"Yeah. But I couldn't have done it by myself."

"Velma?"

"Uh-huh. I know we aren't supposed to think about all the things we've had to do, sort of like it wasn't us doing them, but I still wake up cold sometimes. Velma made the difference."

Murphy watched Pete, his face expressionless. His jaw was quivering like there seemed to be something else he wanted to say, but before he could get the words formulated, Pete went on. "You ever think there might be a hereafter, Murph? Some kind of judgment or something?"

"Nawh." Murphy quickly shook his head, his opening in the conversation gone. "I don't think about it. I just do what I have to do. It's my job."

"It was mine, too," said Pete, "but I still thought about it a lot. I thought about it even more once I retired." He paused. "But, what the hell, I know you didn't come in here to apologize or discuss theology."

"No. I came in here to ask you not to continue this mission."

"But you need me."

"I'm still the boss. I could order you to go home."

"But you won't."

"And you, you stubborn bastard, wouldn't listen to me if I did."

"No."

Murphy walked to the door of the room's tiny bath, flicked the half-smoked Camel in the commode, immediately lit another, his head bowed, his back to Pete. When he turned, he was once again the same old Murphy—all business.

"Our status has gone to hell. We've lost at least thirteen hours and the damned thing's all over the news this morning. About the damned airliner, I mean. It looks like we were right. The Russians shot it down over open water and it probably went in just off the tip of Petropavlovsk. The goddamned press is screaming bloody murder.

"Of course, the liberal bastards still think Flight Eighteen was an innocent airliner and, with any kind of luck they'll keep on thinking it. Amazingly enough, they haven't started in on our own government yet. But they will. The President has issued a statement denouncing the Russians and the Russians are still giving the whole incident the old clam treatment.

"We have infra-red photographs from a Blackbird, an SR-Seventy-One out of Clark Air Force Base that overflew the area three hours ago at eighty-five thousand feet. The ocean just south of Petropavlovsk in the Kurils is suddenly filthy with Russian airplanes and ships. We don't know if they've found anything yet. Probably not, but they'll sure as hell make our slipping in undetected more difficult, if not impossible."

Pete nodded agreement.

Murphy went on. "A couple of our own Navy's ships are standing by off the coast; most likely some U.S. subs are in the area too, but, naturally enough, they haven't been allowed inside the Russians' precious twelve-mile coastal limits to help with the search. The Soviets aren't dumb."

"Which makes haste all the more urgent on our part," Pete said.

"Jones is being replaced by an operative out of California named Harris," Murphy said. "He's on his way. Sonar and electronics expert, I'm told. I don't know the damned man. He's to arrive within three hours and we're to brief him on the way.

"I tried to get HQ to replace the girl too. She makes me nervous as hell. But they wouldn't go along. Probably listening to their goddamned computers again.

"I guess I'm just a chauvinist, Pete, but there's something about her I can't quite put my finger on, a gut feeling. Maybe I'm just not used to women spooks."

Pete nodded. "I can't agree with you about Sheena. She seems highly competent, but a lot of things are changing in the old outfit, all the uniforms, women operatives, computers. Pretty soon, they aren't going to need a couple of old war-horses like us."

Murphy's face darkened slightly. "That's damned easy for you to say, Pete. You got a wife and family. You got a home. I don't have any of that. INTEL-five's the only home or family I ever had and I hate watching the goddamned liberals and politicians drag it to hell. Damn it, Pete. . . ."

"You got a problem, Murph, you'd better share it," Pete said quietly, very much aware that something was bothering Murphy more than just the uncertainly of the mission.

"No. No. Nothing I can't handle. I guess the crash just shook me up. I'm not as young as I once was."

"Neither of us are, but I never thought I'd hear you admit it."

Murphy looked at Pete and what for Murphy passed as a smile crossed his lips.

"You're a goddamned good friend, Pete. I wish I hadn't needed you on this last one, but you're the only man I could trust to get me into the Kurils in one piece. You can still quit if you want to. I think I can make it and I can see the outfit knows I forced you out."

"Have I ever left you holding the bag, Murph?"

Murphy breathed out heavily. "No, Pete. You haven't."

"And you've always played straight with me?"

"I shouldn't have dragged you along on this one. I just wish you'd go back to goddamned Florida and your wife and house and family. That's all." Murphy's voice was angry.

"I sure as hell intend to, Murph, as soon as this gaggle's over." Pete was getting a little irritated at Murphy, his references to this mission being the last one. That was the way so many of his retired neighbors talked about each year's vacation or Christmas holidays. "Right now," he said, "I'm hungry as hell. They got any grub around this joint?"

"There's a cafeteria down the hall," Murphy said resignedly. "They got breakfast if you want—positively awful—but it's hot. I've already eaten so I'll go out and check on loading." Murphy turned and walked out of the room. Pete followed.

"We should shoot for leaving by oh-nine-hundred local," Murphy said as the two men walked down a drab hallway toward the cafeteria. "We can refuel in the Aleutians and still get into the Kamchatka area during darkness. That'll give us time to set up a good base camp of some sort before daylight. I don't know where we'll be exactly, so we'll just have to play it by ear."

Pete was vaguely relieved to hear Murphy back to discussing the mechanics of the mission instead of bellyaching about his lack of home and family. After all, Murphy had made the choice himself. "With any kind of luck," Pete said, "we should get in and out in a day or two and if I remember the area right, that should be plenty. This time of year the north Pacific's not fit for penguins, much less people."

"Yeah," said Murphy. "Not fit for people." He paused. "Just for once, why couldn't we and the damned Russians have gotten into a pissing contest over something in Tahiti or somewhere. Someplace where there's lots of broads."

Pete laughed. "If I see a suggestion box, I'll stick it in for you."

# 6

MOSCOW—The Soviet Union acknowledged late yesterday that one of its fighter aircraft intercepted an "unidentified" airplane in Soviet far-eastern airspace, but the government stopped short of admitting it shot down the Trans-Pacifica Airlines jumbo jet with 246 people aboard.

Breaking nearly 24 hours of silence on the incident, Tass, the official Soviet news agency, printed a three-paragraph report that neither confirmed nor disputed United States charges that the Soviets tracked the airliner, a Boeing 747, for more than an hour before attacking it with a heat-seeking air-to-air missile.

*The New York Daily Mail*
December 27, 1993

**T**he brightly lighted cafeteria, with its rows of sparkling white Formica-topped tables and brilliantly colored plastic chairs, was nearly deserted when Pete entered. Behind a steam line displaying an assortment of greasy breakfast entrees, a fat cook was busy cleaning a grill with salt and a block of soapstone. He did not look up from his work as Pete entered. From the size of the cafeteria Pete guessed the Wrangell INTEL-5 complex must have had at least a hundred permanent employees by then and at least that many more transients like themselves.

Pete's eyes swept the room. It was the day after Christmas, and only a few early risers were present. At one table sat two slim young men in baggy orange flight suits, busy going over a flight plan spread out between them. If they were to be the team's pilots, they gave no indication. At another table were three middle-aged women whom Pete assessed, by their clothing and mannerisms, to be stenographers or lower level computer operators.

Against the far wall, seated alone at a small table, sat Sheena. Without saying or doing anything, she seemed to dominate the room. She was dressed in a dark green nylon jumpsuit that accentuated her excellent figure and a pair of lightweight Gortex hiking shoes. Around her neck, tucked inside the collar of the jumpsuit, was a bright yellow bandanna. Her hair was fastened tightly to the back of her head. She looked up and smiled as Pete entered.

Pete returned her smile and pointed at the coffee urn. "Coffee?" Sheena nodded.

Pete filled two cups and carried them across to where she was sitting. He set both cups down on the table in front of her. "Mind if I join you?"

"Sure. I can always make room for a guy who saved my life, not once, but twice."

Pete blushed lightly. He wondered who had told her he had dragged her out of the airplane, probably the co-pilot. He shrugged, strangely embarrassed. "Damned shame about the pilot and Jones."

"Yeah." Sheena slid a saucer with an English muffin to one side to give Pete room on the table.

"Jones a friend of yours?"

"No," said Sheena. "I'd just met him yesterday. At first I thought he was a friend of Murphy's. At least I got the impression that Murphy had pulled a few strings to get him on the mission. I don't know why. They didn't act much like friends." She studied Pete's face as he sipped his coffee. As he raised his head, she turned toward the grill. For the first time that morning Pete noticed the ugly blue bruise on the left side of her forehead.

Sheena realized Pete was staring at the bruise and gingerly raised her long, slender fingers to feel it. "I must have bumped my head when we hit the drifts," she said. "You think I'll get a Purple Heart or something?" she asked in mock seriousness, her eyes laughing.

Pete chuckled. "Not likely in this outfit. Is it sore?"

"Sure, but I think I'll live. You seen Murphy this morning?"

"Yeah. He came to my room. You?"

"He was in and out of here. Gulped two cups of coffee practically straight from the pot and ran out. Didn't say much. Just 'Good Morning.'" Sheena paused, as if unsure whether she should go on. "Last night, I mean, does he go wild like that very often? They said he dragged out both pilots and was going back in to get Jones, even after the airplane was burning."

Pete shook his head slowly from side to side. "No. Not often. He used to be a lot worse than he is now. Murphy is probably the closest thing to a perfect field operative you're ever likely to see, although he considers himself pretty average. His only failing is expecting everyone else to live up to his standards. I wouldn't worry about it, if I were you. You must be pretty darned good to have been picked for this mission."

Sheena laughed lightly. "I wouldn't say that. I was just unfortunate enough to have taken a little Russian in college so they figured I was a natural for north Pacific duty. Most natives on the Kamchatka speak less Russian than I do. As for Murphy picking me, he didn't. He raised all sorts of hell over my going along, but somebody upstairs overruled him I suppose. He doesn't seem to care much for women operatives. He's made that pretty clear."

"No. He doesn't dislike women operatives; he just doesn't understand them. I don't guess I do either, really, though I try. Back when Murph and I learned the business, women were used as temptresses, bait, or sexual payoffs, but were seldom given full field operative status. I can only think of a few. One of the best was an underwater demolition expert from somewhere in Iowa, of all places. She was killed during the Bay of Pigs thing."

Pete glanced at Sheena's empty coffee cup. She had drunk the scalding black liquid almost as fast as she had said Murphy did. "You want a refill?"

"No, thanks." Sheena drained the final drops from the cup. "Too much coffee makes me nervous. Especially after last night. Whoever fixed our plane did a pretty damned good job."

"Any ideas?"

Sheena looked at Pete before she answered, searching his face. "No. You?"

"Nothing."

Sheena nodded. "So what's our plan now? Murphy say?"

"The same as it was before, pretty much. We're going to refuel in the Near Islands, at a little Air Force station on Shemya Island."

"Air Force?"

"Yeah. An old World War Two bomber base, but you'd be damned hard pressed to put a modern bomber down on it. I don't like the idea of going into an Air Force station either. The Soviets monitor those things closer than's safe for us, but the jet can't carry fuel for a complete round trip from Wrangell, especially since we may have to take the scenic route. Funny thing about pilots, they prefer a round trip to a vacation in Russia." Sheena laughed.

"Of course, we'll be a scientific party as far as the flyboys on Shemya are concerned," Pete went on, "stopping only long enough to fuel. We're to pick up a replacement for Jones before we leave here, a sonar and electronics expert named Harris out of California. He's on his way."

Sheena's coffee cup suddenly clattered loudly against the table as her hand involuntarily jerked when Pete mentioned the name Harris. She put her hand to her mouth and started coughing uncontrollably. The cook looked up from his grill and the two pilots turned from their charts. Pete, fearing she would choke, leaned forward to offer help, but she waved him away. "It's all right," she managed to say finally. "I just choked on a mouthful of coffee. I really shouldn't drink the stuff."

She fished in her pockets until she found a handkerchief with which she dabbed at her eyes. In a few seconds the cook went back to scraping his grill and the pilots returned their attention to the charts.

Pete rose from his chair. He glanced at Sheena's cup; as he suspected, its bottom was bone-dry. "Sure you won't have another cup?" he asked, trying to catch her eyes. She looked down at the table and shook her head.

He walked over to the coffee urns, drew a fresh cup, then returned to the table. He sat back down in his chair and slowly pulled a dish containing packets of sugar and powdered coffee creamer toward him. He carefully tore open three packets of the white, powdered creamer and poured the contents of each into his coffee, one by one. As he did so, he studied Sheena's face. It had suddenly turned into a pleasant but blank mask like that of a fashion model or a stripper. She noticed him staring at her and let a small smile flicker across her lips. She was about to say something, but didn't.

First Murphy was acting strange and now Sheena. Maybe the crash had rattled them all. It had sure as hell shook him, no doubt about that. That must be the answer. There was, after all, little doubt in his mind, and probably in the minds of the others, that the crash had been anything but an accident and that whoever had caused it was still out there somewhere.

Pete stirred the powdered creamer into his coffee with a spoon, then added three packages of sugar, once again, one at a time to give himself time to think. When he had finished, he looked self-consciously at the pile of empty packets he had created. "I really prefer my coffee black," he said, "sort of a way to jump-start the old cardio-vascular system in the morning, but my ulcers insist at least the second cup be diluted." He laughed at his own condition and lay his spoon on a napkin just as the telephone mounted on the wall behind the cook started buzzing. The cook reached for it with one hand while he kept on scraping the grill with the other.

He spoke a few inaudible words into the receiver, then turned and looked directly toward Pete and Sheena. With a quick lift of his head, he motioned that the call was for Pete. Bewildered, Pete walked over to the cook, who kept the mouthpiece covered with his palm and said, "Some guy in Anchorage wants a Doctor Shafer. He says it's urgent. You wanna talk to him?"

At first Pete started to refuse the call. He had not known anyone in Alaska for several years and no one outside INTEL-5, including Velma, was supposed to know he was in the state, much less how to get in touch with him at a highly secret outpost, even to pinpointing the exact room he was in. There weren't supposed to be ten people in Anchorage who knew the facility even existed. None of them would have called him here in this manner. However, something inside, some instinct developed over his years in the business, quietly whispered that the call could be important. True, it would confirm his location, but the caller apparently already knew that.

He nodded to the cook and took the receiver. It smelled of rancid grease. "Yes, this is Doctor Shafer," he said quietly, shielding his mouth with his hand, a practice as revealing of his trade as an experienced combat soldier instinctively cupping the flame of a cigarette lighter.

"Hello, *Doctor* Shafer," said the voice on the other end of the line. Pete quickly gathered from the caller's voice that he was a young male in his early twenties, white, probably from somewhere in the south, Texas, maybe Oklahoma.

"Now, don't talk—just listen. I have some information you need, but I have to give it fast. There're a lot of people I can't trust and a lot of them are in INTEL-5."

"But—"

"Please. Just listen. I have to talk fast. Your outfit is probably trying like hell to tap this call and figure out how I broke your security."

The voice was insistent. "I know who you are and where you're going. I could hazard a pretty good guess why.

"I assume you know that Flight Eighteen had more black boxes on it than most B-fifty-twos. Now, it's not unusual for civilian airliners in this part of the world to be equipped with a little spy gear now and then, most of them are, whether the airlines know it or not, but this baby, Flight Eighteen, was hauling more crow paraphernalia than the average bomber. Radar jamming devices, false image generators, that sort of thing. I worked on Buffs in the Air Force so I know the stuff when I see it.

"One of my hobbies is electronics and computers. What you'd

call a hacker. A person's got to do something up here in the winter time or you'd go nuts. I've got a small satellite dish I built myself. I have it hooked up to an old Apple Two-e that I got cheap before I left the states.

"About a year ago I figured out how to monitor satellite communications, just for fun. That's when I found out about your INTEL-five, purely by accident.

"You folks seem to have quite a set-up, but your satellite communication security is sloppy as hell. It took me six months to break the KGB codes. Yours, I cracked in two weeks.

"Anyway, I've been following this Flight Eighteen thing pretty close, since it was obviously something bigger than usual. Of course, when your little jet bought the farm last night, I knew about it almost immediately.

"I'm sure you know your gear and engine problems didn't just happen by themselves. KGB most likely. Classical move for them. Clumsy bastards. There was talk back and forth about it. In code, of course. Sounded pretty proud of themselves."

Pete tried to interrupt the caller, but the man kept talking in a rapid-fire voice.

"Now, two things you probably don't know. I didn't have time to check it much—damned co-pilot kept giving me the bum's rush—but one of my instruments showed that Flight Eighteen was spewing radioactivity like it was going out of style. Carrying that much hot cargo on a passenger aircraft is very definitely against both FAA and international regs.

"Secondly, one of your team members—you're the only one I've eliminated, don't ask me how—is sending messages via the satellite to someone in D.C. other than INTEL-five. Nothing substantial, just position reports so far. I have reason to believe it's—"

The caller's final words were abruptly cut off by a sudden loud buzzing on the line. Then there was a click and the buzzing was replaced by a dial tone.

Pete replaced the telephone receiver into its bracket on the wall. He looked around for the cook, but he had disappeared, leaving his grill still uncleaned.

Pete stood staring at the telephone. His mind reeled from the call. Somehow the man's voice had had a definite note of honesty in it, but you could never be sure in this business. You could never be sure of anything. You always had your crackpots, your, what had the man said? Your hackers? But someone, probably someone inside the complex, had definitely disconnected the call when the man had started to reveal a name.

But again Pete had known a lot of young operatives who had never lived to be old operatives, acting on tips from strangers. That sort of thing was for spy novels and television; real operatives didn't work that way.

And why had the man bothered to call at all? Was he really just a computer hacker, as he claimed, eager to show off his expertise? The caller could also have been any one of a number of people who had somehow found out about their mission and wanted it to fail by planting suspicions in the team itself.

How did Pete know that the others had not received similar calls? Should he ask them flat out? And yet the man hadn't sounded like a crackpot. A crackpot would never have broken INTEL-5 security in the first place. Neither did he have the artificially slick style of an old-line KGB man, laced with out-of-date slang and jargon. KGB men, women too—say what you want about the KGB, they had pioneered the use of women as spys—generally talked too much, told you so much they began to sound like a script.

Somehow or other the man had found him here and then broken through one of the most sophisticated telephone systems in the world, a system that wasn't even supposed to exist, to contact him. And why him? Why not Murphy? Murphy was the leader of this expedition. Surely the man also knew that. Why would anyone distrust Murphy, for Christ's sake?

"Something wrong?" Pete was startled by Sheena's voice. Then he realized he had nearly bumped into her as she returned from the direction of the bathroom. He had been walking without looking where he was going, mumbling to himself. He shook his head.

"No, no. Just a woman I used to know," he lied, knowing full well that Sheena would not believe him even for a second. "It was nothing." Sheena stared at him quizzically, her face friendly, but clearly indicating she knew that, even if the caller had been a woman, the conversation had hardly been romantic.

Pete realized he had to slip away, clear his mind, check out the wreckage of the Lear for something, anything, that might shed some light on what had happened.

The crash, something about the caller's voice, Murphy's uncharacteristic nervousness, Sheena's strange behavior when he had mentioned the name Harris, had all convinced him that this mission was far more than the welcome break from Florida boredom he had first assumed. He knew he could still back out, of course. Murphy had almost begged him to, almost as if he had, for some reason, had a change of heart about asking Pete to accompany him. Pete needed time to think.

He knew he needed an excuse to get away, a reason for disappearing for an hour or two. He looked across the table at Sheena. Where did she fit into all this?

He leaned over and almost whispered. "Look, I've got something I need to take care of before Murph goes rounding us up and marching us out of here."

Sheena's expression was one of quiet concern. "Maybe I can help," she said.

Pete slowly shook his head. Although something told him he should share his concerns about the mission with her, he still held back. He could not help noticing that her eyes seemed especially green this morning. She smelled slightly of soap and her hair sparkled even in the bland whiteness of the cafeteria. The woman was class from the word go, maybe too much class, he thought. Maybe that was what worried him about her.

Pete had seen his share of women over the years, some professionals, some in other ways, but nothing to match the one seated across from him now.

He smiled as he realized what he was thinking and how under different circumstances he might be tempted to make an old fool out of himself. That Sheena should ever desire a man of his age was laughable at best. His attraction to her was a strange mixture of desire and a fatherly feeling of protectiveness that he could not understand. Perhaps, he thought, she was weaving a spell around him for whatever secret reason. She certainly didn't seem to need much protection.

He picked up his cold cup of coffee and downed it. "See you in a couple of hours. If I'm a little bit late, cover for me, but don't tell Murphy where I've gone."

"What should I tell him?"

Pete searched Sheena's face. "Tell him what I told you. That I went to meet a woman."

"He'll never believe it."

"Any more than you do?"

"No."

"Then what will he believe?"

"That you need time to sort this whole mess out in your mind before you decide whether to go on with it."

Pete slowly nodded his head up and down. "And what do you think I should decide?"

"I guess that's up to you, isn't it?"

"Yeah," Pete said. "Yeah. I suppose it is."

# 7

The President, calling Soviet leaders "barbaric, callous terrorists and flagrant liars," canceled his planned Christmas vacation in Galveston and returned here early this morning by helicopter from Camp David.

Upon his arrival at the White House, the President went immediately to the Situation Room where members of the National Security Council were waiting to give him the latest information on the tragedy in which 246 people, 58 of them Americans, were killed and to discuss options for U.S. action.

The United States has charged that a Soviet fighter shot down the airliner when it accidently strayed into Russian airspace, a charge the Soviets deny.

After the hastily called session ended, a White House spokesman said that the meeting "focused on a measured response that would include U.S. allies in the international community." He ruled out any military action at this time.

IND-TV *Evening News*
December 27, 1993

**P**ete was able to walk out of the underground complex unchallenged. There were a few armed guards at the entrance, but they glanced up only briefly as he passed, obviously more interested in keeping people out than in keeping them in. Wearing a heavily insulated snowmobile suit, huge goose-down mittens, a hooded wolf-ruff parka, fat white "Mickey Mouse" boots, and a pair of clear plastic goggles, Pete stepped out into the pale gray coldness of the outside world. A blast of frigid arctic air struck him in the face like a solid wall of ice and he zipped up the hood of the parka. Alaska's short winter day was just dawning and the air was silent as only the arctic can be silent. It would be night again in less than four hours.

From inside the tunnel formed by the hood's ruff, Pete could see the barren snow-covered landscape that stretched out before him, a gray, gently undulating expanse of stunted bushes and clumps of dry grass. In places the bushes and grass were nearly covered by the constantly moving drifts of snow. Elsewhere the relentless wind had swept the ground clear, revealing the hard-frozen light-brown earth.

Pete had stepped out beside what appeared to be an abandoned hangar at one end of the runway, its main aircraft doors stuck permanently open, allowing the wind and snow to blow inside. Walking past the large open doorway into the pale and weak half-light of the morning, Pete looked around for other buildings that might display more signs of life.

The cracked and broken asphalt of the infrequently used taxiways blended into the dirty and wind-driven snow so that it was hard to tell where the runways ended and the tundra began.

It was ironic, Pete thought, that just below him was a sprawling complex of artificially heated and lighted corridors and rooms where it was easy to forget the arctic winter that waited just above like a hungry tundra wolf.

Several hundred yards away from the deserted hangar, across a snow-swept taxiway, was a tiny tarpaper-covered shed with a rusty sheet metal chimney. A thin ribbon of smoke was streaming skyward from the chimney. The smoke rose, pencil-thin, straight up for several hundred feet into the still morning air before it billowed out into the shape of a tall, skinny mushroom. A few rickety weather instruments and a ragged canvas wind sock identified the building as a meteorological facility of some sort. The air was completely calm but the wind sock was frozen into a half-erect position. Two snowmobilies sat parked on the lee side of the building.

As Pete walked slowly toward the shack, his breath made little clouds of steam that instantly condensed into a thin rime on the ruff of the parka. Even through the thick insulation of the snowmobile suit, he could sense the bitter cold. The stiff outer layers of his clothing creaked and his boots made a crunching noise in the snow as he walked. In the silence the crunching ice beneath his feet sounded as loud as an earthquake. He would have preferred to quietly inspect the snowmobiles, but he knew he would just have to invent a reason for needing one if anybody noticed him and asked. As an operative, he could have checked out any equipment he desired, but doing so would have aroused questions he couldn't answer just yet.

As he neared the shack Pete saw a large plastic thermometer tacked to one of the outside walls. Although the weather station was probably real, INTEL-5 maintained its own comprehensive worldwide weather information system, including highly accurate scientific thermometers. But in the strange rationale of human beings someone had still nailed up this give-away instrument that gave an easily decipherable reading in the most unscientific degrees, Fahrenheit. Although probably reliable enough, its main purpose was not telling temperatures but advertising a brand of Kentucky bourbon. Pete squinted at the short column of mercury. The air temperature was nearly twenty degrees below zero.

Voices were coming from inside the shack. From the muted conversations and occasional laughter, Pete realized that he had not attracted attention. He scanned the two snowmobiles parked beside the building. One was an ancient yellow Ski-Doo hooked to a sled half loaded with firewood. The other was a new Polaris 440, low and fast.

Without hesitation Pete chose the Polaris. It would be little trouble for him to hot-wire the ignition by stripping two wires coming out of the ignition switch with his pocketknife then twisting them together. It would only take fifteen seconds. Besides, the men inside the shack would not be expecting any trespassers in broad daylight. They would be off their guard.

He quickly straddled the machine, feeling the crackling of the cold vinyl seat between his legs. He gently rocked the snowmobile back and forth to make sure it had not frozen to the ground during the night. It moved sluggishly but wasn't frozen down.

The thin, white layer of hoarfrost on the snowmobile's hood told him the engine had not been started for at least several hours, certainly not that morning. He considered trying to push the snowmobile away from the shack, but decided against it. The second the engine started he knew the men would come out of the shack. He would just have to make a run for it. The question was would the Polaris start fast enough to allow him to get away before the occupants of the shack heard him.

Pete tried to remember the last time he had operated a snowmobile, it had been in Canada, ten years ago. The machines had changed a lot since then, but a scan of the machine's dashboard revealed no unusual equipment. Slowly Pete pulled the plastic knob marked choke out as far as it would go. Then, holding the choke knob with one hand, he touched the blade to his pocketknife across the contacts of the ignition switch with the other. The cold battery, threatening to die at any second, turned the engine over slowly for the first few revolutions. Then the engine picked up speed as the oil-gas-alcohol mixture lubricated the inside of the engine's cylinders. It popped twice, as first one cylinder and then the other fired.

Suddenly the engine roared to life in a cloud of smelly silver-gray exhaust smoke. Pete twisted the throttle on the right handlebar twice, revving the engine. Then he released the brake and the Polaris lunged forward, nearly stalling. Its heavy steel skis lifted free of the ice, threatening to flip over backward, forcing Pete to hang onto the handlebars to keep from being spilled off the seat. He hurriedly backed off the throttle and the Polaris shot ahead, leveling out and rocketing across the snow in a blur of speed.

Pete got just a quick glimpse of the three men who ran out of the shack, waving their arms in the air and shouting something he could not hear above the high-pitched roar of the speeding snowmobile.

Snowdrifts and stunted trees flashed by as Pete drove the snowmobile eastward. He glanced down at the speedometer. It showed he was doing nearly fifty miles per hour. From the snowmobile's low seat, his feet less than two inches from the snow hurtling beneath him, it seemed much faster. As he raced along the cold air licked at every crack and crevice in his clothing and Pete remembered that, at this speed, the wind-chill factor made the air equivalent to fifty degrees below zero.

Once he had gotten several thick clumps of arctic alder between him and the airstrip building, Pete chose an area of packed snow where tracks would be harder to find and turned back toward the crash site. He slowed the snowmobile to forty miles per hour for better control since he was now out of sight of the complex. He needed time to think, to inspect—not speed. His mind reeled with all that had happened in the past twenty hours. Someone had gotten to the jet through INTEL-5's tight security. That could have even been an inside job. Murphy was acting strange—like he had asked Pete along but, for some reason known only to him, had suddenly decided he didn't want his help. And Sheena. What was she anyway?

For the next several minutes Pete passed through some of the most hauntingly beautiful country in the world but he saw none of it. He could only think that an unprotected human, even equipped with arctic gear, would not survive long if he were suddenly stranded in such a place. Unforgiving was probably the best word to describe the arctic. Pete had spent more than a little time battling against this region and the desperate people who inhabited it—from Point Barrow to Siberia to Hudson's Bay. Like in the business of espionage, the arctic allowed no second chances, no room for carelessness or accident.

He slowed to walking pace as he eased across some snow-covered debris. Off to his right the land began a steep but even drop in elevation and Pete saw the frozen white flatness of a large river stretching away to the east.

Ice-covered rivers were the freeways of the north, used by animals and humans, but the frozen highways were often treacherous, concealing currents and eddies that created paper-thin coverings of ice to dispense quick justice to the careless or arrogant. Where there were rapids or waterfalls the rivers turned deadly. As Pete drove along the faceless snow was broken only occasionally by the tracks of snowshoe hares and arctic foxes. At one place a small pack of wolves had traveled along his path for a few hundred yards before turning back toward the river. Just beyond where the wolves had been, Pete spotted the low, gray, wooden shacks of an abandoned or seasonal Indian fishing village. As he neared he could see it was deserted.

In the distance he spotted the runway. As he neared it he scanned the concrete for any signs of skid marks or unusual scratches and tire tracks but saw nothing out of the ordinary. He knew this had to be the place where the Lear had hit the snowbank, but there were no telltale signs. There was no disruption of the high wall of snow, no crater where the jet had burned, nothing. It was as if the crash had never happened.

He drove the snowmobile slowly along the edge of the runway, his eyes searching the snow. Perhaps he had been wrong. Perhaps the crash had occurred farther along. Then he saw the tiny fragment of white aluminium that the clean-up crews had missed. This was the place all right. But why had INTEL-5 gone to so much trouble to cover the evidence?

Pete's thoughts were cut short by the roar of snowmobiles approaching from behind. He looked back in the direction he had come just as four snowmobiles came into sight around some bushes about a quarter of a mile away. The roar of their engines increased when they spotted him idling ahead of them. Something about the four men driving at top speed made Pete doubt they were going to be friendly until he could convince them that he was a fellow member of INTEL-5. He turned back toward the buildings on the far side of the runway. Explaining would be a lot easier back at the complex. But the four men were not just trying to catch up with him, they were actually trying to herd him away from the complex!

Cutting straight across was impossible. Pete decided he was going to have to circle around and lose the men, who he was suddenly beginning to doubt were connected to INTEL-5 at all. He hunkered down on the Polaris and twisted the throttle hard. Soon he dropped onto the river and flew along it, the other snowmobiles in hot pursuit and slowly gaining.

Pete glanced at the speedometer. He was doing well over a hundred! Damn, but this thing would run! He felt the adrenaline pump into his blood stream as the chase got underway.

As he raced along the landscape to either side turned into a gray-white blur. Pete glanced in the rearview mirrors mounted on the machine's handlebars. Although he had the Polaris's throttle twisted full-open, his four pursuers were closing the gap. They were only a couple hundred yards behind him now. Pete considered leaving the river and trying to outmaneuver the four other snowmobiles in the bush, but he knew they were probably more experienced on snowmobiles than he was and knew the country too.

He was just about to stop, take a chance that the men were from INTEL-5 after all, and explain about his need for a snowmobile, when a shot cracked behind him and he heard a bullet go whistling past his ear, then another, even closer. Pete had been foolish to venture out alone without telling anybody where he was going. Although he knew the KGB usually kept an eye on U.S. installations, he had never expected them to be here. Yet, he was convinced now that the men behind were just that.

He veered quickly left and then right again to present a harder target, each time feeling the outward ski lift free of the snow. He twisted the handlebar throttle as far as it would go and his wrist strained to wring even more speed from the machine as his pursuers narrowed the gap between them.

The tachometer needle was shoved hard against the far side of the red arc and the speedometer needle had swung past its last increment marking at 120. The Polaris's engine screamed and threatened to disintegrate and he still lost ground as the four snowmobiles behind drew even closer. They were now within a hundred feet of catching him.

One of the four shot out in front of the pursuing pack and drew up beside Pete on the right. Pete got a quick glimpse of the rider, outfitted in solid black, his face hidden behind a black-tinted Plexiglas bubble shield.

The black rider slowly raised his left hand, hanging onto his machine's handlebar with his right. The blue steel of the pistol barrel glinted in the pale light of the early morning sun, just now fully breaking free of the southern horizon.

Pete did not hear the report of the shot over the scream of the five snowmobiles, but he saw the white puff of smoke and the jerk of the black rider's arm from the recoil.

There was a solid thump as the bullet hit the thick insulation of

Pete's snowmobile suit and grazed his shoulder blades. He suddenly felt the icy knife of the outside air rushing in and hot, sticky blood running down the small of his back.

The black rider slowly lowered his pistol for another shot, but before he could fire all five men heard the roar of the approaching airplane.

It was close behind them, coming low and fast. A bright orange, ski-equipped Cessna 180, its skis barely clearing the snow. Even with the snowmobiles at full throttle, the airplane was easily overtaking them.

Before the black rider could aim and fire again, the airplane was on him. He tried to veer out of the airplane's path, but the front point of the airplane's ski caught him squarely in the back and shoved him and the speeding snowmobile sideways.

As the airplane flew past the chase and climbed free, the black snowmobile skidded sideways out of control across the snow at well over a hundred miles an hour. The heavy machine hit a patch of rough ice and bounced into the air, flinging the rider away from it, and came crashing down hard in an explosion of orange fire and black smoke as the red-hot engine ignited the gasoline from the ruptured fuel tank.

Pete gained almost a hundred yards on the other three snowmobiles as they veered wide to miss the thick cloud of black smoke and their fallen comrade who lay limply on the ice, but then they quickly began to close in. The Cessna had climbed and circled so that it was once again behind the chase and coming up fast. Suddenly, above the screaming of the snowmobiles and the steady drone of the airplane, Pete heard a strange noise—the roaring of a waterfall and rapids ahead of him—and realized that the ice was about to end as the quiet frozen river turned into rapids. He looked quickly from side to side only to see, too late, that he was flanked by dark and swiftly flowing water that cut off his escape.

His hand remained frozen on the throttle, allowing the machine to continue hurtling toward the swirling white water, which was now less than five hundred yards in front of him. He knew he was trapped and to try to stop the snowmobile and shoot it out with only his tiny 7mm would be futile.

In the rearview mirrors he saw the flash of the orange Cessna closing the gap, coming low, its skis almost touching the ice. This time, however, the airplane raced past Pete's pursuers and pulled alongside him, slowing and expertly matching its speed to his until both the snowmobile and airplane seemed to be hovering motionless side by side in white space.

The Cessna's right ski hung just beside Pete's left hand, so close he could have reached out and touched it, had he dared loose his death grip on the snowmobile's handlebars.

The Polaris bounced and shuddered as it hit the first of the broken ice.

The dark foaming water raced toward Pete. The spray from the rapids struck him in the face and instantly froze on his goggles.

The combined roar of the airplane and snowmobile and, above all, rapids was deafening.

Pete felt the skis of the snowmobile leave the last slivers of ice and start to hydroplane across the open water. The heavy rear started to sink. Above the sound of the water he could not hear, could not see, could not think.

He took one look at the dangling ski of the airplane beside him and leaped.

He fought desperately to hang on as the Cessna's engine roared to life and the airplane shot up to clear the rocks of the rapids. It banked steeply as it climbed, risking a high-speed stall to avoid a snag sticking from the water. Pete's lower legs were soaked with spray thrown up by the airplane's prop that nearly touched the water. The spray turned instantly to ice as they cleared the top of the falls by inches. Even hanging on for life and nearly frozen, Pete knew there was one hell of a pilot at the controls.

Pete's fingers and body were rapidly turning numb as the airplane climbed clear of the low trees and leveled out, the skis still barely clearing the branches, the pilot closely following the contour of the land. The rush of air threatened to tear Pete loose at any second from the cold metal ski to which he was clinging. Somehow he managed to drag himself up until he was lying on the top of the ski, braced against the airplane's undercarriage.

Although his right hand was still raw from touching the frozen metal the night before, it was now numb from the cold. Where the bullet had sliced across his back, however, was a different story. Even hanging onto the airplane for dear life, Pete felt the pain cutting him like a knife and he wondered how much blood he had lost.

There was a clank above his head and he knew the pilot had reached over and unlatched the airplane's right door from inside so he could fight his way inside. Pete knew that if the pilot tried to land with him clinging to the ski, he would be knocked off and certainly killed. He had to get inside.

Pete also knew he had to make the door, and quick, if he was to avoid getting so cold that he would lose his grip on the airplane and fall to his death.

Slowly, painfully, he reached up and hooked his fingers inside the door. Twice he nearly slipped and fell, but finally he managed to drag himself into the cockpit. He twisted into the seat and sat, gasping for air, his lungs nearly frozen by the cold.

Across from him, the pilot, dressed in a heavy parka much like his own, reached across and pulled the door fastened. Pete could not see the pilot's face inside the parka's hood, but right then he didn't care who it was.

When his fingers thawed out enough to remove his mittens, Pete pulled back his hood and looked over at the pilot. From the side he could see nothing.

Then the pilot raised a gloved hand and tossed back the parka's hood.

Pete had to blink hard to be sure of what he saw.

"That was a damned fine piece of flying" was all he could say, blurting out the words through still-blue lips.

Sheena smiled. "My old daddy was a Mississippi crop duster. Couldn't even write his name, but he knew how to keep his wheels down in the cotton."

Her voice was as calm as if she were on a drive to the beach. "But he did teach his only kid to fly pretty damned good, didn't he?"

# 8

WASHINGTON—The U.S. State Department released transcripts early this morning of radio conversations that it claims will prove the Soviets deliberately shot down Trans-Pacifica Airlines Flight 18.

The transcripts are of tapes obtained from unidentified intelligence sources that were monitoring Soviet radio communications during the time in which TPA Flight 18 was allegedly shot down.

According to the transcripts, a Soviet pilot called his base and said, "I see the target and am preparing to fire my rockets."

The transcript continues to say that after about thirty seconds of radio silence, the pilot came back on the radio and reported, "I have fired my rockets. The target is destroyed."

*The Washington Chronicle*
December 28, 1993

"**F**irst one of you steals a god-damned snowmobile, for Christ's sake, then the other rips off an airplane!" Murphy growled, pacing rapidly back and forth the width of Pete's room at the complex. Sheena cleaned and bandaged Pete's back, paying little attention to Murphy. "If you wanted to inspect the crash site, all you had to do was say so, Pete. Hell, I'd have gone with you! You ought to know the goddamned Russians watch our installations like hawks. You're getting sloppy in your old age, Shafer. Damned sloppy!"

Pete, sitting backward in a straight-backed wooden chair, winced as Sheena doused the ragged gash across his bare back with alcohol. He yelled theatrically as the alcohol stung the wound, but Murphy's words hurt him more than either the bullet or alcohol. He had done a very foolish thing and he knew it. "Damned bullet didn't hurt that bad!" he protested, biting his lower lip at the very real pain.

The shallow flesh wound was painful and messy, but otherwise not serious. The bullet had barely grazed Pete's back, peeling off a strip of skin. His shirt and the inside of his parka were soaked with blood, but the projectile had missed any bones or major muscles.

Murphy went over and inspected Pete's wound. "Serves you right," he announced, once he was sure that the injury was more painful than serious. "Now if that damned Harris would hurry up and show, we could get on about our business." He took one last look at Pete's injury, then left the room mumbling beneath his breath about idiots and snowmobiles.

Sheena quickly covered the clean and no longer bleeding wound with white cotton gauze and taped the bandage into place. "All done. You were real lucky you had that snowmobile suit on. The padding probably deflected the bullet a little and slowed it down, but it didn't save your shirt." She held up a piece of the ripped and blood-soaked garment she had cut off his back. "It looks like those guys out there really meant to do you in. Any idea who they were?"

Pete shook his head. "Plenty of ideas. Nothing positive. I must be getting too old for this business. I really screwed up leaving the complex here."

"Not necessarily. At least now we won't have them to worry about for a while. Think they were KGB?"

Pete shrugged. "Could have been. Could have been a lot of people."

Sheena reached for a box she had brought into the room with her. "You want your thermal underwear? Norwegian wool fishnet, really good stuff."

Pete nodded and took the box. He pulled out the one-piece pair of underwear, examined it, and paused.

Sheena looked at him and laughed. "Oh, all right. I'll leave the room if you're that modest."

"Just a little old fashioned, I guess."

"Nothing wrong with that." Sheena touched him lightly on the shoulder. "You remind me a lot of my dad. Of course, he was a lot older," she added quickly, smiling.

"Thanks, I guess."

An hour later Harris had still not arrived. Pete and Sheena were sitting in the same small cafeteria where they had been earlier. Pete was nursing his fourth cup of black coffee. Sheena, having failed to engage either Pete or Murphy in conversation, studied detailed maps of the islands surrounding the Kamchatka Peninsula.

Murphy, who had just returned from checking the heavily guarded airplane that was to take the team to Kamchatka, paced around nervously, glancing at his watch and picking at his fingernails with a small pocketknife. He had been in and out of the cafeteria several times during the past hour. He was looking more and more frustrated each time he returned.

He was just about to check with the complex's command center for the third time when two uniformed guards walked through the cafeteria door and headed toward him. He stopped pacing as they approached across the floor.

"You Murphy?" one of the guards asked.

Murphy nodded cautiously.

"We got something you probably ought to see outside," said the other guard. Murphy glanced at Pete and Sheena. "If you'll just follow me," said the guard. Without waiting for a reply the two guards turned and headed for the door.

Pete and Sheena followed Murphy and the guards out of the cafeteria, grabbing up their parkas as they went. They were led down a hall, then up four flights of stairs and out into the snow. The sun had nearly set and a cold wind kicked up a fine spray of ice crystals into the air.

The guards walked quickly around a low concrete bunker-type building to where two other guards stood staring at a body lying at their feet.

On the ground close beside the building the dead man lay face up in a pool of blood that had frozen so fast it had not had time to darken. The horrible open gash across the man's throat told Pete nearly all he needed to know except: who?

No attempt had been made to hide or cover the body. It appeared to be lying exactly where it had fallen, as though the murderer wanted it to be found as soon as possible. On the hard-packed snow there were no signs of a struggle, no footprints. He had apparently died silently and without a struggle. The job had all the marks of an experienced pro.

Sheena, who had lagged a little behind, came up beside Pete and Murphy. Pete instinctively started to hold her back from the gruesome sight until he remembered who, what, she was. From what he had seen of Sheena so far, Pete would not have been surprised if she was equally as good with a knife as the unknown assailant.

She gasped when she saw the body and Pete thought momentarily that he could have been wrong in his assessment of her fortitude. A flicker of horror crossed her face, but it was quickly replaced by the expressionless mask Pete had seen earlier that morning when she had pretended to be choking on coffee. He had not been wrong.

He was still surprised to see her quickly wipe at one of her eyes with the backside of her hand. He knew it could have just been the cold making her eyes water, but he doubted it. Pete suddenly had little doubt in his mind that the dead man at his feet was the Harris they had been waiting for, and that somehow Sheena and Harris were connected.

Murphy quickly dropped to one knee and went through the dead man's pockets for identification. The body had already started to freeze and Murphy had to tug hard to open the jacket—stiff from the frozen blood—but none of the coat's outside or inside pockets yielded papers of any sort. Murphy's face registered disgust as his hands slid down inside the dead man's shirt and trousers.

But if the man had been carrying a wallet, any sort of identification at all, it had already been removed. The only thing Murphy found was a small amount of pocket change, a set of car keys, and a tiny .25 Beretta. Nothing more.

Murphy rose from his gruesome search, then looked questioningly at the four guards. They shook their heads. "Nothing," one of them said. "We just thought he might be one of yours."

Murphy stood. "I don't like this," he said, glancing around. "Harris or no Harris, we're getting the hell out of here."

# 9

MOSCOW—The Soviet Union today blamed the CIA for the crash of Trans-Pacifica Airlines Flight 18 with 246 people aboard.

The official Soviet news agency, Tass, speaking for the Soviet leadership, issued a statement, couched in indignant terms, that said the airplane had crashed in Soviet waters for "unknown reasons."

The statement further labeled the intrusion of the airplane into Soviet airspace a deliberate provocation designed to "smear the Soviet Union" and "cast aspersions on Soviet peace-loving policy."

The Soviets also called the President's remarks about the disaster "impudent" and "slanderous."

*The Los Angeles Daily Press*
December 28, 1993

**T**he specially modified Lear 25, except for the outline of the underbelly jump door and a small radome beneath its nose, was configured much the same as the airplane that had crashed the night before on the same runway from which they had just taken off. There was, however, one outstanding difference in appearance. Where the earlier aircraft had been painted solid white, the present one was a dull, flat black with a total absence of exterior markings, because there was now no one to fool that it was anything other than a spy plane.

Inside the airplane was vastly different from a standard corporate jet. There was no attempt to disguise the cabin as belonging to a business jet, unless, of course, the business you were in involved slipping into and out of extremely hostile and heavily armed nations. A solidly braced tier of metal shelves against the forward cabin bulkhead held an array of black boxes that contained computerized inertial navigation equipment, LORAN "C" receivers, and satellite navigation systems. The stacks of electronics also contained various pieces of STEALTH equipment and false image generators, only a few of which Pete recognized.

All but three of the passenger cabin's seats had been removed and the floor was piled high with equipment and parachutes. Two large bundles attached to cargo parachutes attracted Pete's eye. He couldn't help thinking that there was enough gear aboard to launch a small army. He picked up a clipboard that held an inventory sheet for the two cargo chutes. It listed two Zodiac inflatable boats complete with inflation cannisters and a thirty horsepower Evinrude outboard motor for each boat that could push it along at up to thirty knots, weapons, food, camping equipment, and a host of other supplies. For the most part the equipment was evenly divided between the two parachutes.

The original plan for the boats had been for the team to split up into two search parties. Now, however, with the absence of Harris, they would use the second boat as either a spare or one that one of them could search in alone, a dangerous proposition in the rough seas of the Kamchatka.

Stacked along one wall of the cabin was an assortment of scuba gear. The thin but highly efficient black Insulite wet suits would be sorely tested. Although moderated somewhat by the warm currents coming up out of Japan, the water around the Kurils, especially in the winter, was hardly conducive to recreational swimming.

Pete had been a young man the last time he had actually been on the Kurils in the dead of winter. At the time the United States was expecting to get into a shooting war with the Soviets at almost any minute. Pete had been assigned to scout out forward listening post possibilities on the islands. He had slipped ashore from a submarine alone onto Iturup, an island in the southern Kurils that had been under Japanese control during World War II, but that had gone to the Russians after the Japanese surrender.

It had been a boringly routine mission other than for the normal natural hardships of cold, loneliness, and fatigue, especially for a young operative itching for action. The only other human beings he had seen for the entire two months he spent skipping northward from island to island were a couple of native trappers who had come ashore to look for mink sign. They had run away in terror when they saw him, probably thinking he was a Russian soldier. Even long before the present Soviet regime, the natives of the Kamchatka had suffered at the hands of Russians and were, in fact, the last natives to be subdued after the Communist revolution. The experience with the two trappers was his first realization that he had embarked upon a career of loneliness where even those people he might try to help would keep their distance. When he got home, Pete proposed to Velma—a high-school sweetheart—and she accepted. Two days after they were married, he was gone again.

Later Pete got his first taste of action, but it was far away from either his new wife or the Kamchatka, in a swampy little rat hole of a country that was still full of Frenchmen. They called it Vietnam. The American public didn't even know it existed then.

Leaning against one of the piles of scuba gear in the Lear's cabin was an assortment of weapons. Pete recognized most of them. There were two automatic 9mm carbines, a small, wicked-looking 30-caliber submachine gun, and a long-barreled, German-made .357 magnum automatic pistol with a long silencer and a detachable aluminum stock that would allow the pistol to be fired from the shoulder like a rifle. It could be very useful for taking out a guard or two with the minimum amount of fuss when making a mess wasn't a problem. Of course, as had been so deftly illustrated less than an hour before and as Pete knew from personal experience, a razor-sharp assault knife, expertly wielded, assured total silence and a quick and efficient death. Done by a pro, the method was also much cleaner except for an occasional bit of blood beneath the fingernails, a minor annoyance at worse.

The only really exotic weapons in the stack were two pneumatically operated dart rifles. They used a blast of pressurized gas to propel a tiny needle-dart that contained a synthetic curarelike poison that was one hundred percent effective. It paralyzed the victim's vocal cords instantly and the thirty seconds it took to kill were even more agonizing because the victim was denied the final luxury of being able to scream. The dart rifles worked almost equally as well underwater as on the surface.

Also in the pile were two nondescript but heavily padded canvas knapsacks containing plastic explosive charges and detonating devices for blowing up the monitor once it was found.

All in all Pete estimated the gear and weapons to weigh over a ton. In the old days operatives often penetrated a hostile country with only the equipment they could carry on their backs. Given the old-style military parachutes they had used then, an operative loaded down with nearly a hundred pounds of gear made some pretty hard landings.

But even the parachutes were different now. Miracles of modern technology, each canopy was equipped with an onboard computer that allowed it to deplore itself at a preselected altitude, unassisted by the jumper, then home in and automatically steer itself to a beacon located either on the ground or attached to the lead parachutist, in this case, Pete. The parachutes could even glide horizontally three feet for every foot of fall. This allowed the drop vehicle to stay well outside the Russian twelve-mile coastal limit while the operatives glided in undetected.

Each parachute was equipped with an oxygen bottle since the jumpers would be spending several minutes well above the ten thousand foot level, an altitude that had once been impossible.

Even the cargo chutes were equipped with homing devices to follow the lead parachutist down. Pete estimated that all the equipment on the floor, taken together, had cost well over half-a-million dollars. Espionage didn't come cheap any more.

Sheena, who had been forward inspecting some of the gear, walked back to Pete's seat. Her movement startled him because, although he had not realized it, he was drowsy from the pills he had taken to relieve the pain of his bullet wound and his aching back. "Pretty impressive," he said.

"What?"

"The gear. It's pretty impressive."

"Oh, yeah." Sheena seemed withdrawn, distant.

"Now if they could just get some robots to fill in for us, we'd be all set."

Sheena smiled slightly at Pete's attempt at levity. "How's the shoulder?"

Pete shrugged and the movement caused him to wince with pain. "I'll live, I guess. None of my transistors were damaged, just stripped the insulation off a couple of wires. Don't let anybody kid you—this being a bionic man's not the cakewalk it's cut out to be."

Sheena settled into the seat across from him. She did not laugh at his joke. Instead her expression was more one of deep concern.

The second leg of the team's journey was uneventful, the landing at Shemya routine.

The black jet touched down easily, then taxied to a small cluster of low corrugated iron buildings where a fuel truck sat waiting in the white glare of portable floodlights. Overhead the night sky was clear and the wind almost non-existent. The northern lights ribboned the horizon with shimmering bands of pink, orange, and blue.

When Murphy opened the forward passenger door of the airplane and stepped down to the runway, a blast of frigid arctic air rushed inside the heated cabin. The fuel truck driver immediately went about his task of topping off the jet's fuel tanks as Murphy stood on the apron. Pete imagined that he appeared to be waiting for someone, but decided he was just being vigilant. Almost at once, however, a heavily bundled man came out of a nearby building and walked across the tarmac to where Murphy stood.

Pete noticed the man's approach and signaled Sheena. She glanced outside, then grabbed up a carbine and tossed another to

Pete. Hidden in the shadow of the airplane's open doorway, they trained their weapons on the intruder. It soon became apparent, however, that the weapons would not be needed. The man walked up to where Murphy stood, saluted smartly, and stuck out his mittened hand. He then handed Murphy some documents, which he quickly examined and returned. Pete glanced at Sheena and noted she was watching the transaction outside the airplane with extreme interest, a worried look on her face.

Murphy and the stranger exchanged a few words that although he tried Pete could not make out. Then the two stood closely together talking as the fuel man finished his job, climbed into the heated cab of his truck, and drove away.

Murphy led the new man toward the door of the jet and ushered him inside. Without saying anything Murphy closed the door behind him and the stranger, then signaled the pilots the team was ready. The jet began to roll.

Pete and Sheena stared at the man who had just come aboard with Murphy. He was six foot four if he was an inch and even beneath his heavy arctic gear it was obvious he was powerfully muscled. When he pulled back the hood of his parka, they could see his face was squarely built, his nose crooked where it had been broken some time in the past. His hair was cropped too short and his expression was the sort of half grin one normally associated with a person who is slightly retarded or who is Hollywood's stereotype of a Mafia hit man. He looked at Pete, sizing him up, then grinned broadly as his eyes swept Sheena, making no attempt to hide his appraisal of her body. She returned his glare without blinking. Pete steeled himself for fireworks.

Murphy glanced at the two of them. "Pete Shafer, Sheena Lawrence," he said, motioning to each. "I'd like you to meet Field Operative Harris."

# 10

TOKYO—Amid rumors that Soviet ships have located the wreckage of Trans-Pacifica Airlines Flight 18, United States and Japanese aircraft are continuing their search along the airliner's estimated flight path. However, the assumption now is that the 747 went down in Soviet territorial waters. The Soviets have steadfastly denied requests to be allowed to search within twelve miles of the Russian mainland.

A ship, bearing nearly fifty survivors of crash victims, was turned away from the area by Soviet gunboats.

A great many of the victims were Buddhist, a religion that requires at least a scrap of cloth from the body for the burial ceremony. It now appears that the Russians are going to deny the survivors even this small consolation.

*Newstime Magazine*
December 29, 1993

**T**he solid black, totally lightless Lear lifted off easily from Shemya, climbed just high enough to clear a few low-lying islands of the Aleutians, and headed northwest, keeping low to the water.

The distance from Shemya Island to their intended landfall north of Ostrov Karaginskiy on the Kamchatka Peninsula was just over six hundred nautical miles. At the jet's cruising speed of 420 knots they would cross the Bering Sea in a little under an hour and a half. With the exception of a few uninhabited rocky islands, their flight would be over open water.

The jet was flying direct VFR, with all exterior lights extinguished and blackout curtains on the windows. Navigation was strictly by dead reckoning and LORAN "C." Anything that might emit a signal of any sort—radar, Doppler, inertial—had been turned off, and the two pilots closely monitored several radios for any sign they had been spotted. Like Pete and Murphy, both pilots spoke and understood Russian. As they neared the drop area several hours later, Pete would join the pilots in the cockpit and steer them by landmarks. For now it was a beautiful clear night for flying and the two experienced combat pilots had the Lear well under control. They gave the impression of men who truly enjoyed their work.

Somewhere ahead of them across the black ocean was one of the roughest, coldest pieces of real estate south of the arctic circle.

As the Lear approached the most narrow part of Kamchatka, at the small native village of Kichiga, the pilots climbed slightly to clear the low saddle of land between the village and the west side of the peninsula. They planned to cross to the west side before turning south since most of the Soviet radar would be aimed east—not back toward the Russian homeland. Also their flight had been well-planned to avoid Soviet installations.

A few lights flickered below them as they zoomed past at nearly the speed of sound, but for the most part the peninsula was a great, low, gray-white mass stretched out beneath their path.

Flying about five hundred feet above the terrain, the dark forms of trees and rocks were clearly visible against the snow.

The Lear's rapid passing would probably cause no alarm. The natives, huddled around small fires in their huts below, had long ago grown used to the sound of patrolling Russian jets and even if they had seen the Lear, it was unlikely they would have known it was American or would have reported it if they had. As the Lear banked steeply and turned south, Murphy left the jump seat that had been installed just behind the pilots' chairs. He walked back through the dimly lighted cabin.

Harris busily studied a map by the pencil-thin red beam of a tiny flashlight, his brow wrinkled in concentration. Sheena adjusted the harness of her parachute. Pete, loading ammunition into a long curved clip of one of the 9mm carbines, glanced up as Murphy approached. "Everything looking okay?"

"So far. We're about an hour from the DZ. You'd better get suited up so you can help guide the pilots in case they need it."

"Right." Pete finished loading the clip and checked the action of the carbine. Satisfied, he laid it across the pile, and picked up one of the wetsuits. Quickly he stripped to his wool fishnet underwear and donned the garment that would keep him from freezing to death in case he landed in the ocean. He was careful to seal all the seams of the wetsuit with Velcro tape, knowing that the tiniest amount of exposed skin would rapidly freeze. Pete pulled his silver and gray camouflage fatigues over the wetsuit with some difficulty. The overall effect made him appear to have suddenly gained fifty pounds.

Over this he placed the parachute harness to which he would clip the parachute when they neared the drop zone. He sucked the straps tight between his legs. Then he stretched his arms over his head and let them fall, testing the fit of the harness. He made a few minor adjustments and nodded. He next picked up the 9mm and laid it alongside a black jump helmet to which was attached an oxygen mask, its hose dangling, ready to be connected to the jump bottles built into the parachute pack.

Pete looked around the cabin. Both Harris and Sheena had started to outfit themselves. Harris, however, had stopped dressing and was standing motionless, staring at Sheena as she stripped to her wool underwear. Harris noticed Pete watching him and quickly resumed dressing. Pete looked at Murphy and quickly motioned toward the front of the cabin. Murphy nodded that he understood.

Once Pete had gotten Murphy as far away from Sheena and Harris as possible, the two men turned their backs to the cabin. Pete spoke as quietly as he could and still be understood. "How close did you check Harris's ID?"

Murphy started, almost imperceptibly. He searched Pete's face for several seconds before he spoke. "As close as I could, given the circumstances. Everything checked. He knew the code words. Of course, a computer check was impossible. Why?" Murphy seemed agitated, almost hostile, that his judgment was being questioned.

"Lawrence acted awfully strange when he came on board, as if she knows more than she's letting on. And when she saw that dead man back there on Shemya she was trying too hard to keep her cool, if you know what I mean."

Murphy nodded. "I noticed that, too, but I was sure you'd just accuse me of being prejudiced if I mentioned it. What'd you think?"

Pete glanced around. Sheena was watching them closely. Harris was staring at her again.

"I don't know. Probably nothing, but my nerves're acting up. You did get a printout on Lawrence, didn't you?"

Murphy shook his head. "She was already in the complex when I met her. I assumed she'd been checked. Maybe that was a bad assumption. I should have checked her out myself."

"Too late now to matter. If she was smart enough to penetrate the D.C. complex, she'd surely have had everything else set up too."

"You think she had something to do with the crash?"

"Not likely. She was on the plane, too, remember."

"Yeah, but suicide missions aren't unheard of."

Pete shook his head. "No. She's too smart for that. Anyway, it's more the guy I don't trust."

"Harris? Now look, goddamn it, Pete. If you think—"

"I don't think anything. It's just a lot of little things suddenly don't quite add up."

Murphy hesitantly nodded agreement. "It'd be damned hard to scrap the mission now. We're less than half an hour out."

Suddenly Pete spun around. The man called Harris was two feet behind him, bent over, pretending to dig in a pile of gear.

Pete's first impulse was to grab the man and interrogate him on the spot, but Harris's huge bulk deterred him. Harris did not look up and gave no sign that he had been caught eavesdropping.

Pete got his anger under control. "Murph, I think we'd better get all this stuff strapped down in case we have to take any evasive action," he said loudly. He turned toward the cockpit. He got a brief glimpse of Sheena slipping the .357 automatic into a holster she had fastened to her belt.

It hurt him to have to distrust the woman. Pete disliked not trusting any of a team's members, but he could take no chances. Until he had sufficient reason to believe otherwise, Pete knew he was not going to be able to trust either Sheena or Harris. Neither seemed to be exactly what they claimed to be. Pete wondered if he was getting jumpy in his old age. That's what Murphy would have said.

Pete climbed into the cockpit and closed the small door that separated it from the cabin. The cockpit was lighted only by the faint glow of the instrument clusters surrounding the pilots. An overhead radio was crackling with static but was relaying no traffic. Pete knew the pilots would have it tuned to scan the Soviet's aircraft frequencies so they would hear if the Lear had been spotted and interceptors were being scrambled to come after them.

The captain, in the left seat, looked up as Pete climbed into the jump seat. "We've just passed Belogolovoye," he said, pointing to the right. Pete noticed that he pronounced the long Russian name perfectly.

"Our ETA to the drop zone is thirty-seven minutes," said the co-pilot, checking a small folded chart on a lighted clipboard that was secured to his thigh. I'm getting a wind of two hundred eighty-seven degrees at about eight knots. Of course, up higher, that'll be different, but it should hold pretty close."

"Thanks," said Pete. A light wind from the northwest was more than he had hoped for. It would give the parachutes maximum glide distance.

He turned his attention outside the windshield. "Much company out tonight?"

The pilot shook his head. "Nothing. We haven't even hit any radar." He tapped a small black box, attached to the dash, that resembled the traffic radar detectors used by truck drivers. It was infinitely more sophisticated than the average gear-jammer's "bird dog." It afforded 360-degree coverage on several bands at once.

"Too damned quiet," the co-pilot muttered. "I'd feel a hell of a lot better if this wagon had a couple of canons." His voice had a noticeable southern twang.

The captain laughed. "Don't mind Smitty. He got that way flying Thuds over 'Nam. He's harmless, really. Just breathed the fumes off so much Shake 'n' Bake he got punchy."

The co-pilot shrugged. "I just said they'd be nice, that's all." He checked his watch and turned to Pete. "Thirty-four minutes to DZ. Your guys ready?"

"Ready as we'll ever be. We want to go at about fifteen thousand if we can so we'll have room to maneuver."

"You can leave the babe with us if you want," said the co-pilot.

Pete laughed. "Sorry 'bout that fellows." He pointed to a radio receiver on the console between the two pilots. "That on Flight Eighteen's locator frequency?"

"Yeah, but we haven't gotten a thing yet." The co-pilot handed Pete a headset. "You can play with it if you want."

Pete slipped on the headset and adjusted the volume control. The co-pilot was right. The radio was receiving nothing but steady static.

"We should be getting something by now, shouldn't we?" he asked.

The pilot answered. "Hard to say. If it's underwater, its range would be greatly limited. Atmospheric conditions, shape of the battery, all have a lot to do with it. You don't even know for sure the locator wasn't destroyed in the crash."

"I don't think so," said the co-pilot. "Crash locators are tougher than hell. It'd take a direct hit to knock one out."

Pete held up his hand. "I think I'm getting something." He twisted the volume knob and adjusted the squelch.

The faint but unmistakable klaxonlike sound of a crash locator could be heard in the headset. Pete twisted another knob on the radio, trying to get a direction to the signal, but it was too weak to swing the pointer.

"We're still seventy miles out," said the pilot. He started to say something else, but was cut short by what sounded like a burst of thunder directly overhead. The Lear bounced violently like it had just flown through a hard updraft.

Pete had to grab onto the jump seat to keep from being flung against the ceiling of the cockpit. Almost as quickly as it had bounced, the Lear smoothed out.

"Jesus Christ!" shouted the co-pilot. "What was that?"

"I think we just flew through the turbulence of a couple of MiGs," said the pilot. "They must have come between those two ridges over there to the left. We probably missed a mid-air by seconds."

"You think they spotted us?" asked Pete.

"Not likely," said the pilot. They were probably four or five miles west before we came by and MiGs don't usually fly with their radar aimed behind them. The Russians are pretty slack unless they're looking for something in particular. Lot of young guys draw Kamchatka duty. Sort of like the Air Force sends our boys to Minot. More than likely a training mission of some sort or a routine patrol."

"I wouldn't be so damned sure of that if I were you," said the co-pilot.

The pilot laughed nervously. "There you go again, expecting the worse."

"Expecting the worse kept me out of the Hanoi Hilton for eighty-seven missions over Thud Ridge."

Pete whistled quietly. Eighty-seven missions over the heavily fortified mountain range south of Hanoi, called Thud Ridge, was certainly some kind of a record. He was flying with a man who knew his business. And this guy was just the co-pilot! Pete had just begun to speak when the radar detector started buzzing.

"I knew it," said the co-pilot quietly. They've turned and spotted us. He reached for the instrument panel and flipped a switch. A square cathode ray tube in front of him leaped to life.

The co-pilot pointed to two black dots at four o'clock on the CRT. "There they are. Damn! What I've give for a couple of good sidewinders right now!"

"Be glad you don't have them," said the pilot quietly. "Even if you managed to get these two, the Russians have plenty more where those came from. Unless I miss my guess, these are a couple of MiG-23s that carry at least six missiles apiece and can fly three times faster than we can. Our only defense is our maneuverability." He turned to Pete, but he didn't need to. Pete was already yelling into the cabin for the others to strap in.

The pilot quickly rolled the Lear ninety degrees and slipped left. Suddenly the radio crackled alive with Russian as the two interceptors gave chase. From the excited voices of the MiG pilots, even had he not spoken fluent Russian, Pete would have known the Lear pilot had been right. They were relatively inexperienced pilots, probably not combat veterans, but certainly not rank amateurs or they would never have been trusted with the new and highly sophisticated MiG-23s or Su-15s that were a staple aircraft on the Kamchatka.

The two Russian pilots conferred hurriedly back and forth. One wanted to notify their headquarters immediately, but the other cautioned against it. He argued that if they were mistaken about sighting something, they would be punished if they scrambled the squadron. The other reluctantly agreed.

The Lear, already flying low, dived and zoomed just above the treetops. "Hot damn!" yelled the co-pilot as the ground rushed by at better than seven miles a minute.

Pete breathed a bit easier. At least it wasn't too likely the pilots would risk firing a missile without permission from their base. His relaxation was cut short by a stream of tracer bullets that suddenly went zipping past the cockpit window.

The pilot rolled right and the two MiGs zipped past them at nearly twice the Lear's speed. For a few seconds the cockpit was illuminated by the fiery blast of the fighters' engines. They were, as suspected, swept-wing MiG-23s.

"They aren't going to be such bad shots next time," said the pilot. "We gotta get the hell out of here!"

"What do you suggest? We sure as hell can't outrun the bastards." The co-pilot reached for the controls of a jamming device on the ceiling above the Lear's windshield.

Pete reached out and tapped him on the shoulder. "Wait." He turned to the pilot. "Our best bet is to have those two guys lose us completely, so they don't go calling out their buddies. Slowed down, how tight a circle can this bird hold?"

The pilot looked over his shoulder like Pete was crazy. "At just above stall speed, about two miles. Why?"

"There's a volcano twenty miles off to our left if I remember correctly. It's got a crater that's about four miles across and five hundred feet deep. May be hairy in the dark. You game?"

"Fly into a volcano? What are you, nuts?"

"Why the hell not?" asked the co-pilot. "At least our friends back there couldn't get down in it with us."

"It's goddamned crazy. That's why!"

Another string of tracer bullets went by the windshield, closer this time. "Our boys are getting better," said the co-pilot. "They're only missing by a hundred yards now." As he spoke the Lear rocked and swayed. The right wing took a hit out near the tip. A fuel gauge for the right tip-tank showed it emptying quickly. "Damn! They got a tank."

"Where's that crater?" demanded the pilot. Pete pointed east.

They rolled east then swooped low and hugged the tops of trees as the land gradually sloped upward. Just as they neared the top, the Lear shook again as more bullets hit the right wing.

As they passed the crest of the volcano's rim, the pilot cut the power and dived into the crater. The MiGs flew over and past them, missing the Lear by feet.

The pilots fought the Lear down to a speed of 120 knots using flaps and lowering the landing gear. The jet strained and shuddered at the sudden deceleration. The inside of the crater was flooded with a stark, white moonlight. The sinuous piles of lava around the crater's rim cast harsh, jagged shadows that made the flat black-painted Lear almost impossible to spot from above.

The inside of the crater was as Pete had remembered. It was about four miles across and approximately five hundred feet deep. It was impossible to tell much about the bottom, but here and there little clouds of steam and hot gasses splurted skyward. The smell of sulfur filled the cockpit. On one side of the crater a long wicked-looking crack glowed red, showing that the cauldron was still very much active.

"Damn!" said the co-pilot. "You didn't say this was a live volcano!"

"Would it have mattered?"

The co-pilot laughed. "No. Thud Ridge. Golan. Hell. It's all the same to me. A few more hours in the old logbook."

As the pilots got the jet into a steady holding pattern two hundred feet below the crater's rim, Pete listened intently to the radios for the two Russian pilots to speak.

"Let's hope those two guys decide they didn't see anything," said Pete. "There's a good chance they won't want to admit shooting at something without permission first."

Almost as if in answer to Pete's statement, the radio crackled to life as one of the pilots spoke. "I don't like this," he said.

"Neither do I," replied the other. "I could have sworn we saw something."

"Me, too. Should we report it do you think?"

"It'd be a lot of paperwork."

"Yes. And explaining to do if it wasn't found."

"Is this channel monitored?"

"Yes. But we are out of range of our base and they can't hear us."

"Good. I say we continue our patrol as if nothing happened. Kamchatka duty is rough enough without getting in trouble with the colonels or being branded trigger-happy."

"I'm with you. This crate's colder than hell. My heater doesn't work. How is yours?"

"The same. My toes are freezing."

Their voices trailed away as the two MiGs turned and headed northward. Inside the cockpit of the Lear there was a collective sigh of relief.

"We'll give them a few minutes and then beat it," said the pilot.

When the Lear left the crater and resumed its intended course, Pete checked the pilot's charts. With a pencil he pointed to a tiny unlabeled speck in the ocean that was almost due south of the occupied island of Paramushir. The pilot glanced down at where Pete pointed on the chart. "Doesn't look like much."

"It's not. Couple of hundred acres. A few low trees, bushes, a lot of rocks. Hopefully no Russians."

Murphy stuck his head in the door. "How we looking?"

"Fine, now that we've shook our boys back there." Pete turned to the pilots. "You guys handle it now? I got to go check my luggage." The co-pilot gave him the thumbs up. "Sure you fellows wouldn't like to come along?"

"No way. You know the old saying about jumping out of a perfectly good airplane, don't you?" said the co-pilot. "Besides, it's colder than hell out there. Thanks anyway."

Pete laughed and followed Murphy out of the cockpit, closing the door behind him.

Sheena and Harris were already suited up and waiting. Their bulky parachutes were strapped to their backs like backpacks. They had slipped on their helmets and had their oxygen masks hanging ready to be connected to the jump bottles. Sheena had the 30-caliber machine gun slung across her chest in addition to the holstered .357. A wicked-looking black steel survival knife was strapped to her right thigh.

Harris was dressed pretty much the same as Sheena, except he was armed only with one of the 9mm carbines and a survival knife.

The two cargo chutes had been pushed to the back of the airplane where they would be kicked out first when the special drop ramp was opened.

As Pete and Murphy helped each other hoist on their parachutes, Pete felt the jet turn and start to climb. They were rounding Mys Lopatka.

He plugged his helmet's headset into his chest pack, did a quick radio check with the others, then called the cockpit.

The co-pilot's voice came through Pete's headphones loud and clear. "Seventy-five hundred and climbing. Fifty-five seconds to green light."

"Roger," replied Pete. "Clear of jump door."

"Roger. Jump door coming down." Across the rear of the ceiling a row of red lights started flashing and the aft six feet of the cabin's floor started to slowly open downward like a huge metal jaw. The rush of air and roar of the jet's engines made it impossible to hear. Pete pressed his helmet close to his head and turned up the intercom's volume to hear the co-pilot as he went through the jump checklist.

"Twenty-five seconds."

Pete got a firm grip on a stanchion and braced one foot solidly against the first cargo bundle. At the ten second mark he gave the bundle a shove with his leg. The bundle rolled a few feet and fell free. Behind it the other followed.

"Five, four, three, good luck, folks, two, one." Overhead, the red flashing lights turned to green. "Green light!"

Pete ducked to clear the doorway and took two short steps before he felt nothing under him but air. He rolled over into deployment position. In the darkness the three black specks of Murphy, Sheena, and Harris appeared one after another, as the barely visible shape of the airplane rapidly receded.

Slowly he counted to ten when the parachute would open automatically. Although he had jumped countless hundreds of times, Pete still felt relief at the tiny tug as the pilot chute deployed, pulling with it the main that burst into black square flower above him, and jerked him to a near stop.

He glanced down at the small rectangular package of radio gear on his chest. Two tiny green pinpoints of light told him the radio and homing equipment were operating perfectly. A small lighted digital compass showed him heading almost due north. Reaching above his head, he grasped the control shrouds and swung the canopy until the compass gave a heading of 220 degrees.

On the horizon, slightly off to his right, Pete could see the lights of Paramushir. Ahead of him, barely visible against the black of the ocean, about four miles away was a tiny speck that was the team's destination. His altimeter showed he was drifting through 8700 feet. Finally something on this trip was going right.

Behind him and to his right Pete could hear the roar of jet fighter aircraft being scrambled from Petropavlovsk. The Russians had at last picked up the Lear on their radar. More than likely the pilots had let themselves be spotted on purpose to take attention away from the team. Of course, the small jet was by now already far out over international waters and beating it back to Alaska by the shortest route. By the time the Russians thought of looking for parachutes, the team would be safely down and hidden.

As he drifted peacefully through the cold night sky, Pete started to laugh out loud inside his oxygen mask. "Fifty-one years old," he told himself, "swinging from a parachute a mile over Russia and, like a goddamned fool, enjoying every minute of it."

# 11

UNITED NATIONS—The United States and the Soviet Union angrily exchanged charges yesterday in some of the harshest words heard at the United Nations since the Reagan administration days.

U.S. Delegate Harrison Springfield said that the Soviet Union in refusing to accept responsibility for the downing of TPA Flight 18 "is showing its true face to the world, a face that hides behind the word 'peace,' of which it doesn't know the meaning.

"Russia is a ruthless, lying totalitarian state," said Springfield, "that enslaves other nations and kills its own people just like it murdered the innocent people aboard Flight 18.

"Russia's goal," Springfield continued, "is to eventually enslave the world."

*The New York Daily Mail*
December 29, 1993

**T**he island below Pete measured about three quarters of a mile long in its north-south direction and at its widest point approximately a half-mile across. He scanned the island for any signs of life, any lights or fire, but there were no indications anywhere that the island was occupied. The perimeter for twenty or thirty feet back from the black water was composed of jagged, ice-glazed rocks that shone whitely in the moonlight, giving the rugged little island the effect of being surrounded by a glowing mother-of-pearl collar.

Where large rocks protruded above the bushes and grass, the wind had drifted snow on their east sides so that each appeared to have a long white tail, a pale east-pointing weathervane showing the prevailing winds. Except for the drifts and a thin layer of snow that had filtered through the undergrowth, the often savage, almost constant wind had swept the island clean. Tonight, however, the wind was little more than a gentle breeze, although icy cold.

Pete landed standing up, expertly unclipping the parachute canopy as it billowed behind him in the light breeze. A few seconds later Murphy landed nearby, also standing.

Sheena was next. She came in almost horizontally, tacking across the wind to avoid hitting a clump of bushes. She landed a bit harder than Pete or Murphy, falling on her side, but she jumped up, unhurt.

Pete searched the sky for Harris. At first he did not spot their fourth team member and felt a wave of relief at the thought that Harris, for whatever reason, may not have jumped. His relief was short-lived, though, for he suddenly heard the whistle of air rushing beneath Harris's canopy almost straight out in front of him.

Harris had somehow fallen short and tried desperately, amateurishly, to stretch his glide the final few feet to avoid landing in the surging water. He lifted his feet for the final few yards, and his knees crashed hard into the ice-coated rocks, and he crumpled as he hit. His canopy settled into the ocean and the waves tugged at it, threatening to drag him in.

Pete ran toward the shore, tripping over roots and rocks in the darkness as he went. Murphy and Sheena followed. Harris was lying almost unconscious, half in the icy surf, his parachute still attached. He had ripped off his oxygen mask and was gasping for breath.

Pete tried to release Harris's chute but the clips were frozen fast. Whipping out his survival knife, he slashed the shroud lines, allowing the canopy to float free. Then he and the others dragged the helpless Harris over the rocks, repeatedly slipping and falling over each other in the darkness as they struggled with the heavy man.

"He's soaking," said Sheena. "Even in a wet suit, he'll chill fast if we don't get him out of those clothes."

"I saw one of our cargo chutes hanging in the bushes just west of where we landed." Murphy shouted. "I hope it's the one with the sleeping bags and camping equipment." He crashed up the bank in the direction they had come, leaving Pete and Sheena alone to drag Harris away from the shore.

They were both soaked to the waist by the time they had rescued Harris from the surf. Pete removed the man's constricting parachute harness and examined him for injuries. He found none. "He must have just hit his head so hard that he was knocked out in spite of the helmet," said Pete. "He'll come around."

Sheena stood, looking over Pete's shoulder. "I somehow get the feeling he'd never jumped before," she said. "He seemed scared to death up there."

Pete held up Harris's oxygen mask and pointed to a knob on its front. "Looks like he didn't even know how to turn his oxygen bottle on. It's a damned wonder he didn't die up there. Damned computers! Who picked him for this mission? I wonder."

Sheena took the bottle from Pete and opened the valve. Nothing came out. The bottle was empty yet the gauge still showed it as being full.

"Someone must have gotten to Harris's oxygen," Pete said. But why just Harris, he wondered. Why not the rest of them as well.

"Or he used it up himself," said Sheena, "then turned the bottle off and pretended to be in trouble."

Pete looked at her. She seemed rather sure of her diagnosis.

The pale moonlight played on her face, but it held no further answers. He knew he had to find out some things, and the sooner the better. He feared the aura of mistrust that was springing up in the team. He had seen such mistrust arise before and the results had always been disasterous. He had a strong feeling that something was very wrong with this mission and he wondered how Sheena fit into his building uneasiness. Yet, it was Harris, not Sheena, that worried him the most. The man had all the markings of a bumbling fool—only he had more of the markings that a genuine bumbler would have.

He could still hear Murphy crashing around in the brush, searching for the cargo parachutes. At his feet Harris groaned slightly like he might be coming around. Sheena watched him closely, resting her hand on the handle of the .357.

Pete motioned for Sheena to help him bundle up the parachute harness and carry it up the bank. Taking a final look at Harris, Sheena followed Pete. When he had led her out of Harris's hearing, Pete braced himself for the confrontation. "I want to know what you know about Harris," he said, his voice low, but steady and commanding.

Sheena breathed in deeply before she answered. "You don't know?"

Pete shook his head. "Know what?"

Sheena let her hand slide up her leg until it was poised, ready, just above the .357.

Pete saw the movement. "You seemed nervous as hell every time the name Harris got mentioned yesterday and your reaction to that body on Wrangell was pretty damned obvious. You're hiding something and I think I can guess what it is, although I don't know why." He motioned at Sheena's hand near the .357. "Now, I suggest you quit thinking about using that piece, and tell me what it is that's bothering you so much."

"And if I don't?" Her hand tightened around the weapon.

"Then neither one of us will ever get to the bottom of all this."

Sheena let her hand drop. Then she looked all around her to assure herself that they were out of earshot of both Harris and Murphy. She stepped close to Pete until their bodies were nearly touching.

She started to speak, paused as if unsure of whether to go on, then said, "That man down there isn't Harris. I thought you knew that."

Pete nodded. "No, but I suspected as much. Who is he then?"

Sheena shook her head. "I don't have any idea. He's sure as hell not one of ours, I don't think."

"You should have told Murphy at Shemya."

"I don't trust him. I know you guys go back a long way, but I still don't trust him. He was too ready to accept that man as Harris, like he knew him from somewhere else."

Pete glanced up as the sounds of Murphy returning through the brush became louder. Quickly he said, "How are you so certain he isn't Harris?"

"Because the other one was." Sheena looked at Pete nervously as Murphy's silhouette appeared on the skyline, carrying a large bundle on his shoulder.

"The body?"

Sheena took a step up the bank. "We'd better look like we're on our way to help," she said, turning, then added under her breath, "Yes."

Pete grabbed her wrist and held her back. "Are you sure?"

Sheena spun angrily around and faced him, jerking her wrist free. Even in the pale moonlight, her green eyes flashed fire. "I slept with that man for three years before we split. Anything else you want to know?"

Pete shook his head without answering and started up the bank. Sheena followed.

Murphy dumped the bundle to the ground and paused to catch his breath as Pete and Sheena met him. "I found one of the cargo chutes," he said. "The other probably made it too. We'll need to find it before morning or it might be spotted.

"There's a sort of cliff back up there. Looks like it may have some caves in it we could use." He opened the bundle and pulled out a compacted bedroll that contained a sleeping bag.

"Let's get Harris up here and into this, then go check out the cliff."

They found Harris sitting up, trembling violently, but conscious. They helped him struggle to his feet, but even with the three of them assisting it took fifteen minutes to get him stripped of his wet fatigues, into the sleeping bag, and out of sight beneath some low bushes that grew just above the high-water line. Pete dug in the bundle Murphy had brought and found two chemical heat packets. He activated them, shoving one down deep in the bag on each side of Harris. Murphy zipped up the sleeping bag and ordered Harris to lie still and wait for them to return.

Then Pete and Sheena followed Murphy across the island to the cliffs he had described. The going was extremely rough and they slipped often, Murphy cursing quietly each time he fell. The cliffs were really more a line of jumbled granitic boulders than actual cliffs, but they had numerous overhangs and in one place a giant slab of rock had fallen across several other rocks, forming a roof over a bedroom-sized space in which they were able to stand without stooping.

Shielding a small flashlight in his hands, Pete surveyed the inside of the cave. It was protected from the wind and snow on all sides except the front by the rocks. The floor was for the most part flat stone, but near the front a thin layer of soil and leaves had blown in and a few strands of dead grass showed that the wind had also carried in a few seeds. There were some old animal droppings in a far corner that appeared to have been left by a fox or wolf, an evaluation bolstered by the presence of several well-gnawed bones scattered about. The bones were dry and old. Here and there, in the pile of boulders that formed the room's back wall, were small passages between the rocks that looked as if they might be the entrances to small animal lairs. A few appeared large enough that a human could crawl into them and hide if necessary.

"Caves give me the creeps," Pete said.

"Not so much as nosy Russian airplanes," replied Sheena, glancing at her watch. "We have about three hours in which to find our other cargo chute and get out of sight for the day. Unless I miss my guess, our Soviet friends are likely to figure the U.S. might have sent in some searchers and they'll be keeping an eye out. This looks good enough for a base camp."

"Right," agreed Murphy. "The first thing we ought to do is get Harris up here where he'll be out of sight until he warms up enough to help. Then we can spread out and find our gear."

Harris was sitting up with the sleeping bag pulled around his head when Pete, Sheena, and Murphy returned. He was still trembling but appeared nearly back to normal. With their help he managed to walk to the cave, still wrapped in the sleeping bag.

Harris protested when Murphy ordered him to remain in the cave until they returned with the gear, but he reluctantly obeyed.

Pete checked the 9mm carbine that he had carried down with him for damage, found none, and chambered a round. Murphy did the same with another of the carbines. In addition to the .357 attached to her belt, Sheena equipped herself with the small machine gun.

"You two can check out as much of the island perimeter as you can before daylight or until you find something," Murphy instructed Pete and Sheena. "Be especially alert to any signs of a Russian landing party. I'll go get the rest of the gear from the parachute I found and then start looking for the other one. We better plan on being undercover by dawn." He looked at the night sky. "It's going to be a clear day. Good for flying. Bad for us."

Pete and Sheena left Murphy at the cave and headed toward the north end of the island across the mass of jumbled boulders. After nearly an hour of this, they finally came out on more solid ground, hard-frozen where the wind had swept the snow away.

Although for nearly two hours they searched the tangled undergrowth of the island, interspersed with open spaces made by wind or fire, they found as much as they said to each other— nothing of any consequence at all.

To the southeast the sky was beginning to lighten. Pete knew they should probably start heading back to the cave to help Murphy and Harris establish a base camp, but he wasn't yet satisfied that the island was uninhabited.

He looked at Sheena. Her breath made clouds of silvery-white steam in the minus twenty degree temperature. Her height had made crawling through the tunnels of brush especially hard. Not once, though, had she complained.

Sheena saw Pete watching her and smiled slightly. "Damned rough in there," she said.

"Sure is. Maybe we can find our way back by an easier route. It'll be full daylight in an hour. We should probably try to get back and make sure Murph and Harris found the other cargo chute."

Sheena nodded. "Look, I didn't mean to get down on you back there about Harris. I'm really on edge right now. There was no offense intended."

"None taken. I guess I'm just getting like Murphy in some ways. All these computers and stuff make me nervous too. In the old days we usually got to pick our own team members out of people we knew and trusted. Now the computers do that for you. It's become impersonal.

"Maybe it's better that way. You don't go developing personal loyalties and conflicts; therefore you tend to put the mission above the lives of operatives you didn't even know the day before yesterday, but I still don't like it."

"I guess I understand. I like to be able to trust my team members too." She paused. "Just who do you think our Harris is, anyway?"

"Not who he wants us to think he is, that's for sure. Of course, after you've been in this business as long as I have, you get to where you automatically assume that. It's all a matter of mirrors— the only question is how many."

"And Murphy? Is he who he seems?"

"Yeah. Whoever Murph thinks he is at the moment, that's who he is."

"It's all very confusing."

Sheena started to walk down a path that appeared to lead toward the shore. Pete fell in behind her. "That's why they call it espionage," he said.

The half light of dawn made the going somewhat easier, and they soon broke out of the bushes onto the open shoreline. Between the ice-glazed rocks of the beach and the almost solid wall of bushes, there was a narrow strip of hard-packed dirt and gravel on which travel proved to be considerably easier. The sky was rapidly brightening. About twelve miles out to sea Pete thought he saw the shadowy form of a large ship of some sort. Although he could not tell at that distance, Pete hoped it was American. He would have to find a pair of binoculars in one of the cargo bundles and check. If, he thought, no, *when* the mission was completed, they might be able to make it to the ship if their own pickup, the Geisha Lady, did not materialize.

They had walked for nearly half a mile before they located enough of a beach to launch the Zodiacs, a tiny patch of rocky sand between two larger boulders that sat partly submerged by the low surf. It was littered with bits of driftwood that had washed up. Sheena stopped, careful to step from stone to stone so as to leave no tracks that would betray the team's presence. Then she saw something partially buried beneath a tangled pile of wave-tossed rubbish at the water's edge.

Still taking care to leave no tracks, Sheena made her way the few feet to the object and yanked it free from the other trash. It was soggy and heavy, but she managed to hold it up. In the center of the airplane seat cushion was the Trans-Pacifica Airlines symbol of a rising Phoenix against a rayed sunburst. If there had ever been any doubt that Flight 18 had crashed in the ocean, there wasn't now.

Keeping an eye out for any airplanes that might pass overhead, Pete and Sheena spent the next half-hour searching the shore for more debris from Flight 18. They found few bits of cloth and insulation. They could not be sure the fragments were from the Trans-Pacifica 747, but in such an isolated part of the ocean they were unlikely to have come from any other source. They were just about to abandon the search and return to the cave when Sheena bent over and picked up a small child's Nike tennis shoe. The tiny pink shoe was ripped nearly in half.

Sheena held the shoe away from her and looked at it sadly. "I just hope she didn't suffer much," was all she said.

Before they could search further Pete and Sheena heard the roar of an aircraft approaching from the north. They ducked into the bushes as a lumbering Russian cargo airplane, almost identical to an American C-130 Hercules, passed overhead at an altitude of about four thousand feet.

After the airplane had passed, Pete stepped out from the bushes and scanned the western horizon. "Damned sky will be full of planes before long," he said. "We'd better get back."

They tossed the bits of wreckage they had collected beneath a thick tangle of alder. Then Pete led the way in the direction of their landing site, keeping close to the shoreline. Twice other airplanes passed overhead, forcing Pete and Sheena to stoop motionless beneath the bushes until the aircraft had passed. Their silver-gray and white mottled fatigues blended almost perfectly with the stark colors of the leafless alders, but their fatigues would give them no protection from heat-sensitive infra-red cameras. Apparently, though, the Russians weren't anticipating finding any warm bodies on this particular island. They appeared more interested in the American and Japanese ships that Pete suspected were hovering just beyond the twelve-mile coastal limit.

When Pete judged they were abreast of the cave, they turned inland. After about a hundred yards of bushwacking, Pete struck a narrow path leading toward the cave. The path wandered into one of the island's open areas, a room-sized vale, half covered with drifted snow. At the windward side of the clearing the snow appeared to be about waist deep with a hard glazed ice coating where its surface had been briefly thawed by the sun and refrozen.

Pete led the way around the patch of snow when a gasp from Sheena stopped him mid-stride. He spun, flinging up his carbine, and looked where she pointed.

Against the far side of the clearing, blending into the gray sameness of the alders and vines, was a neat row of four crude crosses fashioned from bits of driftwood and broken twigs lashed together with fragments of wire and shoelaces. Whoever had completed the morbid task had thrown his grave-digging tool, a jagged piece of aircraft aluminium, into the brush.

The snow around the makeshift graves was trampled by two distinct sets of footprints; a larger set, obviously those of a man, and a smaller set that could have belonged to either a woman or a child. At one point the tracks led away from the graves and disappeared into the underbrush.

Pete and Sheena did not disturb the graves or crosses. They could yield little to help their mission, although they might later reveal what had happened to Flight 18. Instead they tried to follow the tracks leading into the brush. For nearly two hundred yards they were able to distinguish a trail leading toward the cliffs but then the two sets of tracks emerged into a rocky clearing and they lost the trail. Although Pete and Sheena circled the area twice, they were unable to find it again. They returned to the cave.

Murphy looked up as they entered. "I was beginning to get worried about you," he said. "We didn't find the cargo chute. Any luck?"

Pete shook his head no and then told him about the four graves and the footprints leading inland.

"Not good," Murphy said. "If there are still survivors on the island, they'll be trying like hell to attract attention—anybody's attention. That's just what we don't want. Are you sure you can't find the tracks again?"

Pete glanced at Sheena, who was watching Harris sort the

weapons with great interest. "I don't know," he said. "We have to try. I don't see how anyone could have survived the crash, much less gotten ashore and then kept from freezing to death." He paused. "We owe it to them to at least look. If they're still alive, we have to help them if we can."

Murphy, who had set up a small alcohol-fueled stove, looked up from his pot of boiling water. "Sure," he said. "If we can." He paused while he dumped another handful of snow into his pot. "But need I remind you that the mission comes first?"

# 12

The President announced today that long-range missile talks with the Soviets have been canceled indefinitely.

Citing the downing of TPA Flight 18 as his reason, the President told reporters that further discussions would be worthless.

"The Soviets respect only one thing," he said, "and that is strength."

He went on to advocate the immediate resumption of plans to install a cluster of "super-missiles" in Western Europe, a plan that has been stalled in Congress and strongly resisted by NATO.

However, in an apparent bow to the powerful American farming lobby, the President said that prior grain deals with the Soviet Union would be allowed to stand, although he ruled out any future sales of wheat until the Soviets "make restitution" to the families of the passengers aboard Flight 18.

WUSA Radio News Report
December 29, 1993

**P**ete and Sheena joined Harris in sorting out and inspecting the gear from the chute they had recovered. Although there was still hope of finding the other cargo bundle, Pete noted with alarm that, in addition to the second Zodiac, the missing bundle contained most of the team's food except for a few emergency combat rations, all their spare clothing, the tents, and their first aid box. They hoped the last item would not be needed, but if it was they would be hardpressed without it since it contained their entire supply of sutures, antibiotics, and other drugs. Also missing were two of the scuba tanks. Their portable radio transceiver for making contact with their rescue vehicle, however, was in the recovered bundle.

As they worked, Pete attempted to engage Harris in conversation by commenting on the equipment. Twice he made comments that were obviously incorrect, just to draw Harris out or test his knowledge. But, if Harris noted Pete's deliberate errors, he showed no signs. His only responses were grunts and noncommittal nods.

Before long, the gear had all been inspected and found to have survived the drop in perfect condition. Then Pete helped Harris set up the radio and rig an antenna out of wire strung between two rocks just outside the cave while Sheena studied underwater maps of the nearby ocean floor. From somewhere Murphy produced four plastic cups and a small cellophane container of instant coffee. He passed around the cups and then the coffee, cautioning them that it had to last until they found the other cargo bundle. Only Pete realized that Murphy's distribution of his precious personal coffee supply that he always carried with him was a great sacrifice. With instant coffee and a few packs of Camels Pete believed Murphy could have survived and been contented anywhere.

A little eddy of air whipped up some light ice crystals in front of the cave and sent them spinning inside, causing the Svea's flame to splutter and threaten to go out. Sheena held her rapidly cooling cup of coffee between gloved hands. "I've been studying the charts of the ocean floor," she said, "and that monitor could be in anything from a few feet of water to well over a hundred leagues, in which case we could never reach it using scuba gear. In fact, it could have fallen into one of the many fault cracks in the area. Some of those things could be ten, fifteen miles deep."

"In that case," said Murphy, "it'd be out of reach of the Russians, too, which would save us the trouble of having to blow it up. We don't necessarily have to destroy it, just so long as the Russians can't get to it." He finished his coffee and stood up. Then he walked to the entrance to the cave and looked out. Pete accompanied him.

As they stood looking out at the rapidly darkening sky, Pete sniffed the air. It had a musty smell to it that told of an approaching storm, which would, at least, make flying difficult, if not impossible. But this slim advantage would be offset by rough seas, which would endanger the team's small Zodiacs. They could be swamped and sink in seconds.

"I can't decide if the weather's cooperating with us or the Russians," Murphy said. "But storm or no storm, I think we have to get the one boat we have set up and ready to go. We can cover it with a camouflage tarp and tie it down if the wind picks up."

Sheena and Pete carried the deflated boat and Murphy and Harris brought as much as they could carry of the other equipment. They made their way from the cave to the beach Pete and Sheena had discovered. By the time the team had wrestled the heavy boat and the other equipment from the cave to the water's edge, both Pete and Murphy showed signs of exhaustion.

"What say we let the youngsters go get the motor and fuel cans," Murphy suggested. Pete readily nodded agreement.

"Sure," grunted Harris. The single word was the most he had said for over an hour. He turned and started to trot briskly back up the bank. Sheena stretched and adjusted the belt inside her parka that held the holstered .357. She had left the machine gun that she had been carrying all morning in the cave so her hands would be free to carry the boat. After a backward glance at Pete and Murphy, she followed Harris.

"Not much love lost between those two kids, it doesn't look like," Murphy said when Harris and Sheena had disappeared into the bushes.

"She claims he isn't Harris," Pete said.

Murphy tightened. "Was she serious?"

"She seems to be."

"Damn, Pete!" Murphy spat on the ground. "I wish you'd told me earlier."

"Frankly, Murph, I haven't had a chance. Besides, you seemed pretty damned sure of Harris's ID."

Murphy stood for several seconds, deep in thought and staring out across the island. Finally, he waved his hand in front of his face and laughed as if to dismiss the whole idea. "Ah, he probably just tried to get in her pants or something. Hell, I would if I was younger."

Pete chuckled at Murphy's comment. There was snow on the mountain, but fire still in the furnace. "No," he said, "I think they genuinely distrust each other."

"And you and I, buddy, had best distrust them both until we're sure just who the hell they really are."

"KGB, you think?"

"Hell, no! CIA more likely. Or just a couple of kids the goddamned computer pulled out of somewhere. Of course they aren't the strangest operatives we've ever seen, huh?"

Pete nodded, aware that Murphy wasn't going to let himself be drawn into a discussion of their two companions. Even with Pete, Murphy had always been pretty closed-mouthed when it came to his real opinions about his fellow agents, despite the fact that he was usually more than willing to complain about anyone or anything but in general terms. "Yeah," Pete said. "Remember the one-armed fellow who stole the camel outside Tehran?"

Murphy actually laughed out loud. "Claimed a crocodile ate his arm in Egypt? Yeah. I remember that one. His name was Highland or something. Englishman."

"What else?" He walked over to the heavy rolled-up boat and loosened the straps that held it. He gave the deflated boat a shove with his foot. It unrolled stiffly. In the cold even the special combination of rubber and nylon had grown almost rigid.

Inside the package was a yellow cannister, about the size of a small fire extinguisher, that contained compressed air. Pete unfolded the roll of material sideways until it resembled a small boat about ten feet in length, slightly pointed at the bow. Permanently attached to the stern was a black painted piece of plywood for mounting an outboard motor. Two inflatable seats from side to side across the boat divided it into three almost even sections.

Pete checked all the boat's air valves to make sure they were closed and looked around for anything on the ground that might puncture the rubber and nylon skin as it inflated. The boat was equipped with a manual air pump for use in case of emergencies, but to inflate a completely flat boat with the manual pump would take at least thirty minutes. The compressed air charge would do it in forty-five seconds.

Pete screwed the top of the yellow canister into a brass connection in the side of the boat. Although the boat was designed to be inflated from one place, it divided into five compartments, each separated by one-way valves. Should one air compartment be punctured, the other four compartments would hold their charge of air.

By the time Pete was finished inflating the boat, the wind had picked up considerably. The sky had become completely covered with thick, gray-black clouds and the temperature had plummeted another ten degrees. The wind blew thin icy snowflakes horizontally across the island, stinging Pete's face, his only exposed skin, like tiny needles.

He and Murphy set about arranging the equipment in the boat. They did not talk as they worked, both knowing from long experience what had to be done. Everything was in place except for the motor and fuel cans that Sheena and Harris had gone to fetch. Pete and Murphy covered the boat with the thin nylon-canvas camouflage tarp to keep the boat from filling up with snow and to further conceal it from prying eyes, although the rapidly gathering storm would probably preclude any more flights. The ocean waves had increased in size, even on the lee of the island. Angry little whitecaps flicked menacingly at the tops of many of the waves like sharp silver claws.

Pete glanced at his watch, then toward Murphy. "They should be back with the motor by now," he said, shouting above the noise of the approaching storm.

Murphy looked up from the lines he was using to tie the tarp over the boat, his face beet-red from exertion and the cold. "Maybe they got lost," he shouted back.

Pete finished securing his side of the tarp to some rocks so the wind wouldn't pick it up, then joined Murphy in tying down the other. "Not likely. We'd better go check. They may need help."

Without waiting for an answer from Murphy, Pete grabbed up the 9mm carbine he had leaned against a bush and headed up the bank toward the cliffs. He did not sling the weapon over his shoulder but, instead, carried it ready for action in his gloved hands. Murphy grabbed his own carbine and followed.

As Pete neared the crest of the low ridge, he ran headlong into the fifty knot winds. He had to crouch low as he ran to make any headway. The black stratus roared not far above his head like a gigantic hellbound freight.

Pete knew from experience that the storm could blow over by morning or could go on for days. It was no accident that even the Russians considered the Kamchatka the end of the world. As he rounded a pile of jumbled rocks that broke the wind, Pete saw the cave less than a hundred yards in front of him across an expanse of rugged, now ice-coated, rocks. He allowed the carbine to dangle across his back by its sling so he could have his hands free to negotiate the slippery rocks. With the weapon out of immediate reach of his hands, he felt unprotected should he suddenly encounter an enemy. He started cautiously across the ice-coated terrain. Several times he lost his footing and he regained his balance only by grabbing frantically at the slippery rocks. By the sounds coming from behind him he could tell that Murphy was having an equally rough time.

At last, after what seemed like hours of struggling against the storm, but was in reality only a few minutes, Pete found himself standing on dry rocks on the lee of the cliff. The cave, if he had remembered correctly, was just around the corner of the large boulder to his left. He breathed deeply, cupping his gloved hands over his mouth and nose, allowing his cold-ravaged lungs to warm. The crevices between the rocks were dark now, as the storm-hastened night rapidly consumed the little remaining light.

Pete shivered slightly, partly from the cold, but more from the ominous shadows that created a thousand hiding places all around him. He cradled the carbine in his arms and advanced around the boulder.

He was nearly bowled over by a huge figure coming fast from the opposite direction, running blindly through the stormy darkness. Pete flung up his carbine and Harris was within a split-second of death before Pete recognized him.

Harris shook his head frantically from side to side when he saw Pete and Murphy just beyond. He waved his arms wildly in the air. "Don't shoot! Don't shoot!" he cried out.

In one hand was a coil of dark silver nylon climbing rope. "It's Lawrence," he shouted. "She fell off a cliff!"

# 13

Pentagon sources have revealed that United States forces have been placed on alert status and that "essential" personnel have been called back from Christmas and New Year's leaves.

While the source, who refused to be identified, admitted that the alert is related to the Soviet downing of TPA Flight 18, he denied rumors that some sort of military retaliation is planned.

When asked if one of the options was a total United States blockade of Cuba, the source neither denied nor confirmed that such a move was being discussed.

The alert status is seen by Pentagon-watchers as little more than a show of strength; however, several members of Congress have expressed fears that the President's policies might be leading the United States toward a dangerous confrontation with the Soviets.

IND-TV *Evening News*
December 29, 1993

**P**ete and Murphy followed Harris across the boulder-strewn slope, past the entrance to the cave where the team had stashed its gear, toward the edge of a low cliff that Pete had seen earlier.

"We heard a noise and went to investigate," yelled Harris as he ran. "She slipped on the ice. I tried to catch her, but couldn't." His panic-filled voice was nearly lost in the roaring wind.

On the top of the exposed ridge the icy wind seared Pete's face and lungs as he scrambled across the rocks. The amount of snow in the air had increased until the horizon on all sides was hidden behind the wind-whipped wall of snow. Already the island was in darkness. Only the shapes of the nearest trees and rocks were discernible.

Ahead of Pete Harris stopped abruptly and pointed downward. Pete looked over the cliff. He thought he heard a low, moaning sound somewhere far below, but it must have been the wind rushing among the rocks of the cliff face. The bottom of the cliff appeared to be about a hundred feet below them, but in the darkness any estimation of distance had to be suspect.

Pete took a small emergency light from an inside pocket of his parka and shone it downward. Its small but powerful beam cast a tiny circle of white light on the rocks and bushes at the foot of the cliff. He swept the circle back and forth while Harris tied one end of the silver climbing rope to a jagged edge of a large rock and tossed the remainder of the coil past Pete, letting it fall down the face of the cliff.

Pete picked up the rope, wrapped it around his waist for rappelling, and backed slowly toward the edge of the ice-glazed cliff. Then he paused a few feet from the lip of the rocks to test the rope. Bracing himself solidly, he gave the rope a hard jerk then another. On the third jerk the rope fell limp in his hand. The knot that had held it around the rock had come untied.

Dangling the end of rope in his hand, Pete stared at the dark figure of Harris standing just out of his reach. The huge man appeared to be cowering, but Pete did not miss the fact that

Harris's hands were tightly grasping a carbine. Harris was either one of two things; incredibly stupid and incompetent or just the opposite. Either way he could turn out to be extremely dangerous. Pretending not to notice Harris's grip on the carbine, Pete walked past him and retied the rope to the boulder, making sure the knots were securely tied in a form of tautline hitch that would prevent their being untied while the rope had weight on it.

"Good thing I checked your knot," Pete said to Harris, controlling his voice. He tested the rope for the second time. "In this cold it's not easy tying a good knot—especially with gloves on." He backed quickly to the cliff and rappelled down its face, leaving Harris and Murphy standing on the top, Harris staring after him, Murphy glaring at Harris.

A few feet from the bottom, Pete stopped and took out his small flashlight again. With its beam he searched the ground for Sheena.

The rubble at the base of the cliff was thickly covered with a low, thick mass of vegetation that closely resembled some species of blueberries. Knee high it formed a mat so thick and springy that a person could have nearly walked on the top. For the most part the ground beneath the low bushes was covered with what appeared to be about a foot of drifted snow. Among the bushes, however, were sharp edged granite boulders that had broken away from the cliff.

Sheena had fallen on the bushes and snow, missing the rocks by inches and had rolled back toward the cliff under an overhanging ledge. She lay crumpled on her side in a fetal position. She gave no indication that she was aware of his presence, even when the flashlight's beam crossed the side of her face. His heart leaped into his throat as he saw the bright red blood stains on the snow.

Remembering the faulty knot that could have sent him, too, plummeting down the cliff either by accident or on purpose, he drew the rope tight and secured it around a protruding finger of rock. That way if anybody above tried to mess with his rope, he would know. Right now he had no time to consider whether Harris was just an incompetent knot tier or something more. It was an issue that he knew he must address, but for the moment his first concern was Sheena.

As Pete approached, Sheena rolled over and sat up at an awkward angle, braced against the rock face. In the glare of Pete's flashlight Sheena's pain-filled eyes flashed green fire. With both hands she tightly gripped the .357 out in front of her, her finger on the trigger.

Pete stopped in his tracks as he found himself staring down the evil-looking barrel of the weapon. "Easy," he shouted. "I've come to help you." Suddenly he realized he had come down the cliff without the carbine he had been carrying. He had foolishly left it leaning against a rock after redoing the knot that Harris had tied.

Sheena looked past Pete into the snowy darkness. Wedged against the rocks, her eyes betraying the horrible pain that she was suffering, she made Pete think of a beautiful wild animal, wounded and cornered. After she seemed to have assured herself that Pete had come alone, Sheena nodded upward, questioningly.

"Still on the top."

Sheena breathed a sigh of relief and lowered the .357. As she did so, she involuntarily let out a low moan and a spasm of pain crossed her face, which was ashen white. Pete knew something was desperately wrong.

He took two steps forward and knelt beside her, watching the pistol that she still gripped firmly in her left hand, trigger finger still inside the guard.

Pete knew he had to work fast to prevent Sheena from being immobilized by shock. Beneath the thick arctic clothing, it was hard for him to tell the extent of her injuries. "Where do you hurt?" he asked. There was no response. "Where?" he repeated louder. Again nothing. Sheena stared at him with blank, pain-numbed eyes.

He pointed to her legs and shouted, "There?"

Sheena shook her head. Pete knew she was sinking fast. He leaned over and touched her shoulders and she cried out weakly. Pete unzipped her parka and felt beneath it.

At first Sheena tensed then relaxed beneath his touch. As she relaxed, her eyes began to close. Pete's worse fear was confirmed as his fingers touched the swollen flesh, felt the grating of the shattered right collar bone and arm socket. Sheena must have fallen on a rock after all. She had actually been holding up a five pound pistol with that! If he had ever doubted it, the doubt was completely gone. She was no ordinary person.

"Got to find it first," she murmured weakly. "Got to stop them from finding it, they, he pushed, no morphine, got to stop them."

Her voice trailed off as her eyelids completely closed. Her face was rapidly paling; her skin was cold and clammy.

Pete pulled her parka shut and zipped the hood tightly around her face to conserve as much of her body heat as possible. What did she mean? "Got to find it." Find what? And stop who? Harris? The Russians? Pete knew that unless he worked fast, she might never be able to tell him.

Taking a desperate chance that she had no spinal injuries, Pete straightened out Sheena's legs as best he could and propped them up against the cliff, swinging her body around and letting it lie flat against the snow. It was a temporary measure at best, but elevating her feet would let blood circulate back to her head. As he moved her, he saw that the blood on the snow had come from her elbows and knees where the thick layer of arctic clothing had been ripped away by the rocks. She had lost one glove, and her uncovered hand was already turning blue from the bitter cold. She must have fought desperately to catch herself as she slid and fell down the hundred-foot cliff in the darkness. Although it had cost her some skin and blood, her clawing at the rocks had broken her fall, probably saved her life—at least for a little while. Pete knew that unless he could get her sheltered and warm very, very soon, her painful struggle would have been for nothing.

Pete ripped off his own heavy parka and draped it over her. The shock of the cold wind cut through the rest of his clothing. Lying on the ground, Sheena was sheltered, temporarily, from the icy wind. Pete knew he had to ascend the cliff and bring back something to build a shelter and what supplies he could find. Why couldn't it have been the other cargo chute that was lost? The one that didn't contain the first aid kit?

There was no time to worry about it now or to try to get Sheena to the cave, even if he could have got her up the side of the ice-glazed cliff in the pitch blackness and the storm. If he could have counted on Harris, it might have been possible, but without him Pete knew that he and Murphy would only struggle in vain, using up precious time that Sheena did not likely have in her rapidly deepening state of shock.

Pete checked to see that Sheena was as comfortable as possible, her feet and legs still raised, then he started back to where he had secured the rope down the cliff. Just as he was about to reach for the rope, Pete stopped and returned to Sheena. He gently reached inside her parka and removed the holster. Then he took her .357. Its silencer was still attached. He strapped the holster belt around his own waist and checked the clip for cartridges. It was filled with Winchester hollow-points. Then he returned to the rope, checked that it was still tight, and started the climb upward. Several times he slipped, but each time he caught himself and continued to progress, hand over hand. His hands and fingers were becoming numb from the cold, although he was sweating heavily inside his fatigues from the exertion. Near the top, the cliff veered outward creating a slight overhang and for what seemed like hours Pete dangled only by his arms as he pulled himself the final twenty feet over an abyss of total blackness. His muscles threatened to give way as he pulled himself up the wildly swaying rope. When he finally crawled over the lip, the dark shape of Murphy grasped his shoulders and pulled him to safety. Off to the side was the dark, hulking figure of Harris. Pete wanted to question the man, at gunpoint if necessary, but there was no time for that now. Instead he started shouting orders.

"I need sleeping bags—two of them—heat packs if we have any more and something I can use for a tarp," he barked at Harris. "Murph, see if you can't find something to use for bandage material. Slash me off four or five yards of nylon from one of the parachutes—not Harris's—a dry one."

"Hadn't Harris better stand guard?" shouted Murphy as Pete started back toward the cave. "He said they heard noises."

"Can't risk it," Pete shouted back at Murphy over his shoulder. "I'll explain later. Right now, we need everything we can get or that girl's going to die of shock and exposure."

Inside the cave Murphy quickly lit a small plumber's candle. Its flame flickered, revealing their equipment was as they had left it. Pete dug in the piles and came up with several items that he wanted and crammed them into a canvas rucksack. What he would give for the first aid kit! But there was no thinking about that now. He had to do the best he could without one. Murphy and Harris located the items that Pete had ordered them to find, Murphy, quickly and efficiently; Harris slowly and, Pete felt, reluctantly.

Everything was piled onto the section of parachute and tied in a bundle, which Pete ordered Harris to sling over his shoulder. He and Murphy followed Pete back to the top of the cliff. Harris dropped the bundle heavily on the ground. Pete glared at him in the darkness. "Easy with that!" he ordered. Harris did not respond.

The wind and snow had now whipped into a full-fledged blizzard. Tying one end of a rope about his waist and securing the other to a small tree, Pete went to the edge of the cliff and began lowering the nylon-wrapped bundle down the cliff by a piece of thin nylon shroudline, keeping an eye on Harris as he did so. When he felt the rope attached to the bundle go slack, he stepped away from the cliff and went to where Harris stood.

"I'll be needing your parka," Pete said calmly. Even in the darkness Harris had no trouble seeing that Pete's hand was resting on the butt of the .357.

"But I'll freeze to death," he protested.

"No, you won't," Pete assured him, gripping the pistol. "As long as you stay in the cave in your sleeping bag you'll be fine, and that's exactly where I want you."

"Give him the goddamned parka," Murphy ordered. "Like he said, you'll be all right until morning when we can get this mess straightened out."

Reluctantly Harris peeled off his parka and tossed it on the ground in front of Pete, who picked it up without taking his eyes off Harris or his hand off the pistol. Without bothering to put his arms in the sleeves Pete flung the heavy parka over his shoulders. He then picked up the carbine, wrapped the rope around himself, and backed to the cliff's edge. "When I get down," he told Murphy, without bothering to get out of Harris's hearing, "I want you to untie this rope and drop it. I'm afraid I don't much trust your man, Harris. You'd better watch him yourself." Murphy started to protest, but before he could form his words Pete had stepped over the edge of the cliff and disappeared into the darkness.

When he was again at the bottom, Pete slipped Ensollite pads under Sheena to insulate her body from the frozen ground and wrapped her in a sleeping bag. He activated two heat packs and slipped them down inside the sleeping bag beside her. A quick check with the flashlight showed him that her face hadn't got much paler, an indication that raising her feet had at least slowed the effects of shock. Of course, he knew her rugged constitution had a lot to do with it. Her breathing was still ragged and uneven but seemed steadier. He knew he was going to have to do something about her shattered shoulder, probably just immobilization, all he could do, but that would have to wait until later. For now it was imperative that he construct some sort of shelter against the raging wind and minus twenty degree temperatures if either of them was going to survive the night.

He set about constructing a lean-to shelter over Sheena by anchoring a large square of the parachute canopy to the cliff with pieces of shroud line tied to the rocks' jagged edges. Using the lid from an ammo box, he shoveled snow on the bottom of the tarp, stretching it tight against the wind. He then wrapped the ends around and anchored them the same way, creating a tight, nearly windproof cocoon beneath the protection of the overhanging ledge that would deflect any stray rocks that might happen to be dislodged above. He heaped snow all around the tent to break the wind until he virtually had a snow cave. He was careful to leave ventilation holes.

When he was satisfied, Pete crawled in beside Sheena, dragging the gear with him and pulled the end flap closed. Inside the shelter was slightly larger than a good two-man mountain tent. It was possible for a person to sit up, but not to stand. He soon had a plumber's candle lit and the Svea stove roaring beneath a small English billy kettle into which he heaped handfuls of snow. In his pocket he had some more of Murphy's coffee. Pete knew that the candle and stove would make the tarp glow from the outside, creating a beacon for any enemies that might be abroad, but he knew he had to chance it. Sheena needed the warmth desperately. There was little danger of detection, for the icy blizzard that raged outside was not conducive to movement, even if there were hostile forces on the island, which Pete doubted. More likely, he thought, the only hostile individual on the island right at that moment was shivering in his sleeping bag in the cave. Pete hoped Murphy would be on his guard. Still, Pete leaned the 9mm carbine against the cliff where he could reach it easily should it be needed and kept an ear out for any strange sounds from outside, although it was unlikely he could have heard anything above the storm.

After he had fed snow into the billy, Pete checked Sheena for any other injuries from her fall. The inside of the shelter had warmed up enough now that he felt safe uncovering her long enough to examine her broken shoulder. Although the scrapes on her knees, elbows, and palms were horrible to look at, they had already clotted. Her shoulder, however, was worse than he had expected. It was badly swollen and discolored from the tissue damage beneath the skin. He checked her right palm; it was warm and pink. At least, at far as he could tell, the major arteries to her arm had not been damaged. Yet. Her shoulder would have to be immobilized as best he could until she could be moved to a regular medical facility. God only knew how long that would be or even if it could be done at all. If it took more than a few days, she could lose use of the arm; if it took significantly longer than that, unless they found the first aid kit with its antibodies, gangrene might set in and cost Sheena her life.

Pete knew that he would have to move the shoulder, at least a little, to get it into a position where he could immobilize it. In doing so, he would risk aggravating the shock, from which she seemed to be recovering, but he knew he had no choice but to chance it.

If she tried to move, a splintered piece of bone could cut a nerve or major artery. Better, he thought, to get it done immediately.

He peeled back Sheena's fatigue shirt, exposing as much of her shoulder and arm as he could without removing the shirt, but realized it had to be cut away to give him room to work on the shoulder. He split the shirt's sleeve and side. Underneath, Sheena was dressed in a plain khaki T-shirt. What he needed right now was morphine, and then antibiotics, but they were in the first aid kit. Sheena moaned as he touched her.

Working urgently with his swollen and nearly frostbitten fingers, Pete ripped the parachute section into strips, then used the strips to lash Sheena's upper right arm tightly against her side, her lower arm across her chest. He was careful to allow for blood circulation in the limb. When he was satisfied that he had done all he could do, he wrapped the sleeping bag back around her and checked her wrist. Her pulse was steady and even now, a sign that the initial shock had been arrested in time.

As he held her hand, Sheena began to stir. She opened her eyes and tried to lift her head, but Pete placed his palm gently against her forehead, preventing her from doing so.

"Where?" she demanded.

"Shh, it's only me," he said quietly. "It's all right."

Pete realized, of course, that Sheena's condition was far from all right. With her shattered shoulder she was going to be of little or no use in the team's mission. In fact she was going to be a hindrance. Not only that, but unless she could be transported in a very few days to a hospital with surgeons and antibiotics, her chances of keeping the arm, even her life, would become increasingly minimal. There was no way that Pete could accurately access the internal damage to Sheena's shoulder, but he knew, from the discolored flesh and the swelling that was already straining his crude bandages, that it was extensive. Any movement could cause more damage.

A blast of wind shook the makeshift tent. The candle flame flickered in a draft and Pete reached out with his hand to shield it. Even above the roar of the wind as it struck the cliff face above them, Pete could hear the crashing breakers over a quarter-mile away. That was one consolation, at least. There wouldn't be any patrols out tonight on land, on sea, or in the air. Anyone with any sense, even the most diehard Russian officer, would not dare taunt the fury of Kamchatka until the storm abated.

Beside Pete, Sheena tried to move but froze in place, her face registering the wave of pain that the movement caused. When the pain had subsided, Sheena lifted her head slightly and tried to look down the length of her body, her eyes betraying her confusion brought about by the pain and shock. It was then that she realized for the first time that her right arm and shoulder were tightly bound. She rolled her eyes toward Pete questioningly.

"How bad is it?" she asked, her voice weak, apprehensive.

Pete started to lie, but then realized there was no use. The look in Sheena's eyes told him she knew that her condition was bad. "Not good," he said. "Your shoulder is broken. We're going to have to wait here until morning or until this storm blows over before we can safely move you to the cave. From there we'll have to try to make radio contact with a U.S. vessel, then slip you out to sea where you can get medical attention."

"You can't!" she blurted out. "You can't!" The sudden movement caused her whole body to shudder with pain and she fell back trembling, her face losing some of the color it had gained. The violent pain threatened to plunge her back into shock. Her breath came in short gasps.

Pete leaned over and tucked the sleeping bag back around her. He felt her forehead with the back of his hand. It was clammy and cold again. "Just rest now," he said, "and we'll decide what to do in the morning."

"Promise you won't let Murphy try to keep me from going with you," Sheena pleaded, grabbing at Pete's sleeve.

He took her outstretched hand in his. It felt so very small and cold and vulnerable. "We can take it from here," he said. "You're in no shape to dive. If that monitor's out there—we'll find it."

Pete could tell that Sheena was quickly losing consciousness again, partly from the pain and partly from her exhaustion.

"You aren't one of them, are you?" she muttered, almost delirious. "You really don't know that it isn't . . ."

"Shhh." Pete lay two fingers gently across her mouth to silence her. "Rest," he said quietly, smoothing back her hair. "All you need is rest."

As Sheena relaxed beneath his hands, Pete desperately wished he believed his own words.

# 14

WASHINGTON—The President's tough language against the Soviet Union after the disappearance of Flight 18 has sent his popularity with the American public soaring.

In the results of a poll released today, the President's foreign policy approval rating jumped from 39 percent to 62 percent.

This figure, with a margin for error of plus or minus 5 percent, reflects the percentage of voting-age Americans who fully approve of the president's foreign policies.

The poll also showed that 35 percent of the people questioned favored even harsher policies toward the Soviets, including limited military action.

*The Los Angeles Daily Press*
December 29, 1993

**M**orning came with agonizing slowness, a bitter cold, depressingly gray half-light. Pete shivered inwardly as he struggled into wakefulness from a fitful sleep that had been laced with half-awake dreams. During the night, Sheena had snuggled close to Pete for warmth and her head rested in the crook of his arm.

In the dreams, however, the woman beside him had not been Sheena but a dark-eyed Egyptian girl that he had known only by the name of Phaedra. Even though it had been nearly twenty years since he had last seen her alive, running down a Cairo alleyway, her body and face still stuck in his memory as clearly as if it had been only the day before. Only afterward had he realized he was in love with her, only after he saw her dead body lying crumpled in the filthy sewage ditch where the Moslem extremists had left it with her breasts cut off as a warning to any other Egyptian women who might entertain thoughts of cooperating with the hated Yankee dogs. The sight had made Pete lose his head and he had gone hunting the woman's killers. They weren't very hard to find and he would have joined her in the ditch had not Bill Murphy shown up just in the nick of time. It was the first time of many that Murphy had saved his life. It was also the first time Pete had ever seen Murph work over a crowd with a Thompson submachine gun. From that moment Pete knew the power and strength of Murphy's loyalty.

Several times during the night Pete had been awakened by Sheena's rapid, tortured breathing beside him. Other than trying to keep her warm, there had been little he could do. Twice he had checked her forehead with his hand, each time finding her cold and clammy to his touch. With no antibiotics, no pain killers, her suffering must have been extreme and could only get worse. Pete knew he had to get her to help—and soon.

She moaned in her sleep, but did not wake up as he slowly crawled out of the shelter, tucking the ends of the tarp back down to preserve as much of her body heat as possible. At least it was no longer snowing and the wind had stopped. Above him the cliff

— **151** —

face looked even more formidable in the weak light of morning than it had in the darkness, the rocks shimmering from their glazing of ice. Without ropes or climbing gear it would be impossible to ascend the cliff itself. Fortunately, though, the cliff was not one unbroken line, but turned into a jumbled mass of boulders a few hundred yards to his left where a section of the face had collapsed.

But even there Pete found the going difficult and dangerous. Several times he slid backward, wrenching his back and ankles painfully before he found himself at the top. He stood for several minutes, trying to catch his breath. The frigid air seered the inside of his mouth and lungs, but beneath his heavy arctic gear he was sweating profusely.

He scanned the horizon, looking for any signs of movement, but saw none. Even the ship that he had spotted lying far off the coast the day before was not visible. This alarmed him. If the ship had been American, as he had suspected, it was his best hope of getting medical care for Sheena. He told himself that it was not gone, that it was only hidden by the low clouds. Although the wind had died down considerably, the sea was still very rough. Long waves crashed relentlessly against the shore. It would be difficult to launch the Zodiac.

Pete looked in the direction of the cave where Murphy and Harris had spent the night. There was no smoke but he thought he smelled burning wood. Carefully he made his way to the opening of the cave. As he approached the final few feet, he deliberately kicked his feet on the ground and rattled the frozen bushes to alert Murphy and Harris of his presence. There was no sense in risking getting shot as an intruder.

As he had expected, Murphy met him just inside the cave, holding a carbine. He relaxed when he recognized Pete and returned to feeding twigs to a small fire that he had burning beneath the billy. On the floor, sitting up in his sleeping bag, with his back against a rock, was Harris. The big man looked thoroughly miserable. Pete remembered he had left Harris's parka at the foot of the cliff.

"So how is she?" asked Murphy without looking up from the fire.

Pete shook his head. "Pretty bad, I'm afraid. Her shoulder's broken and the arm joint's shattered. She keeps going in and out of shock from the pain and internal damage. We're going to have to get her out of here somehow."

Murphy poured Pete a cup of instant coffee and handed it to him. "That may not be easy, and besides, we have to complete our mission first."

Pete started to protest, but Murphy cut him off. "Now, I know what you're about to say, that we could get Lawrence to one of our ships and then come back and continue the mission, but we can't risk it. We only have one boat and three people left and we can't take a chance on losing any of them. Lawrence will just have to wait until we're finished." Murphy returned his attention to the fire that was spluttering hopelessly and beginning to smoke from the wet cedar wood.

"I'm at least going to look for the other parachute," said Pete. "Maybe the antibiotics in the first aid kit would buy us a day or two."

Murphy nodded. "Suit yourself, but don't take all day. We have to get started searching for that crash locator. Last night's storm kept the Russians in, but they'll be out again in a few hours or I miss my guess."

Pete gulped down the remainder of his coffee, which had already grown cold in the cup, then started to walk out of the cave. Harris's voice stopped him in his tracks.

"Wait!" Harris was struggling free of his sleeping bag, slapping his hands together and shaking. He was still fully clothed, even down to his combat boots. "I'll go with you. We can get my parka and then I'll help you look for the parachute."

"Sure, if you want." Pete had no desire at all to be accompanied by Harris. Pete didn't like the idea of having to take a chance on turning his back to Harris, but he could tell from the man's voice that it would be useless to object to his going along. Anyway it might give him a chance to find out just what or who the hell Harris was. With Harris stumbling along behind him, Pete headed for the cliffs.

When the two of them got to the edge, Pete led the way along the cliff-top until he found the place where he had climbed up earlier. Before starting down, he stopped and allowed Harris to catch up. Some inner sense told him that it might be a good idea to keep Harris away from the helpless Sheena. Had he really pushed her over the edge of the cliff as she had mumbled in her delirium? Had she just imagined it or had she just slipped on the icy rocks in the dark? In her shock Sheena could have imagined anything had happened, yet there was the incident with the rope to think about. If Harris had indeed tried to kill Sheena, he would surely try again, unless it looked as if Sheena was going to die anyway.

Pete stopped and looked at Harris as the hulking man stumbled along behind. He was clutching one of the carbines and the coil of climbing rope that Pete had carried up with him. He was already shivering uncontrollably in the cold. His breath made little white clouds of steam. Pete wondered if he knew how to use the rifle. Where in the hell INTEL-5 got such an operative he could only guess. In any case he would definitely bear watching.

Sheena had seemed convinced that the man could not be Harris. But, if he wasn't Harris, then who in the hell was he? How had he gotten Harris's identification?

It was unlikely that the bumbling giant had managed to ambush the real Harris at Wrangell and do such a professional job of slitting his throat then somehow beat the Lear to Shemya. At least it appeared unlikely. Maybe that was the way it was meant to appear. Maybe he wasn't an INTEL-5 operative at all. But, somehow or other, he had convinced Murphy he was.

"Damn, it's cold!" Harris mumbled as he drew alongside Pete.

Pete nodded. "Colder than hell. Those rocks are slick. You want to wait up here while I go get your parka and check on Lawrence?"

Harris shook his head vigorously. "No way! The sooner I get that parka, the better." He tossed the coil of rope on the ground, expertly flicking a bowline around an upjutting piece of rock. "That will give us something to hold on to, at least," he said.

"Well, be careful," Pete said, not sure of the meaning of what he had just seen. "One accident's more than enough."

He started the slow, hazardous climb, using the rope to balance himself on the icy scree between the boulders. He slipped often but finally managed to stand up at the bottom.

Pete looked back up the slope behind him. Harris was still negotiating the rockfall, slowly, but with surprising competence. When Harris noticed Pete watching him from the bottom, he slipped and fell heavily on his rear, sliding the final few feet to the bottom. As Harris picked himself up, Pete said, "You did that pretty well for a man not used to climbing."

Harris brushed himself off. "Just lucky I didn't bust my ass," he grunted. "We to that parka yet?"

Pete shook his head. "It's just around here," he said, pointing. He waited until Harris passed him and then followed along the base of the rocks. He knew that he didn't want Harris behind him with a carbine.

The makeshift tent was still as Pete had left it earlier. Keeping an eye on Harris who was standing off to one side cradling the carbine in the crook of his arm, Pete pulled back the flap. Sheena mumbled in her sleep, but did not wake. Although her face was still cool to the touch, a little color had returned to her cheeks and she seemed to be breathing easier. The sleep would do her more good than anything Pete could manage without the first aid kit. He quietly removed Harris's parka and reclosed the flap of the tent.

Harris caught the parka when Pete tossed it to him. He set the carbine on the ground and zipped the coat tightly around his neck. He nodded at the tent. "Any better?"

"No." Pete stared at Harris. "What the hell happened out here last night anyway? You said you heard something?"

Harris picked up the carbine. "Lawrence said she did. I didn't hear anything." He casually slung the carbine over his shoulder and started walking into the brush. As he followed Harris, Pete nonchalantly unzipped his parka, slipping his trigger finger out through the slot in the palm of the glove, ready for action. The butt of Sheena's .357 loomed just inside the coat, within easy reach.

"She said something else too."

Harris stopped and turned without touching the carbine. "What did she say?" he asked. His eyes swept Pete, paused momentarily on the open parka and the hand resting innocently just inside as if Pete was searching for a cigarette in his shirt pocket. Harris's eyes told Pete that he wasn't being fooled.

"That you pushed her." Pete's hand crept upward. Ready.

Harris laughed. "Weak. Really weak. That all she said?"

"Yeah." He watched Harris for any flicker of movement that might betray him. "What would give her that idea?"

Harris raised his hands in a gesture of defeat. "Look, Shafer."

He paused as if thinking. "I guess I'm going to have to trust you. By the looks of that heater just inside your coat, I'd say I don't have any choice." He laughed lightly, then suddenly straightened up and, almost like an actor doing exercises, his whole manner seemed to change. It was as if the bumbling fool had been replaced by a businesslike operative.

"First off," he said, "I was sent on this mission by INTEL-five headquarters. They'd got information that indicated one of you was cooperating with the Soviets to make sure the mission failed. We had good reason to believe it was one of you, but which one we didn't know. I was waiting for you on Shemya and was supposed to convince you to let me go along as a fifth member of the team, but when the real Harris ended up dead, my job was made a whole lot easier. The Russian KGB got him most likely. My real name isn't important and, since the others know me as Harris, I'd like to hang onto the moniker. Okay?"

Pete nodded. His mind reeled with this turn of events. "So that explains the bowline this morning. You were so cold you forgot to play the dunce. Of course, last night you knew I would check my rope before rappelling, so you weren't afraid of me falling to my death?"

Harris smiled. "Of course not. No good mountaineer ever puts his faith in an untested knot, especially one tied by a person he considers an idiot. You are an accomplished mountaineer, of course, as am I."

"And I suppose you speak fluent Russian too?"

This time Harris shook his head. "Unfortunately, no. Greek, German, several dialects of Spanish, but no Russian."

"I'm surprised. I was beginning to think you had gone from village idiot to superspook. But the real question is why you've been playing the dunce. You've been doing it so well you could have killed yourself."

"You should know the answer to that, Shafer. Assuming this operation is infiltrated, we would have to be eliminated for the counterintelligence to succeed. I was given orders to set myself up as bait. The first attempt would most likely be on my life because it could so easily be made to look like an accident, given my 'incompetence.' And, in fact, Lawrence tried to do me in last night. What she said was not true. I didn't push her. She tried to shove me off the cliff, only she slipped and fell herself. I do a lot of things, do them quite well in fact, but killing women, even women working for the other side, isn't one of my fortes."

Pete slowly looked Harris up and down. "So you think Sheena has reason to want the mission to fail?"

"I do."

"Then why didn't you come to me earlier?"

"I wasn't sure about you either until this morning. You two seemed awfully friendly."

"You could have gone to Murphy. After all, he is the official leader of this expedition."

Harris shook his head. "I couldn't trust him either. As you know, he went through a period of alcoholism. He could have been compromised."

So Harris had not had access to Murphy's genuine personnel file! Murphy's "period of alcoholism" had just been a front to trap a British double agent. This did not automatically rule out Harris as an INTEL-5 operative, but it did at least show that he didn't enjoy the complete trust of the organization.

"No." Pete said. "He wasn't compromised. I was with him through his bout with the bottle and he damned well wasn't compromised. I saw to that. If there was ever anybody on the face of the earth who hated communists more than Murph, I'd sure as hell hate to be one and meet him."

Harris nodded. "His reputation in that regard is well known, but still. . . ."

"Still what?" Pete asked.

"Nothing. Nothing," Harris said hastily. "I have no reason to doubt your friend Murphy is all you say he is. What say we look for that chute?"

"Sure," Pete said. "No matter what, we still need that equipment, especially the first aid kit."

Harris nodded. "After all we have to get Lawrence out of here after we find what we're looking for, if only for the satisfaction of seeing her tried and punished."

Pete gritted his teeth at Harris's words. Even if Sheena was a Russian agent, which he still could not believe, he knew he would take damned little pleasure in helping prove Harris right.

# 15

In a blow to United States efforts at organizing an embargo of the Soviet Union for the shooting down of TPA Flight 18, the French have announced that sales of pipeline equipment to the Soviets will continue. This is widely regarded as a slap in the face to U.S. policy.

France's Trade Bureau, however, released a statement to the press that cited contracts already in effect. "If France does not fulfill its obligations," read the statement, "not only would we be legally liable, but some other nation would be only too happy to supply the Soviets with their needs."

There is a widespread belief here that the decision to continue trade with the Soviets was influenced by the powerful French Communist Party.

The West Germans have also expressed an unwillingness to go along with the United State's proposed embargo of the Soviets.

IND-TV *Evening News*
December 30, 1993

The huge man called Harris seemed indefatigable as he and Pete searched the island for the missing cargo parachute. In the minus-twenty degree cold the landscape appeared completely vacant of life, its very existence frozen in time and space. Not even the air moved and the low, gray layer of clouds overhead threatened to shatter into a thousand jagged shards of dingy ice and come crashing down at any moment. The black water of the sea was the only thing that moved at all, surging slowly like some great, all-encompassing, one-celled animal breathing easily in a stage of sleep. Huge chunks of ice, a few of them the size of small houses, rocked restlessly up and down in the water as if they could somehow sense the ultimate futility of struggling against the all-consuming, emotionless black animal that held them in its grasp. Pete shivered and tried to keep up with Harris.

Although in the cold the brush was as brittle as spun glass and the snapped twigs echoed like cannonade in the icy stillness, Harris expertly stooped and dodged the frozen foliage. Although Pete was an accomplished woodsman, his passing sounded like that of a scared dog in comparison, his breathing loud and labored as he fell farther and farther behind. He allowed himself to fall back to his own more comfortable pace, searching the landscape on either side of him as he passed, looking for signs of the missing parachute or the people who had made the pitiful graves in the snow. He saw nothing.

Harris was out of sight somewhere ahead of him when Pete heard the roar of the approaching airplane. He had been so busy searching the ground, with the hood of his parka pulled tightly around his ears for warmth, that the airplane was nearly on him before he noticed. He scrambled across the final few feet of the open space he had been crossing and into the safety of some leafless alders just as the airplane appeared out of the north. He crouched low, his face down, as the propeller driven twin-engined reconnaissance airplane passed slowly overhead at an altitude of less than five hundred feet, its vertical tailfin nearly touching the low underbelly of the clouds. It was flying close to his position. Pete wondered if the airplane's crew had spotted the team's missing cargo chute or a piece of wreckage from the airliner. There was also the possibility that the unknown survivors of the crash had constructed some sort of signal to try to attract rescue before the cold claimed them. It was unlikely they were still alive, but their signal could have survived.

The airplane flew past. Pete carefully turned and raised his head, still shielding his face inside his parka hood in case there might be a rear observer. He knew that there is little that stands out like an upturned human face. Just beyond the island the airplane banked steeply and circled back toward him, descending within a hundred feet of the water. Pete dropped his face again as the airplane roared past in front of him, directly over where he guessed Harris was hiding. It passed so close that the high-pitched sound from the engines hurt his ears. So near was the airplane that he could see the tiny, veinlike black threads of oil emanating from seams in the engines' cowlings. There was a bright new square of aluminium on the side of the fuselage where a hole had been patched. On the airplane's tail was the bright red star insignia worn by all Soviet aircraft.

Pete held his position as the airplane grew smaller and smaller watching for it to wheel and return, but it did not. Instead it disappeared northward in the direction from which it had come. When the sound of the airplane's engines had nearly died, he stepped out from beneath the thin branches of the bush where he had taken questionable shelter then stretched and stomped his feet to restore circulation. Even through the thick "Mickey Mouse" boots, his feet felt cold. He glanced up to see Harris coming through the bushes toward him. The big man made the motion of mopping his brow. "That was too damned close," he said.

"Yeah. By the way they came right to this particular island, checked it out, and then left again, I'd say they were looking for something in particular."

Harris nodded. "Uh-huh. Us."

"Not necessarily," said Pete. "Flight Eighteen obviously went down pretty close to here and whoever dug those graves in the snow could have tried to attract attention, but that still doesn't explain why they'd fly straight to this island, out of all the islands near here. Of course, if our cargo chute is hanging in the bushes somewhere that'd be a dead giveaway, but they sure as hell wouldn't have seen it all the way in Petropavlovsk and come to investigate. The Russians probably suspect, maybe even know for sure, that there's been an insert, but it's unlikely they would know exactly where it took place."

Harris shook his head slowly from side to side. "They know, exactly where we are, who we are, and what kind of weapons we have."

Pete was caught off guard by the calm certainty of the man's voice, almost the kind of movie-spy sureness where the battered but triumphant agent sums up the case for headquarters.

"How can you be so sure?" Pete demanded, not bothering to hide the skepticism in his voice.

Harris reached into one of the inside pockets of his parka and withdrew a flat, black rectangular object. Even before Harris extended the shiny chrome antenna for him to see, Pete knew that what Harris was holding was a miniature radio transceiver of some sort. "I found it in my parka after you got it back from Lawrence this morning. She must have thought it would be safe there. I assume she was asleep when you retrieved it?"

Pete reached out unbelievingly and took the radio from Harris's outstretched hand. "Russian-made?" he asked.

"Of course not." Harris laughed dryly. "Japanese. But I dare say the frequencies are Russian."

Pete turned the radio over and over in his hand. There was no mistaking that it was the real thing. The black leather case was totally unmarked. He unsnapped it and pulled out the actual radio itself. It, too, was unmarked as to make or manufacture. Only when he slid back a tiny panel protecting the radio's crystals did he see the tiny, almost invisible logo that said MADE IN JAPAN. He looked at Harris. "You were right," he said. "It was made in Japan. Not exactly one of your commercial models either." He examined the radio's controls. There were the usual switches for volume, squelch, and channel selection, plus a switch that apparently operated some kind of homing device. It had no speaker, only a tiny earplug at the end of a thin wire. Without a doubt, somewhere in the Russian airplane that had just left, was a receiver tuned to pick up and locate whatever kind of signal the radio beacon transmitted. Pete noticed that the transmit/receive switch was on receive.

He turned it on. "Can't hurt to see if we can hear anything as long as we don't go transmitting, can it?" he asked. Harris shook his head. All Pete could hear, however, was a weak static. A tiny meter showed the batteries were all but exhausted. He turned off the radio, then checked its battery compartment. The batteries were of a strange size that Pete had never seen before. "Can I keep this?" he asked.

"Sure." Harris nodded. "It looks like the damage has already been done. She's probably had that damned locator on since we bailed out yesterday. Probably even broadcast our exact strength and location. I wouldn't be surprised if we get a visit any minute now. If it hadn't been for the storm last night, we'd more than likely be cooling our heels in a Russian stockade already. Or worse."

Pete stuck the radio in his pocket. He shuddered inwardly. Only once had he ever seen the inside of a Russian military holding facility from a prisoner's point of view, and the memory was anything but pleasant. Fortunately he had escaped within a few days, but the experience had been burned indelibly into his mind. Over the years quite a few of his friends and colleagues had disappeared permanently into Russian prisons. Since INTEL-5 did not even admit its very existence to the world, there was little pressure that it could bring to bear on the Soviet hierarchy for the release of captured operatives. Of course, there were the clandestine deals—one of yours for one of ours—but such deals were few and far between, reserved for only the highest ranking or most valuable prisoners. That Sheena Lawrence, if that was her real name, could be responsible for putting him back into a Russian prison at his age was more than he could understand. She had seemed so decent, so American!

"You're probably right," Pete said. "It looks like whoever has been using this radio has nearly worn out the batteries and I'd wager they weren't listening to the Dolphins."

"Dolphins?"

"The Dolphins. Miami."

"Oh, yes. Football." Harris smiled.

Pete stood facing the north, listened for the sound of approaching boats or airplanes. He heard nothing. "We've got to get back to the cave," he said, turning and starting to go back the way they had come. "We'll have to decide what to do and Murphy has to be in on it. We wouldn't have a chance in hell of fighting off a landing party and even if we did they'd just send in another, bigger one. So it looks like we have only two choices, neither of them very good. We can try to get Lawrence up the cliff and into the boat then escape to another island, or we can try hiding out in the cave and hope the Russians get tired of looking for us and go away. We don't have time for that."

As they headed back toward the cave Harris followed behind Pete, nervously glancing over his shoulder at the sky for more airplanes. As Harris fell farther and farther behind, Pete turned and yelled at him to catch up. When he saw Harris increasing his speed, Pete whirled and crashed through some bushes without paying attention to where he was placing his feet. Suddenly his toes caught under something hard and stiff lying across the path. Pete felt himself falling, plunging forward out of control. He flung up his arms to break his landing and caught a glimpse of what had tripped him up as he fell across it. He hit the ground hard, but immediately jumped up in horror at what he saw.

The hard-frozen body of a man lay on his back, eyes staring icily skyward. Through rips in the ragged and burned clothing, Pete could see the ugly wounds and burns that bore mute witness that the man had suffered horribly before he died. In contrast his face now held a frozen, bewildered stare like that of a dead fish in a butcher's case.

Pete and Harris left the body lying where it was and went immediately to the cave. Murphy looked up from the radio transceiver as they entered. "Nothing but static on this god-damned thing," he announced before Pete had a chance to speak.

Harris quickly stepped forward and told Murphy what they had found—the dead body and the portable radio that had been in Sheena's possession. Then he described how the Russian airplane had circled the island.

Murphy looked thoughtful. "I was afraid the team might have been infiltrated," he said. He did not even seem to notice the very marked change in Harris's manner. He walked to the mouth of the cave and stared out northward across the island. "So you think Lawrence is KGB?" he finally asked.

Harris nodded. "I'm pretty damned sure of it—or at least she's a Soviet counteragent. How else could the Russians have found us so easily?"

Murphy turned to Pete. "You were with Lawrence all night. What kind of a chance do you give her of surviving?" he asked.

Pete shook his head. "Not very good unless she's transported to a medical facility within the next forty-eight hours."

Harris shrugged. "Not much chance of that. Our best bet would be to leave her here and get on about our work."

"Now wait just a minute!" Murphy and Harris both turned and eyed him suspiciously as he continued. "First off, we don't know Lawrence is KGB—we only have Harris's suspicions—which I, myself, still don't place a lot of stock in—and secondly, even if she is, I'm not leaving her out here to die as long as there's a chance of her survival."

"But if we don't—" Harris started to say but Pete cut him off.

"Goddamn it, Murph. You owe me one, you said so yourself, and I'm calling it in. We take the girl with us."

Murphy protested but Pete was adamant. "Besides," Pete said, "*if* she has communicated with the Soviets, she has surely told them that we haven't located the submarine monitor yet." He glanced at Harris. Did he see the big man's face brighten slightly?

"You know yourself, Murph, that the Russians would much prefer that we do the work of finding that monitor for them, not to mention that the crash locator is broadcasting on a secret frequency that only you and I know, so it's likely they won't come crashing our party until we find something. Then all they have to do is come capture us *and* the monitor. That'd be a hell of a lot bigger prize than just catching three operatives."

Harris hastily nodded his agreement with Pete's assessment. Murphy looked from Pete to Harris and back to Pete. Finally he agreed that they would at least bring Sheena to the cave if it was possible without too much trouble.

The three men rounded up two pieces of dead wood and some shroud line to make a stretcher. Then they left the cave and started back toward the cliff where Sheena had been left. They were almost to the first of the jumbled rocks at the top of the cliff when Harris suddenly stopped.

"Damn!" he said. "I forgot my carbine. I'd better run back and get it, Murphy, just in case your friend Pete is wrong and the

Russians decide not to wait." He wheeled and headed back in the direction of the cave at a trot before either Pete or Murphy could stop him.

When Harris had gone, Pete turned to Murphy. "I don't trust him. He seemed too ready to believe Lawrence was with the KGB, but Lawrence knew he wasn't the real Harris. Who the hell is he?"

"Or *her*, for that matter? I don't trust either one."

Pete pulled the tiny transceiver from his pocket and stared at it. He slipped the radio's earphone inside the hood of his parka and inserted it in his right ear. Then he flipped the transceiver into the receive mode and turned it on. Although he turned the volume to maximum, the almost-exhausted batteries gave little more than a low static. He played with the squelch controls and flipped through the radio's frequencies. He had almost decided to turn off the transceiver when he heard the faint bits of Morse code. Although Pete had not sent or received Morse code in eight years, he managed to make out the Russian word for *monitor* before the batteries gave out altogether.

# 16

A peaceful protest by Japanese-Americans upset over the United States handling of the Trans-Pacifica Airlines incident turned violent today when police tried to prevent marchers from boarding a Soviet freighter here to unload lumber from Central America.

According to police spokesmen, the protestors were ordered off the dock but did not leave. After repeated orders to vacate, the police moved on the crowd with clubs and a water cannon. A fight ensued that left four policemen and 25 demonstrators in need of medical attention. One of the policemen is listed in critical condition from a gunshot wound.

In all, 42 pople were arrested under various charges.

WUSA Radio News Report
December 30, 1993

**W**hen Pete pulled back the flaps of the makeshift tent, he found that Sheena was awake. She smiled weakly when she recognized him. Her face was still pale from the shock of her injuries, but she appeared a little bit rested at least. Slowly she pulled her left hand out from inside the sleeping bag and Pete saw that she had been grasping her survival knife tightly. She looked at it self-consciously. "I must have lost my pistol in the fall," she said. Her voice was low and seemed a little slurred when she spoke. "Can you find it for me?"

Just then Harris poked his head around Pete. Sheena gasped and clenched the knife, trying to pull her feet back. Harris chuckled at her displeasure. "That was a nasty fall you took last night," he said. "How are you feeling?"

Before Sheena could reply, Pete pushed Harris back behind him. If there was anything that Sheena didn't need in her weakened condition, it was a shouting match with Harris. "Don't mind him," said Pete. "Whatever he says. We're going to get you out of here."

Sheena tried to raise up on her elbows but fell back. "You've got to find it first!" she whispered. She started to say something else, but Pete stopped her just as the tarp was jerked away from over them, revealing the slate gray sky overhead. Sheena blinked several times as the sudden light hurt her eyes. Murphy and Harris stood looking down at her.

"Okay," Murphy ordered Pete and Harris. "Let's get a stretcher made out of this piece of parachute and the poles, then get her strapped on it and up to the cave. We haven't got all day."

The three men fell to work without further talk. Once they had the makeshift stretcher ready, they laid it on the snow beside Sheena, then they lifted her onto it. She groaned as she was tied to the stretcher and the fresh pain of being moved caused her to clench her teeth. She seemed almost too weak to protest.

It took them nearly an hour to get Sheena and the stretcher up through the jumbled, ice-glazed rocks and to the relative shelter of the cave. They watched the sky almost constantly during their struggle up the cliffs, but no more airplanes appeared. Pete thought that was strange for the wind had died and Soviet airplanes should have been out searching for them. Maybe, Pete thought, he and Harris had been spotted when the first airplane had passed over and a boatload of Russian troops were on the way. Or could the Morse code message have something to do with it? Harris *had* been out of sight when he intercepted the transmission, but so had Sheena. And there was no way of knowing that the message had originated on the island. He wasn't even sure now that he had heard correctly. His Morse code was rusty from disuse and there were several words in Russian that he could have mistaken for what he thought he heard. Pete knew he was just getting too jumpy for his own good.

Once they had seen that Sheena was as comfortable as possible, Pete, Murphy, and Harris donned their wet suits. Pete made a final check to see that Sheena was well-covered by the sleeping bag and had a container of water nearby should she wake up. While Murphy and Harris were busy gathering up weapons and gear, Pete bent down and slipped the .357 inside Sheena's sleeping bag, being careful to put the safety on so that she would not accidentally cause the pistol to fire. He knew that what he was doing was a calculated risk. If Sheena turned out to be the enemy, she could turn the weapon on the team but, if she was not, then the pistol might be her only chance of survival. At least, Pete knew she had it and wouldn't be taken by surprise if his faith turned out to be misplaced. He paused, knowing he may have just armed the enemy, but decided to go with his gut feeling and leave the pistol where it was. He stood up, glad that neither Murphy nor Harris had noted what he had just done. Sometimes things were easier to do than explain.

He picked up one of the carbines and the pack of explosives then followed Murphy and Harris down toward the shore. The two scuba tanks and their related masks and swim fins had been placed in the boat earlier, as had the pneumatic dart guns.

The Zodiac was as they had left it. A little snow had blown onto the tarp, making the camouflage even more effective. Harris and Murphy untied the ropes and removed the tarp while Pete readied the outboard motor for starting. With the alcohol-gasoline mixture he knew it should start right away, despite the extreme temperatures, providing the battery had enough strength to crank it over. The men watched the low swells for a brief lull of quiet water then slid the boat into the water. Pete scrambled aboard and took his place at the stern, next to the engine. Now if the outboard would only start before a big wave rolled in and dumped the boat full of water!

Pete's worry was needless, however, for the battery started the outboard engine easily despite the cold. Pete raced the engine momentarily then let it idle while Harris and Murphy climbed aboard. Pete put the engine into reverse, then, once clear of the rocks, he turned the boat and headed out to sea.

Once they had cleared the surf, Murphy pulled one of the team's two tiny directional radios out of his pocket and tuned it to the frequency of Flight 18's crash locator. In appearance it was very much like the Russian transceiver except that it had a tiny speaker in addition to an earphone. Murphy listened to the static emanating from it, trying to pick out the klaxonlike beeping of a flight recorder. Although he turned the miniature radio in all directions, even holding it above his head for a clearer signal, he got nothing. Murphy shook his head. "I don't like this," he said. "If we're within twenty-five miles of that locator, we should be getting a signal."

Pete scanned the horizon. As far as he could see, there was nothing but endless, rolling gray swells. "Let's go out another mile or two and try again," he suggested. Murphy and Harris nodded in agreement then hunkered down in the boat with their backs to the wind and spray while Pete expertly drove the small rubber boat farther and farther from the safety of shore. He knew that should another airplane fly over they would be exposed with nowhere to hide.

After they had been underway for about half an hour, the island where they had left Sheena had almost completely disappeared from sight. Pete checked a tiny oil-filled compass permanently mounted into the Zodiac's rear seat and noted that their heading was approximately northeast. According to INTEL-5's computer estimates, they should be in almost the exact area that Flight 18 had gone down if, as suspected, the Soviets had hit it just before it reached Petropavlovsk. He slowed the boat until the engine was just idling enough to keep it headed into the long, rolling swells. Murphy pulled the tiny receiver back out of his pocket and turned it on. "Any idea how deep the water is here?" Murphy shouted back to Pete.

Pete looked around him. "Unless I miss my guess, it's not much over two-hundred feet," he shouted back. "But there are cracks in the ocean floor that they figure could go down fifteen miles. Earthquake faults. They keep constantly shifting, so they're impossible to map."

Murphy nodded. Although he kept working the controls of the receiver, he was unable to get a signal. After he had tried for about fifteen minutes, he shook his head. "Nothing," he announced.

He was just about to say something when Pete suddenly raised his hand for silence. Then Murphy and Harris heard it, too, the low rumble of an approaching Russian patrol boat. "Everybody get down!" Pete ordered. "There's nothing stands out at sea like something vertical."

Harris and Murphy obeyed by ducking down until their backs were just barely visible above the sides of the boat. Pete bent horizontally and kept the engine slowly idling, expertly holding the boat in the trough of a running wave. Although he could not see it, Pete could hear that the Russian patrol boat, similiar to an American PT, was getting closer. The rhythmic throbbing of its huge diesel engines made it sound like the boat was going to run them over. Although he knew that they wouldn't stand a chance, Pete pulled the 30-caliber machine gun closer. Murphy gripped his carbine. Only Harris had not picked up his weapon. His hands were thrust deeply into his pockets for warmth, as if he realized the futility of their trying to shoot it out with a gunboat.

The boat came closer and closer until Pete felt that it would be nearly on them at any second but then, as quickly as it had appeared, the patrol boat abruptly turned course and started heading away. After a few minutes Pete let the Zodiac crest a small swell and sneaked a glance at the gunboat's departing stern. He noted that its radar antenna was rotating and should have picked them up. Perhaps the radar operator had not been paying attention or had been looking for something larger. After all, a rubber boat hiding in the trough of a wave would present a poor radar target. Pete, Murphy, and Harris breathed an almost simultaneous sigh of relief. "Damn!" muttered Harris.

Pete kept their tiny boat in the trough of the wave until they could no longer hear the patrol boat, then he turned and headed back toward the island while Murphy fiddled with the receiver, still trying, unsuccessfully, to pick up a signal from Flight 18's crash locator. As they neared the island, Pete turned and ran along the shore for about half a mile, scanning the shoreline for any signs of intruders but saw none. When they found the place from which they had launched earlier, he turned and skillfully rode the surf into the narrow beach.

As they pulled the Zodiac up onto the shore, Murphy shook his head. "It looks like we're going to have to head farther north," he said. "I don't think Flight Eighteen made it this far south."

"I wouldn't be so sure of that," Pete said. "Somehow or other those people got to this island, and they couldn't have made it far."

Murphy nodded. "You got a point. They could have had some sort of life raft, but it isn't likely. Maybe we just haven't looked in the right place yet." He glanced at the sky that was rapidly darkening as the short day ended. "We'll try it again, come morning," he said.

After they had secured the boat against storms and prying eyes, the three men walked slowly toward the cave. The wind had picked up and the temperature was plummeting as night came. "I think we can risk a little fire tonight," said Pete. "If we keep it shielded inside the cave and use only dry wood, it's unlikely it'll be spotted. At least I'm willing to risk it."

Harris rocked his head vigorously up and down. "I'm for that." he said. "My feet are freezing!"

Suddenly the three men stopped dead in their tracks. Ahead of them, in the area of the cave, came the long, low moaning cry of a woman. Pete felt a chill go racing along his spine at the sound. Grabbing up his machine gun, he started to run toward the cave with Harris and Murphy hot on his heels.

As he rounded the final boulder before reaching the mouth of the cave, Pete heard the sound again, closer. He raised his machine gun to ready and checked its safety with his thumb as he ran. He leaped around the edge of the cave, ready to blast whatever it was that was causing Sheena to cry out in such agony, be it Russian soldiers or a wild animal. Then he saw a strange person and suddenly realized that the sound had not been coming from Sheena at all.

In the gloom Pete could see Sheena propped up on her left elbow watching the tiny, gnarled figure of a woman rummaging through the team's supplies, picking up and fingering everything before discarding it to the side in a large, haphazard pile. She seemed unaware of his presence. When Murphy and Harris came up behind him, Pete motioned toward the woman. They watched silently, transfixed as the woman fingered certain items with extra care as if they interested her the most. She lifted these items to her face and sniffed them loudly. Most she rejected immediately, but some were set aside in a separate pile. Pete noticed that most of the set-aside items were things in cans—then it hit him. The woman was searching for food. Twice while they watched, the woman threw back her head and emitted the long, wailing howl that they had heard earlier.

After several minutes passed Pete spoke in a loud, friendly voice, "Hello, we are Americans." Then he flicked on his tiny flashlight and shone the beam in the woman's direction. She spun around in a complete circle, searching for the sound, flinging up her hands as if to protect her face from the light. She was dressed in only a torn and burned ski jacket and a pair of ripped blue jeans that flapped as she moved. Even in the cold of the cave the sour stench of burned, already gangrenous flesh was almost overpowering.

The woman turned her face completely toward Pete and the full extent of her injuries and burns registered in his mind as he played the beam of his flashlight on her body. Her face and hands were masses of third degree burns. The heat had blinded her. Her face, what was left of it, was a horrible blackened scar, interrupted only by streaks of congealed blood where she had clawed at her charred skin. Two swollen and watery slits marked where her eyes had been. Her head was hairless except for a few scorched patches, the rest having been seared away.

Through the open front of the ski jacket Pete could see that nearly all of the woman's clothes had been burned off the top half of her body. Her chest was a mass of charred tissue mixed with melted synthetic cloth from what must have been her blouse. How she had lived at all was more than Pete could imagine, much less how she had survived the cold and storms of Kamchatka for nearly four days with only a light ski jacket for warmth. A few pieces of grass and leaves stuck to her clothing and body suggested that she had somehow managed to stay alive by crawling into a small cave or animal lair that was filled with dry grass. Obviously hunger and a desire to be rescued had driven her out.

The woman babbled something incoherent that was half Japanese and half pidgin English, followed by a low version of the howling wail. Although he knew only the most rudimentary Japanese, Pete realized that the woman was deliriously asking for food as she blindly clawed at the cans and boxes. Her face was burned beyond being able to register emotion and, it appeared, she had suffered so much that her entire nervous system had gone into shock. She could no longer feel physical pain. All she knew was hunger.

Pete moved toward the woman and gently guided her away from the team's equipment to keep her from further injuring herself or damaging the gear. At first he tried to comfort the woman in English, but soon realized that, if she had ever understood any English at all, in her weakened, delirious condition, she was not comprehending his words. Falling back on his minuscule Japanese vocabulary, Pete tried to tell the woman that she was going to be fed and cared for, but he suspected that she understood none of what he was saying.

Once he had the woman away from the supplies and had a sleeping bag wrapped around her, Pete built a small fire in the center of the cave, dispatching Harris outside for bits of dry wood. Murphy started the Svea stove and began heating water then dug around in the team's scattered equipment until he had rounded up all of their pitiful stock of emergency c rations. There were three tiny square metal tins, each containing a can of spaghetti, a bar each of compressed cornflakes and puffed rice, a miniature unsweetened chocolate bar, a packet of instant coffee and two packets of sugar.

Murphy opened one of the cans of spaghetti then half submerged it in the boiling water to warm it before he carried it across the cave and placed it in the woman's outstretched hands, if the charred members she extended toward him could still be called hands. He turned back toward the fire intending to find a plastic spoon for the woman when he heard her gobbling noisely, digging the hard-packed spaghetti from the tiny can with her blackened clawlike fingers.

Instead of continuing his search for a spoon, Murphy walked to where Pete was hunkered down feeding small twigs to the fire. As Murphy knelt beside Pete, the two men looked at each other. Murphy shook his head despairingly. "You know she hasn't got a chance in hell," he said, his voice low.

Pete stared across the cave at the woman, who was still digging at the near-empty can, and nodded. "If we just had some morphine."

Whatever else Pete might have started to say was cut off by the clatter of the empty can falling from the woman's hands. Almost at once she began to moan and wail again. In her sleeping bag Sheena stirred and struggled to sit up but fell back exhausted.

Harris walked in with a small armful of twigs and pieces of driftwood, which he dumped on the ground beside Pete. Then he squatted down beside the other two men and surveyed the scene in front of him. After nearly a minute of silence Harris asked, "What are we going to do with them?"

Both Pete and Murphy shook their heads and turned their faces away from the two women. Finally Murphy spoke. His voice was quiet and subdued so that neither woman would hear him. "I don't think it's going to matter much, one way or the other," he said.

Pete glanced over at Murphy. He knew full well that Murphy's words were true about the burned woman's chances of survival and he knew that Sheena was also sinking fast. Her right shoulder had turned into a swollen, blackened mess and she had started flitting into and out of consciousness as her condition worsened. If he could act quickly enough, at least Sheena had a good chance of survival, but Pete knew that he could not leave the burned woman behind to die while insisting upon trying to evacuate Sheena, which he intended to do. He had never deserted a fellow operative and he didn't intend to start now.

Murphy met Pete's gaze and it was obvious from the look that passed between the two old friends that Murphy realized what Pete was thinking. "Let's make them both as comfortable as we can until morning," said Murphy, "then we can decide. We can't do much before daylight anyway now, so there's no sense in rushing a decision."

Suddenly, from behind them, there was the loud rattle of metal and the burned woman emitted a loud, piercing scream. All three men spun around and lunged for their weapons, but there was no need for them. During the few minutes that their backs had been turned, the burned woman had crept across the floor blindly searching for additional food and had somehow crawled into the smoldering campfire, knocking over a heating billy, and catching the left sleeve of her ski jacket on fire. She was screaming and madly batting at the smoking jacket with her right hand, trying to smother the fire.

Murphy sprung across the cave and quickly snuffed out the fire with his gloved hands, but even after the jacket's sleeve was no longer smoking, the woman continued to pound it against the floor—in the process ripping loose some of the charcoaled flesh from her hands, which immediately started to bleed. By talking to her gently, Murphy finally managed to get the woman calmed down and into a corner where he gently covered her up again. He then unwrapped one of the compressed cornflake bars and gave it to her. She immediately started devouring it noisely and Murphy turned away, his face almost as ashen gray as the sputtering, smoking campfire.

While Murphy built the fire back up as best he could with the wet, punky wood, Pete made a cup of instant coffee, which he carried over to Sheena, along with one of the chocolate bars. She looked up at him as he knelt beside her and a flash of recognition crossed her pallid face. "Pete," she muttered weakly. "You have to stop them." Her voice trailed away as Pete slipped his hand under her head and smoothed back her hair. Murphy glanced up when Sheena tried to speak but then returned to feeding the fire. Pete gently cradled Sheena's head in his lap and tried to get her to drink the warm coffee.

She managed to drink nearly half of it before she started coughing. Pete removed the cup from her reach. Then, when she had quit coughing, he tried unsuccessfully to help her eat the chocolate bar. He gave up, then, and just sat gently stroking her tangled hair until he felt her relax in his lap and her breathing become more regular. She slept.

After a few minutes Murphy went over and gently tapped Pete on the shoulder. When Pete turned and looked up at him, Murphy pressed a steaming cup of the precious coffee into his hands then returned to the campfire and squatted down in front of it without speaking a word.

The dim yellow light of the fire cast flickering shadows on the wall of the cave, and for a long time only the sound of crackling wood and the low whisper of the wind outside interrupted the team's temporary respite from action. The burned woman had lapsed into silence, crouched in her corner. Harris was dozing beside the fire, his feet stretched out until they nearly touched the low flames. A carbine was cradled in his lap. After a while he began snoring softly, but neither Pete nor Murphy made a sound. The two old friends sat staring into the fire and saying nothing. Pete felt the exertion of the past three days overcoming him as his mind slowly played over old memories. He and Murphy were young men again—traveling across Egypt in a camel caravan. The sun bore down hard as the rhythmic swaying of his camel lulled him to sleep.

It was after midnight and the campfire had burned down to a bed of dimly glowing coals when a noise snapped Pete awake. Before the blinding white glare of a powerful flashlight hit him, Pete had barely time enough to see the dark figures of the four heavily bundled men, armed with rifles, who had walked uncontested into the cave.

"Do not resist," a voice boomed out in Russian, "and you will not be harmed."

# 17

Representatives of the Heavy Equipment Manufacturer's Council, a lobbying group, are protesting United States cutoffs of heavy construction equipment shipments to the Soviet Union.

Spokesmen for the group met with the President this morning, then emerged from the White House and spoke with reporters. While they did not claim success at getting the embargo lifted, they did state that the President has taken the matter under careful consideration.

Meanwhile, angry laid-off heavy equipment factory workers picketed on the sidewalk outside the White House.

One of the picketing workers expressed the feelings of many of the protestors when he said, "Why should we have to go without work just because the Russians killed a plane-load of Japanese?

"What have they ever done for us but put Americans out of jobs with all their foreign cars?"

PBN-TV *News Around the World*
December 30, 1993

When the soldier spoke, Harris sprang to his feet, wildly fumbling with the mechanism of his carbine, but before he could get off a shot, he was knocked savagely to the ground by the butt of one of the Russian's weapons. As he fell, he lost his grip on the carbine and it went rattling across the ground beyond his reach.

Murphy managed to grab up his carbine but it was kicked out of his hands. Pete, still sitting with Sheena's head in his lap, didn't even attempt to resist. Instead he gently slid out from beneath Sheena's head and lowered it to a pillow made of a rolled-up piece of parachute. Sheena murmured quietly in her sleep as Pete inched away from her and slowly stood up, his hands above his head.

One of the soldiers threw a handful of twigs and dried leaves on the fire and it flared up, illuminating the scene. They had been captured by four soldiers dressed in the heavy green parkas of the Soviet's arctic divisions. By their sparse uniform insignia Pete knew that three of them were the Soviet equivalent of corporals and the fourth was a sergeant. All appeared quite young. He listened for the sound of additional soldiers outside the cave but did not hear any. Apparently the four had come alone, probably in a small boat much like their own Zodiac. The only real question was from where, not that it mattered much now. They would probably find out sooner than they wanted to.

The Russian sergeant motioned to Pete with his rifle, indicating that he should move toward the entrance of the cave. Keeping his hands above his head, Pete did as he was ordered. He knew that resistance, at least for the moment, would be useless.

The soldiers appeared very well trained and disciplined as they silently herded Harris, Pete, and Murphy into a line before the fire and frisked them for hidden weapons. When this was done, the sergeant and one of the corporals quickly examined Sheena and the burned woman. After he had pulled back the top of Sheena's sleeping bag and seen the condition of her shoulder, the sergeant recovered her and stood up shaking his head. Sheena stirred only briefly and did not wake. However when the corporal went to the burned woman and shone his flashlight on her, he jumped back in horror at what he saw. The woman, awakened by his movements, instantly began screaming loudly. The sergeant stepped beside his corporal and his face also registered disgust at what he saw. He quickly ordered one of the other soldiers to bring a small first aid kit out of his rucksack. From this the sergeant pulled a small syringe of morphine. Stepping up to the woman, he pulled away enough of the parachute material to expose her legs. Without hesitation he jammed the morphine needle through her jeans into the outside of her thigh. She screamed but stopped within seconds as the morphine took effect.

Pete was grateful to the man for what he had just done and noted where he had got the first aid kit. Perhaps, surely, it also contained antibiotics. He would try to talk the man out of some for Sheena as soon as the chance arose.

The sergeant walked back to the fire and faced his three uninjured captives. He was a big man, but he did not have the abruptness about him that usually marks the professional soldier. This, coupled with his gentle treatment of the two women, made Pete suspect that the sergeant and his three men were not crack commandos, that they had somehow stumbled upon the foolishly sleeping team of operatives by accident. Had they been soldiers sent from the mainland specifically to capture an INTEL-5 team, it was a sure bet that such an obviously easy-going sergeant would not have been put in charge. While INTEL-5 was practically unknown among Americans, its reputation with the Soviets was formidable.

Slowly the sergeant looked at each of them. Murphy glared back across the fire. Pete remained expressionless. Harris seemed totally confused and disoriented. One of the corporals quickly bound all three men's wrists loosely behind them with a piece of shroud line cut from one of their own parachutes. Harris started to mutter something as he was being tied, but the sergeant ordered him to be quiet before he could speak. Even though he spoke in Russian, Harris obviously understood what the man wanted for he shut up immediately. Once he thought the captives under control, the sergeant spoke.

"Do you know," he began in very broken English, "that you are trespassing on the land of the Soviet Union?"

He paused as if waiting for an acknowledgement of some sort, but when he got none, other than fixed stares, he continued haltingly, apparently struggling to find the correct English words. "Very well then. I am Sergeant Kasmin. Neither I nor my three men wish to harm you in any way, but if you try to escape, then we would have no choice but to shoot you with our guns. Do I make myself clear on this?"

The last question appeared to Pete to be part threat, part honest question. His first instinct, had he been a beginner, might have been to inform Sergeant Kasmin that he need not try to communicate in English, since both Pete and Murphy spoke fluent Russian. Not being a beginner, however, Pete remained silent. There was no need to throw away any trump card, whatever its worth. He nodded to the sergeant that he understood.

Pete watched as the three corporals gathered up the team's weapons and piled them in a corner out of immediate reach. They seemed very interested in the American carbines that made their own automatic rifles seem heavy and awkward in comparison. The sergeant pointed to a place on the ground at the far side of the fire away from the weapons and motioned for Pete, Murphy, and Harris to sit. They did as he ordered then watched as he dispatched one of the corporals outside for firewood. From his instructions in Russian to the corporal Pete gathered that Kasmin had decided not to try to move the captives until morning. Apparently he did not wish to risk capsizing an overloaded boat in the darkness. He did not mention having found the team's own boat.

Soon the fire was blazing high. Its warmth and light filled the cave. From their knapsacks the four Russians pulled some pieces of hard, dark bread and a small block of cheese, which they began to eat, not offering to share with their captives. From their talk and the way they wolfed down the coarse food, it was obvious they had been away from their home-base for several days. The soldiers then passed a small flask of vodka between them, but never took their eyes off Pete, Murphy, or Harris.

Murphy continued to glare at the Russians in his best name-rank-and-serial-number fashion, glancing futively toward the pile of weapons, but at least Pete knew that Murphy would not risk their lives by attempting to escape unless he had a good chance of success. Harris, however, was another case. He worried Pete.

The big man squirmed nervously on the ground, alternately eying the Russians, the weapons, and the entrance to the cave. Twice he made a motion to attempt a foolhardy dive for the entrance, but each time he did not. Such a break would be suicidal. Pete also knew that if Harris foolishly tried to escape, he might not be the only one who got caught in a spray of Russian bullets. Besides that, an aborted escape attempt would only serve to put the Russians more on their guard, possibly eliminating a better chance.

Pete considered attempting to scoot close to Harris and trying to make him calm down but decided not to, fearing the Russians might mistake his action as an escape try in itself. Pete soon realized that this was a mistake.

Apparently the Russian soldiers did not suspect that any of the Americans understood Russian, for they soon began talking loudly among themselves without trying to hide their words from their captives. Although the small flask of vodka was nowhere near enough to intoxicate even one of them, the camaraderie of the shared bottle soon loosened their tongues and they began to discuss the events of the day and evening. It was largely as Pete had surmised. They had not been sent to this island specifically but had been assigned to search as many of the small islands as they could for bits of wreckage from Flight 18. They had been out for two days, hopping from island to island in the freezing temperatures, and were anxious to get back to the relative comforts of their base. They had not been told to expect to find Americans.

The soldiers had put ashore on the island in their small rubber boat, looking for a suitable place to camp for the night when one of them had smelled smoke. They had stumbled around in the darkness for over an hour before they located the cave. The three young corporals were expecting a handsome reward for capturing the American spies, but the sergeant, who was little older than his men, cautioned them against getting their hopes up although he, too, seemed excited about their good fortune.

Suddenly Pete noticed Harris tensing up, but before he could stop him, the man had sprung for the opening of the cave. The big man's sudden movement caught the relaxed soldiers by surprise and he was able to get a large rock between himself and the spray of automatic rifle fire that the sergeant sent after him. In the small space of the cave the burst of noise caused Pete to try to jerk up his hands to protect his ears but he could not because they were tied behind his back. Both Pete and Murphy instinctively flung themselves on the ground, but fortunately none of the bullets ricocheted back into the cave.

One of the corporals grabbed up his weapon and wheeled to cover Pete and Murphy lest they too should try to escape or reach the pile of weapons, a precaution that was fully justified for Murphy was already halfway to the weapons, even though his hands were still securely tied behind his back.

The sergeant and the other two corporals ran out of the cave into the darkness after Harris, the sergeant shouting "Stop!" in English and the two corporals yelling in Russian. There was the sound of crashing brush from outside and curses in Russian as the soldiers slipped and fell in their attempt to run across the slippery rocks in the darkness.

The sound of their footsteps and voices faded away. Then, after what seemed like an inordinately long time, but was only a few minutes, there was a burst of automatic rifle fire followed by silence. Pete suspected that Harris had led them on a good chase, but he had not been able to hide or outrun the powerful beam of their flashlights. And with his hands tied behind him even if Harris had got a weapon somehow he would have been unable to use it. Pete suddenly felt a tightening in the pit of his stomach for Harris, although he had neither liked nor trusted the man.

When Harris had made his dive for freedom, Sheena had rolled over and groaned but not awakened. Now, however, she struggled into consciousness and stared across the cave to where Pete and Murphy still lay on the ground with their hands bound behind them. She looked at them for several moments, blinking as if unsure of what she saw, then switched her gaze to the young Russian corporal who stood over them with his rifle poised. He noticed her watching him from the side but did not seem to pay her much attention. Apparently he did not consider either Sheena or the burned woman any reason for his concern.

Although Pete remembered that he had hidden the loaded .357 inside Sheena's sleeping bag, he hoped that she did not try to use it now. In her very weakened condition she might be able to shoot the corporal, but it was unlikely that she could get the drop on him without firing and, although the weapon was silenced, if the corporal screamed, it would bring his comrades running before either Pete or Murphy could untie themselves for a fight. As he saw Sheena's left hand creeping down inside the sleeping bag and grasping the weapon, Pete knew he had to act fast. He had to take the chance that the corporal did not understand much English.

"Sheena, not now," Pete said quietly without any inflection in his voice that would give his meaning away.

The Russian corporal raised his rifle at Pete and ordered him, in Russian, to be silent, and Pete had found out what he had wanted to know—the corporal did not speak English. Sheena relaxed her arm inside the sleeping bag. Pete knew that the pain of her injuries plus the internal damages had rendered her nearly helpless, but at least she was still capable of understanding. If he could manage to get the antibiotics and morphine, she stood a good chance of surviving for at least a few more days. He hated to think what would happen to her should they not escape. The Russians on the far eastern frontiers did not enjoy a reputation as being especially hospitable to wounded foes, or wounded allies for that matter.

Slowly and deliberately making his Russian sound awkward Pete spoke to the guard. "I am afraid that our woman in the sleeping bag badly needs medical attention," he said.

A flash of recognition, almost a smile, crossed the corporal's face as he heard his language spoken, however badly. Pete knew that the corporal, although he might have never actually spoken to an American before, would be amazed that one should speak Russian. "I cannot talk to you," said the corporal, eying the cave's entrance nervously and speaking in Russian, but slowly and with exaggerated enunication for Pete's benefit. "If you want something such as medicine you will have to ask Sergeant Kasmin." The corporal tried to put a note of finality in his voice that would leave no doubt that the conversation was over, but Pete pretended not to notice.

"But you do have antibiotics in your first aid bag?" he asked in Russian.

The corporal frowned, but the effect on his boyish face was more nearly comical than threatening. It was doubtful the young soldier had yet celebrated his twentieth birthday. Pete thought that he was not unlike his young counterparts in any army in the world, thrust into a situation where he might die for an abstract idea that he couldn't even start to comprehend, much less have any real opinions about. Probably a decent kid, were he not a soldier. Pete started to ask him another question, but the corporal jerked his rifle at Pete to accentuate his words. "Be quiet!" he ordered.

Pete shrugged and smiled at the corporal but obeyed his order of silence. He deliberately kept eye contact until the young soldier finally dropped his gaze to the ground. Apparently satisfied that the captives were not going to try to cause any more trouble right away, he selected a rock close to the fire and sat down, being careful to keep a clear view of his prisoners.

For several minutes the only sound in the cave was that of the fire and Sheena's labored breathing, but soon the quiet was interrupted by heavy, stumbling footsteps approaching from outside. The corporal sprung to his feet and assumed a melo-dramatically alert stance as the footsteps sounded just beyond the entrance.

There were a few muttered curses in Russian and suddenly Harris was shoved into the cave with such force that he tripped and fell heavily on the ground. His cut and bleeding face hit the ground with a sickening thud, missing the fire by inches. His hands were still securely tied behind his back, visibly tighter than before, and his clothes were torn as if he had put up quite a fight before being taken. That Harris had not been killed flooded Pete with a mixture of relief and a strange apprehension. Harris was quickly followed into the cave by Sergeant Kasmin and the two other corporals.

When he hit the ground, Harris rolled away from the fire and lay on his side gasping for breath, his face toward Pete and Murphy. Blood from a jagged cut across his forehead ran in his eyes and dripped to the ground, quickly forming a small, dark red puddle beneath his head. Sergeant Kasmin stood over him, legs spread, his heavy rifle butt poised to strike Harris again should he offer any further resistance, but Harris did not.

Kasmin's eyes narrowed to evil little slits as he glared past the fire at his other captives. Gone was the picture of an easy-going, not-too-professional soldier. Harris's escape attempt had appar-ently made Kasmin realize the seriousness of the situation in which he inadvertently found himself. It seemed to Pete that Kasmin also realized that getting the prisoners back to base wasn't going to be the easy job he had thought.

After several minutes of silence Kasmin strode across the cave and, with the barrel of his rifle, poked the black-draped mound in the corner that was the burned woman. Still out from the morphine, she shuddered slightly, but made no other move.

Kasmin then stepped across until he stood over Sheena. Pete tensed. Although she seemed to be aware of Kasmin's presence, Sheena's eyes were blank. Kasmin looked at the crude stretcher that was still beneath her, then he pulled back the top of the sleeping bag. Bending down, he once again examined her shoulder as if evaluating her chances of surviving travel. Still, he did not pull down enough of the bag to find the .357 hidden inside. He ordered one of the corporals to hand him the first aid kit. From it he selected a small package, removed a single red-and-white capsule, and handed the rest back to the corporal.

When he noticed Pete and Murphy watching him, Kasmin held up the capsule. He laughed wickedly. "No, gentlemen. This is not some kind of horrible Russian torture that your country falsely accuses us of using. It is nothing but a powerful antibiotic that will arrest your fellow operative's deterioration so that she can be taken to Petropavlovsk and interrogated," he laughed again. "As you shall also be. Perhaps *then* you will see the horrible Russian tortures if you do not fully cooperate." Kasmin did not bother trying to speak in English as if he somehow now realized the kind of men he was dealing with and that translation was totally unnecessary.

The corporal, to whom Kasmin had handed the first aid kit, now produced a small flask of a clear liquid that Pete assumed to be vodka. Then, lifting Sheena's head, Kasmin slipped the capsule into her mouth and managed to get her to wash it down with a drink from the bottle. She gagged at first then swallowed. Kasmin lowered her head and stood up.

He then ordered the two corporals that had helped him capture Harris to go check on their boat and make sure that it was secure for the rest of the night. They grumbled slightly about having to go back out into the cold, but a frown from the sergeant sent them on their way. Kasmin followed them out of the cave as if to assure himself that they actually did go tend to their boat as ordered, leaving only one corporal to guard the prisoners.

Harris's face was no longer actively bleeding but was still covered with blood as he pulled himself to his knees and, half-squatting, made his way to the shadows behind Pete and Murphy, where he flopped down heavily into a sitting position with his back against a rock. Pete watched him and, even in the shadows, it was obvious that Harris had taken quite a beating from the soldiers. Perhaps, thought Pete, he would have to change his opinion of Harris.

Kasmin stepped back inside the cave, frowned at the dying fire, and ordered the corporal to go outside for more fuel. The corporal, slinging his rifle smartly over his shoulder, quickly did as he was ordered, leaving Kasmin alone with the captives.

The sergeant glared past Pete and Murphy at Harris's dark shape then smiled evilly. Turning to one of the knapsacks, he bent over and seemed to search for something inside, chuckling to himself as he did so. He had just started to straighten back up when he was suddenly stopped by the sound of a movement behind him.

It was only then that Pete and Murphy realized that Harris, hidden in the shadows, had somehow managed to untie himself and then creep across the cave to one of the team's carbines. So quick and silent had he been that no one—not even Kasmin—had noticed.

A look of hatred, frustration, and fear swept the sergeant's face as he wheeled and found himself staring down the wicked barrel of Harris's carbine, a look that could have been more than a little bit inspired by the memory of the beating that he and his men had inflicted on Harris less than a half hour earlier. Slowly Sergeant Kasmin dropped his automatic rifle to the ground, raised his hands, and stood trembling before Harris.

Harris, however, did not strike the man. Never taking his eyes off Kasmin for even a second, Harris quickly cut the ropes that bound Pete and Murphy who immediately armed themselves. Harris then held the carbine on Kasmin while Murphy relieved the sergeant of an automatic pistol inside his coat and a knife tucked inside his boot. After that Murphy happily knocked Kasmin to the ground and tied his hands behind him. He had just drawn back his foot to kick Kasmin in the face when he was interrupted by the approach of the corporal with an armload of firewood.

Murphy stepped toward the entrance quietly, his carbine ready. But, when the corporal stepped inside the cave, he intuited the situation and flung his armload of dirty sticks into Murphy's face, grabbing for the automatic rifle slung across his shoulder. The Russian's finger never even got near the trigger before his chest was splattered by a burst of bullets from Harris's carbine. The corporal fell heavily forward, a confused look on his face. He was dead before he hit the ground—not even time to scream.

Pete wanted to curse Harris for firing the shots that would surely bring the other soldiers running back, but he knew that the big man had not had a choice. If he hadn't shot, Murphy would have. In any case Harris was already to the cave entrance, yelling for Pete and Murphy to follow him, but Pete remembered Sheena.

"We have to get her out of here too!" he yelled, but Harris was already outside and beyond hearing. Pete glanced at Murphy who shook his head quickly.

"There ain't no way!" Murphy shouted, but when he saw that Pete was not going to leave the cave without Sheena, he tossed a few pieces of equipment onto the stretcher beside her and grabbed the front, cursing Pete vehemently.

With Pete carrying the rear, the two men started from the cave at a near trot, stopping only long enough for Pete to grab the Russian knapsack that contained the first aid kit.

When Pete and Murphy emerged into the darkness, Harris was nowhere to be seen. Without waiting for him, they headed toward where they had left the boat, carrying Sheena between them.

The rough terrain and darkness quickly forced them to a walk, but they were nearly halfway to the shore before they heard the sound of running feet behind them. They put down the stretcher and grabbed up their weapons, Pete a carbine and Murphy the 30 caliber machine gun, but the footsteps were only those of Harris. As he caught up to them, he frowned, obviously disgusted by their insistence on burdening the team with a helpless woman, but said nothing, realizing argument would be useless against Pete.

When they realized that Harris was, as yet, not closely pursued,

Pete and Murphy picked the stretcher back up and resumed their push toward where they hoped their boat was still waiting for them. Harris brought up the rear, keeping a watch back up the trail behind them.

The boat was as they had left it. They jerked away the tarp and readied the Zodiac for launching, sliding it down the bank until the stern was floating. Then they carefully removed Sheena from the stretcher and placed her aboard, lying her across the floor in the center.

Murphy climbed across Sheena and was beginning to start the outboard motor when Pete's voice stopped him. "What about the other one?"

Murphy looked up angrily. "Forget it, Pete! She's too far gone to matter now. We have to get the hell out of here!"

Pete started to reply, but before he could speak he heard the sound of feet crashing through the underbrush, running toward them. There was no doubt that they belonged to the Russians.

With only a clip or two of ammunition apiece the team had no chance in a firefight. He quickly helped Harris slide the boat into the water, shoving it out to where the propeller would clear the rocks. A low, breaking wave crashed down on them from out of the darkness, crashing over the stern and sending several buckets of water sloshing into the boat, soaking their gear.

Giving the boat a final shove, they crawled aboard as Murphy started the engine. It caught immediately, then sputtered and threatened to die just as the flashlights became visible through the brush.

Murphy furiously manipulated the engine's mixture control and choke as the water on either side of the rubber boat erupted in rows of tiny craters as the bullets struck the water. The Russians were running toward them, firing their rifles, and shouting.

It seemed that the Russians were nearly on them when the engine finally sprang to life. Murphy twisted the throttle full-open and the boat almost left the water as it lunged forward up the side of a wave. Bullets whistled past their heads.

Probably because of the cover of night, neither they nor the boat was hit by the shower of gunfire, and within less than a minute they had put a small point of land between them and the soldiers. The four were wet, cold, and minus much of their equipment, but they had escaped, at least for a while.

When he felt the Russians were safely behind them, Murphy turned the tiny boat's bow into the rolling black swells of the icy ocean and headed out to sea.

# 18

Senator Samuel Shunner, long-time critic of the administration's military policies, charged today that U.S. intelligence agencies had ample time to warn Trans-Pacifica Airlines Flight 18 that it was about to stray into Soviet territory.

That such a warning was not given, Shunner said, was just another example of the President's desire to go to war with the Soviet Union.

According to Shunner, both United States and Japanese surveillance activities should have been fully capable of detecting Flight 18's departure from course and warned it in time to correct its path.

Shunner said that the United States has a sophisticated radar at a post in the Aleutian Islands that is so powerful that it can detect a baseball at a range of 2,300 miles.

The White House has refused comment on Shunner's charges.

*AM-American Newshour*
December 31, 1993

**B**y morning Murphy had located another uninhabited island about twenty miles from the one they had escaped. It was much smaller and rockier than the first with only a few sparse clumps of vegetation, but there was a tiny sheltered cove with a smooth, black sand beach that made landing the Zodiac an easy task. To make it even better, to one side of the beach was a small overhanging ledge of dark volcanic rock that was perfect for concealing the boat from prying airborne eyes. And, as if nature had designed this particular island solely to suit the team's purposes, less than a hundred yards from the shore, up an easy, gradual slope, was the island's largest patch of bushes, a stand of arctic willows that was just thick enough for a man to crawl under and hide. The air had also warmed somewhat, although it was still cold. After having adjusted to minus twenty degrees, the near-zero temperature seemed practically balmy to the group. The ground beneath the willows was thickly padded with fallen leaves, a sort of oasis in an arctic desert.

The men quickly got Sheena, her health seemingly improved by the antibiotic capsule, up the beach and safely hidden in the clump of willows. Then they pulled their boat from the water and got it out of sight beneath the overhanging rock so they could sort undetected through their dwindling stock of gear.

The two large piles of equipment with which they had left the Lear jet three days earlier was now one very small pile. Along the way they had lost or left behind in the cave all of their camping gear, extra clothes, main radio transceiver, food, medical supplies (except for the Russian first aid kit), and all of their weapons except for two carbines, the machine gun, and the .357 that only Pete and Sheena knew was still concealed deep inside Sheena's sleeping bag. Most of the ammunition for the weapons had also been lost in the escape.

Fortunately, though, they had stored several items in the boat before the Russians had stumbled onto the island in the dark. These included a small, portable transceiver for finding the crash locator, the two padded containers with the explosives, two of the pneumatic spearguns, their two surviving scuba tanks, enough fuel to run the outboard motor for about another six hours, and a few waterproof flashlights. Attached to an inside wall of the boat was also a small emergency packet that contained a penlight flare pistol, two packets of shark repellent, and a small plastic solar still for making sea water drinkable.

In addition to these items all four were still wearing their thin wetsuits beneath their clothes even though the gloves and socks to the wetsuits had been abandoned in the cave.

Although the morning sky was still as gray as the days before, there was little wind and only a light swell on the ocean. Murphy commented on the favorable flying weather for the Russians and said that he expected the sky to be full of Soviet airplanes soon.

"The damned Russians are going to be madder than hell when they find out we're here," he said.

"I'd sure hate to be Kasmin and have to tell my boss that I let four American spys get away," agreed Harris.

Pete looked at the giant man then at Murphy. He still couldn't bring himself to like Harris. "All the more reason why we'd better do our job and get the hell out of here. The next batch of Russians we see aren't likely to be as easy to deal with."

Both of the other men nodded in agreement.

They worked swiftly and in a few minutes had completed their inventory and decided to resume searching for the crash locator despite the risk of being spotted. When they were ready to shove off, Pete walked up the beach to check on Sheena. Murphy ran to catch up with him, a carbine beneath his arm.

They found Sheena asleep, resting more comfortably than she had appeared in the past several hours although her face was still pale. Murphy watched closely as Pete checked her pulse without waking her up. Satisfied that her pulse and body temperature were close to normal, Pete nodded and stood up, motioning to Murphy that they should leave her sleeping. Murphy seemed satisfied, even pleased, at Pete's decision.

The two men were almost back to the boat before Pete spoke, his voice low as if he feared he might wake Sheena. "Right now, sleep is the best thing for her. God knows, she'll have to be put back in the boat soon enough. I just hope our pick-up's out there."

Murphy nodded agreement as he and Pete helped Harris launch the boat. Soon, with Pete running the boat, they were headed back toward the area where the airliner was thought to have crashed into the ocean.

When they had gone about a mile from shore, Murphy took out the small transceiver and tuned it to the crash locator's frequency. Almost at once he held up his hand for quiet. Pete let the boat's engine slow to an idle.

"I'm getting something!" exclaimed Murphy. He flipped the speaker on for the others to hear and Pete made out the weak, but unmistakable, beeping of a crash locator. Slowly Pete began driving the boat in ever-widening circles while Murphy attempted to establish an exact reading on the locator with the small directional pointer built into the transceiver. Twice he thought he had lost the signal but each time he found it again, stronger than before. At last the pointer locked onto the signal and Murphy pointed northeast. Pete straightened the boat and slowly headed in the direction that Murphy had pointed. After about fifteen minutes Murphy waved for the boat to be stopped. "It should be right below us," he announced.

Pete and Murphy quickly donned the two surviving scuba tanks and, leaving Harris to keep the boat circling overhead, flopped backward into the freezing black water. At Murphy's suggestion they decided not to take the explosives with them on the first dive, choosing instead to find the locator first, then return for the packs. Harris seemed more than a little bit pleased at being left on the surface, even though he would be exposed should more airplanes show up.

For the first twenty feet the water was fairly clear and the two men swam downward easily, but before long it began to darken. Pete checked the luminous depth gauge mounted on his diving belt. They were seventy-five feet below the surface and there was still no sign of the bottom. Murphy paddled downward slowly, still listening intently to the waterproof transceiver through the earphone, following the dimly lighted pointer that showed the way. Without any sort of diving lights, theirs had been lost with the cargo parachute, they would just have to feel their way to the monitor. Their small waterproof flashlights could be used for setting the explosives once the monitor was located but the tiny, weak lights would not help them any in finding it.

The water was almost opaque now, Murphy little more than a flitting dark shadow swimming beside and just ahead of Pete.

Suddenly Murphy stopped and pointed to his left. Even in the darkness, Pete could see what Murphy was pointing at. Among several large fragments of the 747's tail section was a long, round, metal cylinder lying on its side on the ocean floor at the edge of what appeared to be a deep crack in the earth. The crack seemed to be several hundred feet across and it stretched away to either side until it disappeared.

One end of the cylinder appeared to be hanging out over the abyss as if a good solid shove could send it hurtling into the depths. Pete knew that moving the heavy cylinder would not be so easy as it looked. However, he also knew that a correctly placed charge could move it, destroy it, and, at the same time, bury any evidence that it had ever existed.

The device looked quite different from the other submarine monitors Pete had helped plant. It wasn't nearly so heavily armored for one thing, but that could just be the result of changes in design. After all, over ten years has passed since the last monitor had been placed in Petropavlovsk harbor. Still, as he swam closer, his suspicions began to grow that this object was not at all what the team had expected to find.

Murphy reached the strange metal cylinder first then swam slowly around it, kicking up a swirl of black sand from the ocean floor with his flippers. Pete wondered what Murphy could be thinking right then.

The cylinder closely resembled a rather fat torpedo or a large aircraft fuel tank of some sort. It was about fifteen feet long with a diameter in the neighborhood of four feet and appeared to be made from heavy aircraft aluminium with four tail fins that further heightened his ominous feeling. Pete knew there was no way it could be a submarine monitor. For one thing he could see no antenna cones, and for another the device looked incapable of burrowing into the ocean floor. Then it hit him.

A bomb! The goddamned thing was a nuclear bomb!

So Flight 18 *had* been "spewing radio-activity like it was going out of style" as the mysterious caller had claimed! Now Pete knew why.

He quickly swam around the bomb to where Murphy, near the tail, was prying at a hatch cover he had unscrewed. Murphy glanced up when he noticed Pete's approach. Pete formed the word *bomb* with his lips. Murphy nodded then shook his head from side to side in disbelief. The hatch cover popped loose and Murphy shone his flashlight inside, revealing a maze of wires and mechanisms that Pete suspected were timers and detonating devices. Murphy reached inside the compartment and banged on one of the mechanisms with his fist, causing Pete to cringe back, not, he realized, that it would have done any good had the device gone off. But the bomb did not explode and Murphy replaced the cover, using only two screws of the ten that had originally held it in place. When he was finished disarming the bomb, he motioned that Pete should follow him back to the surface. Without waiting he started swimming upward. Pete followed.

When they broke through into the air, Harris was about two hundred yards away in the boat. Murphy and Pete pulled off their masks and yelled to him. Harris drove the boat over to meet them and soon they were both back in the Zodiac, removing the bulky air tanks and catching their breath.

Pete sat on the rubber floor of the boat, breathing heavily. "Murph," he said, disbelievingly, "somebody, for some reason has put one over on us. That's no submarine monitor. That's a goddamned nuclear bomb."

Harris, in the stern of the boat, bolted upright. "IT'S WHAT!" he shouted. His face went white.

"A bomb. Apparently somebody switched a bomb for the submarine monitor, thinking it would go off in Petropavlovsk harbor. Why they should want that, I don't know." Pete paused. "Unless some nut actually wanted to start World War Three. God knows the technology and raw materials are readily enough available. It's a damned good thing you got to it and disarmed the firing mechanism before something set it off."

Murphy scanned the horizon nervously for airplanes but saw none. "It wasn't armed," he said.

Pete breathed a sigh of relief.

"But it is now."

Pete tried to remain calm, but couldn't. "What did you do down there, Murphy? I thought you jammed the mechanism. I thought you knew what you were doing. What a time to screw up!" Pete grabbed his scuba tank. "We have to get to it, disarm it, before it can explode! How hard will that be?" He pulled his diving mask over his forehead and turned to check his air gauge.

When Murphy did not answer right away, Pete thought he had

not heard and repeated the question. When he still got no reply, he finished tightening his weight belt and turned around toward the other two men.

Murphy had not even started putting on his scuba gear. He sat in the stern beside Harris, who had his carbine trained on Pete's chest. He had a nasty snarl on his lips.

"I'm sorry, Pete," Murphy said, his voice almost apologetic, "but I'm afraid we can't allow you to go disarming anything."

# 19

WASHINGTON—A committee of Congressmen
has angrily charged that the State Department's recent release of tape transcripts of
the Soviet's aircraft communications during
the TPA Flight 18 incident has compromised
U.S. intelligence.

The committee also charged several members of the Senate with releasing highly
classified documents.

Whether or not the State Department revealed too much, intelligence experts agree
that such revelations always make them
nervous. But, they say, what the State Department or the Senate revealed would hardly be a surprise to the Soviets.

*Newstime Magazine*
December 31, 1993

**W**hen they got back to the island where they had left Sheena, Harris unceremoniously herded Pete up the beach at gunpoint with Murphy following several paces behind. Sheena was awake and sitting up in her sleeping bag as the three men came into the clump of willows where she was. She started to greet Pete but stopped short when she saw what was happening. Harris glared at her victoriously.

Pete swung around and faced Murphy. "Why?" he demanded. "Why are you doing this, Murph?"

Murphy looked away at first and then at the ground before he lifted his eyes to meet Pete's. "God knows I didn't want to get you into this, Pete," he said. "You remember—in Alaska—that I tried to talk you out of continuing the mission."

"You knew damned well I wouldn't quit."

Murphy nodded. "Yeah, I should have, anyway."

"Well, it doesn't make any difference whether I'm here or not now, Murph. Maybe I'm glad I am. The question is why you want to explode this bomb at all? And who put it here?"

Murphy did not reply for what seemed like a long time. When he did, his voice was cracked and sounded very old. "It wasn't my idea originally, Pete. I just got tired of seeing the country going to hell, and when some of the higher-ups approached me with the idea, I went along. Maybe if you'd still been in the organization, you'd have talked me out of it. But you weren't.

"When you retired, you left me all alone, Pete. You were the last goddamned friend I had. Nothing but damned liberals and computers everywhere after you left, tying everybody's hands behind their backs, letting the Russians get ahead in everything. I knew that if we didn't whip the bastards soon, we weren't going to be able to—only there's nobody left in power with enough guts to start it. But if the Russians thought we dropped a nuclear bomb on them, they'd shoot back. Then our lily-livered politicans wouldn't have any choice but to fight."

Although his voice sounded determined, Murphy's eyes were filling up with tears, a thing that Pete had never seen before. He had known for a long time that, beneath Murphy's hard-crusted facade, there was a streak of gentleness and feeling, but Pete had never seen the man actually cry before. Even when he had had some damned good reasons.

Embarrassed at his own outburst, Murphy looked away from Pete—toward the eastern horizon. "Goddamn it, Pete!" he blurted out. "I've sentenced my oldest, dearest friend to death. But can't you see?! We've got to hit them first! Before they hit us!"

Pete shook his head slowly that he did not agree, although Murphy was still looking away. "Can we disarm it, Murph?" he asked, trying to make his voice sound calm.

He started to step toward Murphy but was brought up short as Harris jabbed a carbine barrel into his ribs. "Keep away from him!" Harris ordered.

Pete turned slowly and stared up at Harris. In the big man's eyes was a hard, cold hatred. There was also fear now that he knew that what he had thought all the time to be a submarine monitor was really a bomb. He jabbed Pete again, pushing him away from Murphy then over to where he stood beside Sheena. She was still lying on the ground in the sleeping bag, watching the developments with a horrified but knowing look on her face as if, through her pain, she had just figured out what was happening.

Harris leered down at the woman and chuckled. "Now let's see you survive, bitch!" he snarled. "You aren't going to have your old boyfriend here to help you this time."

Murphy was still standing with his back to the others. Very slowly he turned and looked at them. His eyes were blank, glazed-over balls inside his head. Pete thought he looked very, very old.

"Murph," Pete pleaded, ignoring Harris's repeated order to be quiet, "you don't want to do this. If there's anybody in the world who knows what war is like, it's you. There's still time, Murph. There's still time! We can disarm the bomb! We can beat the Russians some other way. We don't need a war! Our system's stronger. You know it is."

Sadly Murphy shook his head. "I'm afraid not, Pete. You're starting to make sense—as you always have, damn you—but it's too late. I unjammed the timer mechanism and started it working again." He glanced at his watch. "In exactly forty-five minutes, none of this will matter. We'll all be at the center of ground zero.

I'm sorry, Pete. That bomb is a thousand times more powerful than Hiroshima."

Pete lunged toward Murphy. "Damn it, you can't do this!" he shouted angrily. He grabbed for Murphy's neck, but before he could reach his old partner, Pete felt the stock of Harris's carbine go crashing into his ribs, cracking several and knocking him to the ground. A sharp, violent pain shot through his body.

"Are you going to allow this, Murphy!" Pete cried out. "Are you going to let this baboon do this to me?"

Murphy turned his face away from Pete, who was lying sprawled on the ground. Murphy was now sobbing audibly. Pete knew he had totally lost control of his mind.

"Shut up, goddamn you," snorted Harris, "or you aren't going to last for forty-five minutes!" He turned toward Murphy. "You too, old man. Drop the gun and get over here!"

Murphy wheeled to find himself also looking down the barrel of Harris's carbine. Slowly he dropped his own weapon to the ground. "But, I thought you were one of us. . . ." His voice trailed off.

"Never mind what you thought," snapped Harris. "Get over here with these other two pigs!"

As Murphy obeyed, Harris pulled from his pocket a small radio transceiver that was identical to the one he had claimed to have taken from Sheena's parka. Keeping one eye on the three prisoners, he flipped the radio on and spoke into the receiver in perfect Russian. "Come in, Ivanestky One. This is Red Bear Four."

For a few seconds Harris was silent as if listening to a reply on the earphone that none of the others could hear. Then he smiled grimly and nodded his head up and down, apparently satisfied at what he was hearing. He spoke into the radio again. "Get me a helicopter out here and have a MiG waiting. I need immediate evacuation," he said, his voice almost frantic. "Then I'll need a direct patch to Moscow."

Harris started to give the coordinates of the island, but before he got past the first few digits, there was a low, muffled crack that sounded like a weapon being fired far away.

Harris dropped his carbine and the transceiver, flinging his hands to his face, but his fingers found nothing there—only a bloody crater where his nose and eyes had been. The job of blowing away his face had been done as only a soft hollow-point .357 slug at close range could have done it.

Harris crumpled to the ground and what remained of his head sounded like the thud of a rotten pumpkin as it hit.

Murphy wheeled around and started to grab for Harris's dropped carbine, only to be brought up short by the barrel of Sheena's .357 sticking through the jagged, still-smoking, hole that it had just blown in her sleeping bag.

"I wouldn't touch that gun if I were you, Mr. Murphy," she said quietly.

"You too!" shouted Murphy.

Sheena shook her head. "No, Mr. Murphy. Unlike you and your dead buddy, my job is preventing wars—not starting them." She looked at Pete who was still lying on the ground. "Are you able to dive?"

Pete gingerly picked himself up off the ground, the pain of his cracked ribs evident in his face. A little blood was trickling from his mouth. He spat. "It doesn't look like I have much of a choice does it?"

Sheena nodded. "No. It doesn't. Not unless you want yourself to be atomized. Do you think you can disarm that bomb?"

Pete turned toward Murphy. He understood Pete's unspoken question. "Yeah," Murphy answered. "I'll come show you how." His voice was sad, distant.

Pete's ribs caused him great pain and slowed them down, but he and Murphy managed to help Sheena to the boat. Although her shoulder now seemed even worse than it had before, Sheena downed a handful of pain killers from the Russian's first aid kit and insisted on walking to the boat rather than being carried on the stretcher. Several times she stumbled and once she fell, but she never let go her grasp on the .357 nor took her eyes off Murphy. It was obvious that she still didn't trust him to disarm the bomb.

Sheena settled onto the floor of the boat, the .357 automatic resting across her lap, while Pete went to help Murphy shove the boat out into the water.

Just as they were about ready to climb into the boat, the water beside them exploded as a burst of automatic rifle fire split the silence. Three men were running toward them and shooting for them to stop.

It was Kasmin and the two surviving corporals, who had put ashore on the other side of the island and who had been watching them through binoculars. Pete now knew Harris was the reason they hadn't attacked earlier.

Before Pete and Murphy could grab up weapons and return the fire, a bullet struck the rubber boat which started hissing immediately as the punctured compartment quickly began losing its air. More serious than the punctured boat, however, was the next burst of fire. Murphy jerked and screamed as a bullet struck him in the lower part of his left leg, shattering the bone and turning the water red, yet he did not fall. Instead he grabbed up the 30-caliber machine gun with its one remaining clip of ammunition and returned the Russians' fire.

When they saw the Americans were going to fight back, Kasmin and his two men dived behind some rocks for cover but kept up a constant and heavy fire that pinned Pete and Murphy to the beach. The rubber boat began to float away, sagging on one side where the punctured compartment was located. Even with one air compartment flat, it would still float, but apparently unaware that Sheena was still lying low in the boat, the Russians ignored it, concentrating on Pete and Murphy's position.

Pete glanced at the clip in his carbine and saw that he had only two rounds of ammunition remaining with no more in his pocket. He looked sideways at Murphy, four feet away, cradling the machine gun beneath him. His left pants leg was soaked with blood and his face was twisted with pain.

"How much more you got?" Pete whispered.

Murphy checked the clip of the machine gun then shook his head. "Couple a dozen rounds, max." He glanced up the bank. "I think I can keep them busy long enough for you to make a run for the boat."

"What about you?"

"It doesn't matter about me. Right now, all that matters is for you to disarm that bomb!"

"Then you go. You know more about it than I do."

"No," said Murphy. "I got you into this mess, Pete. I got to stay and try to get you out of it. Besides I can't dive with this damned leg." He pointed to his blood-soaked trousers. "All you have to do is jerk out all the red wires where they run into the main timer."

Another burst of bullets whizzed close over Pete's head from a new direction. The Russians were moving around them for a clear view of the beach. Pete knew that he and Murphy wouldn't last long once they were flanked—especially with so little ammunition—and it wasn't likely Kasmin was in any mood to take prisoners.

"You got to go now!" shouted Murphy. "They're moving around fast."

Pete glanced toward the ocean then to Murphy lying on the sand just out of his reach. He wanted to go to the man, to shake his hand, to tell him—anything! He tried to formulate the words to express his feelings, but before he could speak, another burst of rifle fire kicked up a cloud of sand between them. "See you!" Pete shouted and made a dash for the water.

Pete hit the surf just ahead of a hail of gunfire, dived underwater and swam toward the boat, holding his breath as long as he could. As he dragged himself on board, he found that Sheena had managed to start the engine. He moved to the stern and took over the controls, turning the boat out to sea. Bullets went whistling by his head and kicking up the water behind and in front of the boat. A new hiss of air told him that another compartment had been hit but the boat was still floating.

The last thing Pete saw was Murphy charging up the beach toward the Russians, stumbling along on his knees, drawing their fire toward himself and away from the boat.

As the rubber boat picked up speed, Pete glanced back just as the gunfire reached a crescendo, but he couldn't see anything for the cloud of smoke from the battle.

Then from the island there was nothing but silence. As quickly as it had started, it had ended.

Pete bowed his head. Bill Murphy had been one hell of a man.

# 20

WASHINGTON—The United States has reacted to the Soviet downing of TPA Flight 18 with harsh words and denunciations of Moscow, yet has got little cooperation from its allies.

France has gone ahead with plans to sell construction equipment to the Soviets, as have Germany, Spain, and several other European nations. Only England has actively supported the United States led embargo, but even they are talking of resuming trade with the Russians.

Here at home, wheat and corn farmers have still been allowed to fulfill Soviet orders for their products and a ban against shipment of heavy equipment is due to be lifted next week.

All-in-all, there appears to be little left for the President to use as a bargaining chip with the Soviets.

*World Perspective Magazine*
December 31, 1993

**P**ete grabbed a quick glance at his wristwatch as the Zodiac, one of its sides deflated, struggled through the swells toward where the ticking bomb lay on the bottom of the ocean. He did a quick mental calculation. There were twenty-seven minutes—maybe twenty-eight—before civilization, for whatever it's worth, went up in smoke.

The small transceiver was tuned to the crash locator's frequency and had a good lock on the signal. The beeping was loud and clear at five second intervals. Twenty beeps to the minute. Five hundred and forty beeps to the start of Armageddon.

There was nothing else for Pete to do now but try to disarm the bomb. There was no one to call for help, no one to lend him or Sheena moral support. If he failed, no one would ever know of his attempt—likewise if he succeeded.

There was nobody out here anywhere but Pete and a woman; a woman who was about the gamest female . . . scratch that, about the gamest person he'd ever known. But, with her crushed and swollen shoulder, she couldn't even get a scuba tank on, much less be of any help on the ocean bottom. Well, by God, he'd been bored in Orlando and had wanted an adventure, one last adventure before he got old, and he was sure as hell getting it.

*Beep. Beep. Beep.* The sound of the locator beacon interrupted his thoughts.

The three airplanes seemed to come up out of the water to the north. They were MiG-23s, flying low to the water with an air-to-ground missile slung under each wing and the barrels of a cannon sticking out of their wing-slots like evil projecting eyes. They roared directly over Pete and Sheena, so close that Pete felt the heat from their exhaust.

The airplanes climbed and circled in a great, graceful, deadly, sweeping turn and came roaring back toward the small rubber boat. "Get down!" Pete yelled as the first rows of geysers came streaking through the water toward them, passing so close that they threw a shower of water into the boat.

As they passed, Pete could see the bright orange helmet of the lead pilot, could see the black-glass visor that hid his eyes and the oxygen mask that covered his face, making him look like some sort of robot programmed only to kill.

But behind the trappings that turned the pilot into a faceless warrior, Pete knew, was a man, a young man, most likely, who, unless he failed in his mission to destroy the small, wounded rubber boat bobbing below him, was going to die in exactly sixteen minutes.

*Beep. Beep. Beep.*

The three MiGs turned again and headed back toward Pete and Sheena. Once again the airplanes strafed the water with their cannon but once again Pete was able to veer the boat to the side just in time to avoid being hit. However having to dodge the airplanes was eating up precious time—thirteen minutes and counting.

*Beep. Beep. Beep.*

For a second the radio went silent, causing Pete's heart to stop— then he pointed the radio behind them and the beeping started again. They had passed directly over the locator.

Pete swung the boat around and cut back the engine to an idle. He motioned to Sheena and she dragged herself back to the stern and took the control of the motor from him, keeping the tiny boat wallowing in a trough—holding it as steady as she could while Pete quickly donned the heavy air tanks and scuba gear.

Before he pulled on his face mask, Pete turned to Sheena. "It probably doesn't matter much now," he said, "but Bill Murphy was the best friend I ever had. What he did, it wasn't Murphy's fault. He just got caught up in a system of hate that's bigger than any of us.

"Just in case I don't make it back, I'd ask you to remember that when you file your report. That's all." Sheena nodded that she understood Pete's request but said nothing.

The three MiGs were circling now, about a half mile away as if waiting for something, then Pete saw the small twin-engined cargo plane coming toward him.

It was higher than the MiGs had been, almost a thousand feet above the water, yet it was flying straight for the Zodiac. A jump-door on its side was standing open and Pete could see four black-suited frogmen crowded in the opening, ready to parachute into the water. Pete hoped there were no more inside.

Pete glanced down at his air gauge. It showed that the tank contained enough air for fifteen minutes. If he couldn't reach and disarm the bomb before it detonated, five of those minutes would go unused.

*Beep. Beep. Beep.*

Pete picked up the two packages of explosives from the floor of the boat and noticed one of them was ripped. A bullet had come within a half inch of ending it all for them. As he bent over, his cracked ribs sent a jolt of pain through his body, but there was no time to think about it now. He checked the small timer on the explosives. It had been banged up but still appeared functional.

Pete perched on the fully inflated side of the boat with one of the penumatic dart guns in his left hand, the transceiver in the other, and the two bundles of explosives strapped to his weight belt. He gave Sheena the thumbs-up sign and flopped backward into the icy water just as the first of the four Russian frogmen bailed out overhead.

*Beep. Beep. Beep.* Eight minutes.

The extra twenty pounds of explosives pulled Pete down so fast that his sinuses threatened to collapse from the extreme and sudden pressure, but he knew he didn't have time to worry about his own comfort. Following the dimly glowing direction indicator on the transceiver, he swam steadily downward with sure kicks. In the darkness his shoulder bumped against a large and soft living thing of some sort, but he did not pause to see if what he had touched was a fish or something else. There was no time.

As Pete neared the bottom he swam in almost total darkness with only the indicator dial to guide him. Below him he could see the dim, shadowy ocean floor and then the long, dark crack in the earth that looked like it might go all the way to hell itself. He turned and swam along the crack until he spotted the bomb.

Pete glanced at his watch; six minutes to go. He turned off the transceiver and had started to clip it to his belt when he felt the radio go flying from his hand, hit by a dart from a Russian speargun.

Pete whirled just as another dart zipped past his head in a swirl of bubbles. He knew that the Russian's dart guns were at least as deadly as the American version. He flung up his own pneumatic dart gun and fired. One of the three Russian frogmen threw up his arms then went limp.

Pete quickly fired again, but his second target dodged in time and the paralyzing dart flew harmlessly past him. Both frogmen now took aim at Pete. He dived for the ocean floor just as the two darts hit the mud and debris to either side of him. Pete frantically looked for the fourth jumper. Maybe he hadn't jumped at all, but more likely he was slipping around behind Pete at that very second.

Pete was only twenty-five yards from the bomb now. He could see the shadowy forms of the two Russians as they swam around him, slipping from rock to rock, trying to get between him and the bomb. Pete made a dash for the hulking metal shape then dived behind it just as two more darts bounced off the bomb and deflected upward, leaving a silvery trail of air bubbles. With two strong strokes he reached the control compartment near the rear of the bomb. He grabbed at his leg-sheath for his survival knife to remove the remaining two screws, but it had fallen out somewhere.

Pete sneaked a glance out over the top of the bomb's cylindrical metal surface in time to see the two frogmen swimming toward him, their dartguns poised to fire. Apparently they had not seen him. They were in easy range. Bracing himself solidly, Pete lay his dartgun over the top of the bomb and took careful aim firing at the lead swimmer, who flung up his arms much as the first one had done.

Before Pete could get off another shot, however, the last of the three dived for the bottom and took cover behind a fragment of wreckage from Flight 18. Pete glanced at the luminous dial of his watch. Two minutes to go.

He knew that he was going to be exposed to the frogman's fire if he tried to open the bomb and disarm it, but he had no choice. There was no time now to take him out, even though he hid behind the wreckage in easy dartgun range. Pete knew he had to rip open the compartment and pull out the wires—the red ones—before the frogman could kill him. Once the bomb was disarmed, his own death wouldn't matter.

He dropped the explosives to the ocean floor then, bracing his feet on the bottom, propelled himself toward the compartment. He jammed his thumbnail into the first of the two screws and twisted hard. It was loose!

The second screw proved harder but it, too, was loose enough to turn. Pete yanked away the metal plate and surveyed the mass of wires and devices inside, using the nearly exhausted beam of his small waterproof flashlight.

As his fingers touched the largest box that appeared to be the main timing mechanism, Pete could feel the ticking inside—counting off the seconds until doomsday.

He felt a jolt as a dart hit his air tank and went whizzing away, missing his ear by a fraction of an inch. He turned and saw the frogman bearing down on him from the rear—gun raised for another shot.

Pete spun and fired his dartgun from the hip. The frogman dropped his weapon and threw up his hands as the dart hit him in the stomach, but he had such momentum that he plowed through the water into Pete, who had to shove him sideways. As the Russian passed, Pete could see the man's face inside his diving mask. It was a face frozen in a horrible silent scream as the dart did its work, its quickness being its only mercy.

Grasping the bundle of red wires leading into the main timer, he gave them a hard jerk and they came loose in his hands. He felt the timer with his near-frozen fingertips. The ticking had stopped. His watch showed he had had a full thirty seconds to spare.

Pete quickly looked all around him for the fourth Russian frogman but did not see him. He retrieved the two packs of explosives. Carefully, aware of the damaged timer, he planted them beneath the front of the bomb where the explosion would catapult it into the chasm. He hoped it was deep enough to hide the bomb forever. Packing a few handfuls of mud over the explosives to direct the explosion, he set the timer for two minutes then started swimming for the surface.

Less than thirty seconds later there was a muffled roar behind him as the packs exploded prematurely. The force sent Pete rocketing toward the surface, spinning madly head over heels with a cloud of mud and water. His diving mask and air regulator was torn from his face and knocked away before he could grab it. His mouth and throat filled with icy salt water, and for a few seconds he did not even know if he was still conscious.

Then he felt a strong arm hook around his shoulders and drag him into the rubber boat. Sheena. Beside him in the water floated the dead body of the fourth Russian frogman who had apparently tried to commandeer the Zodiac without taking Sheena's .357 into account.

As Pete lay on the floor of the boat, retching, Sheena climbed across him and took the controls of the outboard engine, revving it until the boat seemed to be flying across the water. Pete was only vaguely aware that another air compartment had been punctured and that the boat was now little more than a limp innertube.

The Russian airplanes filled the air above them as they passed over a large brown splotch on the ocean where the mud and dirt from the explosion still boiled upward. Pete could hear the sound of approaching helicopters overhead.

When he had his throbbing, aching lungs under control, Pete looked ahead of them and saw the outline of the small fishing vessel that Sheena was making for. The small anti-aircraft gun that had appeared on its foredeck from a hidden compartment gave notice that it was no ordinary fishing boat. As they drew closer Pete could see the letters in Japanese written on its bow. He knew little Japanese, but he recognized what the symbols meant. The boat was the *Geisha Lady!*

As Sheena rapidly closed the gap between the two boats, Pete saw the gun cut loose at an approaching MiG. The airplane pulled up as it took a hit in the belly then cartwheeled into the ocean in a brilliant explosion.

They were nearly to the rescue boat when another MiG came diving straight down out of the sky and released its missile. It struck the *Geisha Lady's* pilot house dead center. The small vessel exploded in orange flames and immediately began to sink.

A piece of flying, burning debris sailed through the air and struck the crippled Zodiac in the center, slicing it in half. It collapsed and sank out from under Pete and Sheena.

The ocean was now covered with fuel from the burning *Geisha Lady* and a low sheet of blue, smoky flame raced toward them across the water.

At the last second before the flames reached them, Pete grabbed for Sheena and pulled both of them under as the flames raced overhead. They clung together in the water, sinking. Salt water burned the inside of Pete's mouth, eyes, and lungs. He felt the world going black. He struggled toward the surface, but Sheena's weight kept dragging him down. He refused to let her go.

He felt like he was kicking against something large and round and made of metal, but he knew that it was only his imagination playing a final trick on him before he died. Above him it sounded like there was a full-scale battle going on, but he knew it was only his imagination.

As the gunfire raged overhead, Pete clung to Sheena until his mind went black and he was dreaming a crazy dream that he and Sheena were being pulled aboard a submarine by a young, bearded man with the same southern accent of the mysterious caller in Alaska.

Then everything disappeared and there was nothing.

# 21

WASHINGTON—In a news conference today, the President expressed his desire to reopen arms talks with the Soviet Union.

"Although we intend to deal from a position of strength," said the President, "we are willing to discuss an end to the threat of nuclear war."

The talks have been stalled since the shooting down of an unarmed airliner by the Soviets nearly a week ago.

The invitation to the Soviets to reopen the talks came as a surprise to many observers in Washington.

There has been, as yet, no Soviet response to the offer.

*The New York Daily Mail*
December 31, 1993

**P**ete clawed his way up through the dark water with one hand, desperately clinging to Sheena with the other. The icy water grasped his feet, trying to keep him back. But he knew he must not give up. He could not. How long he had been under water he had no way of knowing. His lungs ached for air. Somehow he managed to keep his legs moving, kicking weakly for the surface.

At first he had not even known for sure if he was swimming for air or if he was mistakingly going deeper and deeper. But now the blackness was slowly turning brighter as he struggled upward. At last the water above him seemed to take on a pink glow. Something was clinging to his legs.

Seaweed!

He summoned all the strength left in him and kicked at the grasping tentacles. With his one free arm he pawed at the water. It was getting brighter. Only a few more strokes and he would be in air. Precious air. With the seaweed still wrapped around his ankles he gave one final burst of effort and broke through.

"Good morning!"

A Navy doctor, in a crisp white captain's uniform, stood smiling down at Pete over his clipboard.

"We had begun to think you were going to sleep *another* forty-eight hours, Mr. Shafer. Welcome aboard the aircraft carrier *Kennedy*. I'm Doctor Gasser."

Pete tried to sit up on his elbows but found his arms too weak to support his own weight. The doctor motioned to a young male nurse wearing the insignia of an ensign. He scurried over with an extra pillow, which he placed under Pete's head; then he pushed a button that raised one end of the bed until Pete was in a sitting position. After the nurse had made Pete comfortable, he went to the foot of the bed and unwrapped the sheets from around Pete's legs where they had tangled in his sleep.

Not sure that he wasn't still dreaming, Pete looked around him.

Except for the gray tile on the deck, the entire large compartment was painted a slick and shiny, almost wet-looking white. The overhead was punctuated by the brilliant blue-white glare of fluorescent lights and along the bulkheads were the usual little carts holding the sorts of things one normally finds in a hospital, but the room's windows were portholes.

He really was in the spotlessly clean sickbay of a ship. The *Kennedy?*

Then, for the first time, Pete noticed the IV tube running into his left arm from a bottle of clear liquid hanging on a stand beside the bed.

He certainly had no idea how he had got aboard an aircraft carrier, but it had to be true. The last thing he could remember was being in the water with Sheena when—

Sheena.

Pete raised up, his eyes sweeping the room, but all he could see were neatly made, empty beds.

He sank back down onto his pillow dejectedly. All of his efforts had not been enough. He had disarmed the bomb but had ultimately failed! Of the team only he had survived.

Doctor Gasser watched him for a few seconds, and then, understanding, said, "If you're looking for your companion, Mr. Shafer, she's fine. We did surgery on her shoulder after you were transferred from the sub that picked you up. She woke up two hours ago and demanded a wheelchair. After she'd checked you out to her satisfaction, she went to the officers' mess and ate, I understand, enough breakfast for both of you plus some.

"I've sent her word that you appeared to be coming around— under threat, I might add, that if I didn't she would feed me a bedpan, a threat that I have every reason to believe her capable of carrying out. She should be along shortly or I miss my guess. God only knows where you picked her up, but she seems to be one hell of a woman."

No sooner had the doctor finished speaking than the door to the sickbay burst open with a bang and Sheena hurtled into the room, propelling the wheelchair with her left arm, her right arm and shoulder in a massive cast.

She was dressed in a pair of blue Navy mechanic's coveralls and her hair was tied up in a sweep with a red bandanna. Although her face was sallow, she looked beautiful to Pete.

A medical corpsman ran in a few steps behind her, trying to

catch up to the wheelchair he had been detailed to push. Behind him came a Naval officer identified by his uniform as a rear admiral.

Sheena spotted Pete sitting up and smiled broadly. "Hey! Look who's awake!" she said, wheeling over to his side and taking his hand. "They tell me you had a touch of pneumonia, but that it's clearing up." She tapped her cast, then looked at Gasser. "The Navy's got some damned good doctors," she announced.

"I'm beginning to see that," he said.

Sheena smiled broadly. "I see that you've already met Doctor Gasser." She turned to the rear admiral. "Pete Shafer, I'd like you to meet Rear Admiral Richard Black."

Black reached out and shook Pete's hand. "I've heard a great deal about you from your young companion here."

Black then turned to Gasser. "I wonder, Doctor, if we might have some privacy."

Gasser nodded. "I'll be in my office if you need me." He tucked his clipboard underneath his arm and left the room.

When he had gone, Black spoke. "Damned fine man, Gasser. And a hell of a doctor. He does good work, but what he doesn't need to know won't hurt him."

Black turned back to Pete. "Mr. Shafer, I am the head of INTEL-five operations in the entire northern Pacific. Although we've never met face-to-face, your exploits were well-known to me long before you retired. Now, Operative Lawrence here tells me that you've almost single-handedly saved us from getting into World War Three."

Pete grew uncomfortable. "Well, I don't know about that," he said.

"Well, I do. Several of us in INTEL-five began to get suspicious nearly three months ago that there were some hard-liners high up in the organization who were getting set to try something, but, believe it or not, we only found out about the bomb on Flight Eighteen after it had left Anchorage.

"We tried to call it back, but either the pilot didn't hear us or he pretended not to. We were left with no choice but to shoot it down before it could reach Petropavlovsk."

The deadly logic made Pete close his eyes and what little strength he had drained from him.

"There were over two hundred people," he whispered.

"I know. Innocent people. But if that bomb had exploded in Petropavlovsk Harbor and started World War Three, even if it was just the work of idiots, two hundred *million* innocent people would have died, maybe even twice that. It was a sad trade-off, but it had to be made."

Black paused to let Pete absorb what he had just heard before continuing.

"We knew, after we'd downed the airplane, that we'd still have to get a team in to destroy that bomb before the Russians found it.

"Two of our best men in the Kamchatka area were reported missing right before this whole thing happened. Right now we don't know whether their disappearance was caused by KGB, as we originally had thought, or whether this small group inside INTEL-five was responsible. But that left Murphy as the most knowledgeable man on that area, even though he was semi-retired. He insisted that you be called out of retirement to go along. We figured that you two guys had about as good a chance of finding what you thought was a submarine monitor as anybody the organization had.

"Incidentally the only person on the team who was told that what you were going after was really a bomb was Lawrence, here. She's my personal assistant and has been our top trouble-shooter in the Pacific Basin for several years."

Pete glanced at Sheena. She smiled self-consciously.

Black continued. "We very stupidly assumed the KGB was ignorant of what was going on until your Learjet crashed at Wrangell. Even then we didn't find out that your team had been infiltrated until you had already left Shemya Island. Although we had our suspicions, we had no positive way of telling which one of you it was. I apologize, but with such a delicate situation, we were forced to suspect each of you."

Black smiled. "At one point, Lawrence tells me, she began to think you were the rotten apple although she knew your official file by heart. She was glad when the real KGB agent turned out to be Harris or whatever his name was. Lawrence, of course, then took care of him in her own inimitable fashion." Black turned to Sheena. "You know, I half believe she enjoyed it."

So! Pete thought, that explained a lot of things. The attempt to kill Sheena then, when that failed, the attempt to discredit her by producing the radio transceiver that was, in reality, Harris's. It also explained how the airplane had found them and then flown away. Harris had told the airplane that the crash locator hadn't yet been found.

When Sergeant Kasmin and his three men had shown up it had almost fouled Harris's plan. He had to lure Kasmin outside by trying to escape so he could reveal his true identity. That would also explain the ease with which they had managed to escape from the cave. Killing the corporal had just been Harris's way of adding a note of realism.

Harris knew he had to contact Moscow before the bomb was destroyed. Without evidence, no one would believe him. Pete would never know how Moscow would have responded to Harris's information. He did know that all the trigger-happy nuts aren't just on the side of democracy. Sheena intervened in the only appropriate way. When Kasmin, watching through binoculars, had seen Harris killed, he decided to attack.

Black walked across the room and stared out of a porthole for a few seconds then returned to Pete's bedside. "It's too bad about your friend Bill Murphy," he said.

Pete looked at Sheena disbelievingly even though he knew she had only done what she had to do. Although Pete knew in his heart that she had filed a full report on Murphy's connection with the group wanting to plunge the world into war, he wished there had been some way to let his old friend die with the honor that had meant so much to him.

Sure. Murphy had fallen prey to his own hatred of the communists, but he had redeemed himself at the end. Pete dropped his head for what he knew was coming next. He wanted to cry out in Murphy's defense, but he held his tongue. Murphy would not have begged himself and he would have hated Pete if he had done so.

Black cleared his throat. "Lawrence tells me," he began, "that Operative Murphy gave his life so that you and she could escape to disarm the bomb. I know his record, of course, and this action was completely consistent with a magnificent career. I am personally putting him in for a posthumous Medal of Honor.

"Although INTEL-five was the only family he ever had, I feel that his actions should be made known to everyone in the organization. We will issue a paper to that effect for all operatives and, as soon as it can be arranged, there will be a world-wide minute of silence in his behalf. Murphy's story will be a real inspiration to the younger operatives."

Pete lifted his head and looked at Sheena. She was smiling.

"Yeah," said Pete. "Old Murph'd like that."

WASHINGTON—The U.S. State Department said today that it has ended its unsuccessful $33.2 million search for the wreckage and flight recorders of Trans-Pacifica Airlines Flight 18.

The jumbo jet was apparently shot down by the Soviets during the early morning hours of December 25, 1993.

The two-month search "is over," said a State Department spokesperson. "United States search units have found no wreckage or traces of wreckage."

The Boeing 747 is believed to have strayed into Soviet airspace near the southern tip of the Kamchatka Peninsula.

All 246 people on board the airplane were killed, including 58 Americans.

*Shippensburg Weekly Gazette*
February 24, 1994